FAT CHANCE

A B MORGAN

Junction Publishing

THE SEARCH BEGINS

JANUARY 25TH

1

THE SEARCH BEGINS

JANUARY 25TH

Konrad sat at the kitchen table scraping the last morsel from half a grapefruit as he pored over his tablet, checking his Twitter feed. The chatter coming from the radio was giving an update on local news, distracting him.

'... And finally, police say their investigations into the severed human thumb, found by local bin men during their rounds on the fourth of January, have stalled. No one has come forward seeking medical treatment and a search of the police database has failed to identify who the print may belong to. Little is known about the thumb other than it is from a male, most likely Caucasian.'

There was a rustle from the newspaper his wife was holding as she stood up and trotted round the sturdy pine table to show him a short article.

'Look, Kon, it says here that Harry Drysdale has gone missing.' She dropped the relevant pages on top of his iPad, obscuring his view and angling for his attention.

'What, our Harry Drysdale? Immaculate Harry?'

'Yes. See.' She pointed out the photograph to the left of the article on page two of the Daily Albion. 'He was due to be leading for the defence in a murder case starting today but hasn't been seen since the Thursday after New Year.'

'Did he fall down a crevasse?'

'Not according to this. He didn't even make the flight to go on his skiing trip and failed to meet up with his lawyer friends in Chamonix for their annual New Year hangover cure.'

Konrad returned to staring glumly at the bowl of pith and grapefruit skin. 'He looked perfectly alright the last time we saw him.'

'I know,' Lorna said. 'But this isn't like Harry.'

The tone of her voice made Konrad pick up the article to read for himself.

2

SIX MONTHS PREVIOUSLY

Ella hadn't seen Val for years. Her face was one from the past, a hazy memory from a part of her life that she would rather forget. However, whether it was by fate or coincidence, Valerie Royal re-entered her world one summer night; the evening she lost her job at the Old Music Hall Bingo Club.

Ella pressed the button and watched the numbers come up on the screen in front of her. All she was required to do was to chant them out loud, clearly and with enthusiasm.

Three years of bingo calling, albeit part-time, was taking its toll and signs of her frustrations were beginning to emerge, no matter how hard she tried to hold herself in check. Under-achievement was eating away at her. On that particular Saturday her ability to put on a show of perky, cheerful, sales patter was being sorely tested, and she finally caved in to her compulsion to entertain.

Ella often breached the club's regulations. Nothing illegal. Insignificant rules, like for example the one about staff uniform. It was drab, so she brightened it up to match her fifties rockabilly hairstyle and reddest of red lipstick. Anything to make her feel alive, and not to conform.

That night, like any other, she was supposed to call the numbers, just the numbers. However, it was repetitive and mind numbing. With her resistance absenting itself, Ella went rogue. She used the vintage bingo calls of yesteryear, and the older players, judging by the gusto with which they joined in the fun, loved it.

'Garden gate,' she called.

'Number eight!' the crowd called back.

Scanning around the dozens of heads, Ella paused briefly to allow for any shouts signalling a winner before the next number was played.

'Top of the shop.'

'Ninety!'

She caught sight of a group of twenty-somethings exchanging questioning and bewildered looks. 'Come on now you youngsters at the front. If you don't know the calls, then make friends with the nearest granny, buy her a drink and she'll teach you. Remember, one lucky winner has already bagged themselves over sixty pounds for a horizontal line this evening, ladies and gentlemen. We have eighty pounds for two lines and a whopping two-hundred pounds sterling for a full house. It could be yours. Eyes down again.' She pushed the button on the random number generator and two digits appeared.

It had to be done.

'A favourite of mine, anyway up, meal for two ...'

Only a handful of voices shouted the reply, 'Sixty-nine!' followed by gasps and giggles from the players sitting imme-diately in front of the caller's desk. To their far left Ella spied a table with two players who couldn't have looked more out of place if they'd tried. They were totally disengaged with each other and with the game. Lesbians, Ella guessed from their appearance. The more masculine of the two wore a black leather biker jacket over a black roll-neck sweater. She had badly bleached spikey hair and an angular face to match, pale and sour. Her pink-haired partner wore a floral print tea dress and silver Doc Marten boots which complemented her tattoos and facial piercings. The rather scrawny, spikey-haired woman was staring at Ella, in preference to her date.

'All the whores ... sorry, that should be all the fours.' A little ripple of pleasure coursed through Ella's body as she witnessed the expressions of surprise on the faces of the players as they laughed at her apparent mistake.

'Forty four!'

'Dirty Gertie ... number thirty.' She'd filled in the blank, as even the most experienced players were unfamiliar with some of her more modern bingo lingo.

'Jump and Jive.'

'Thirty-five!'

'Here!' an elderly man shouted, waving his bingo card in the air.

Standing at the electronic terminal, holding the microphone up to her mouth, Ella congratulated the man on his winnings while another staff member dealt with the process of making sure the claim was legitimate.

'Well done, Derek. If you and Audrey drank less gin you'd have enough for that fortnight in Magaluf by now. He's a lucky man. Wins every week don't you, Derek?' The grey-haired gentleman smiled and waved again. They plainly appreciated the humour, but as Ella's portly manager approached from the back of the hall his wrinkled balding head and dark expression foretold of trouble coming directly her way. In an attempt to prevent him from tackling her about her unorthodox style and inappropriate dress, she hastily announced the next game.

'On the green card, ladies and gentlemen, let's have eyes

down for that elusive big winner. If the magical, full house includes your superstar square, then your winnings will be doubled. It's a Saturday special, ladies and gents. Make your dreams come true.' She swung around extending her arm to encompass every corner of the room.

The biker woman was still staring at her, but now she had risen from her seat and was clapping, a lopsided half-smile on her face. Only then did Ella realise who she was and why she would be staring so intently. Her astonishment resulted in a pause, during which her infuriated manager relieved her of the microphone and instructed her to take a break. He made a brief announcement to the customers using a nasal monotone, redolent of a nineteen seventies disco DJ.

'Your next game starts in seven minutes. Seven minutes, ladies and gentlemen. Place your drink orders. I thank you.'

He turned on Ella, piggy-eyed disgust evident on his moon face. 'What the hell do you think you're playing at? And what the heck are you wearing? You can't wear red shoes, or that ghastly headscarf thing. You've been warned before about this sort of behaviour. We'll be a laughingstock at the National Bingo Callers' finals if this gets out. You're suspended. Go home.'

'I'm not. I quit. You can stick your poxy job.'

WHEN ELLA EMERGED from the staff exit, she had her coat thrown over one arm, and a large handbag swinging from her shoulder. The reality of what her life had become landed with a psychological "flump" like an avalanche at her feet and she was muttering away, giving herself a stern talking to about being potentially homeless in the near future. She was stopped in her tracks by the woman in the biker jacket. It was Val.

'You've pulled. Let's get a drink,' Val said gruffly, lighting a cigarette and walking next to Ella, matching her strides.

'Where's your friend?'

'She's staying. Blind date. Bad idea.' Val shrugged.

Even after nearly eight years had passed, Ella still had to set Val straight. 'You haven't pulled; I'm still not a lesbian, Val, so no funny business. Anyway, where did the rest of you go? I hardly recognised you.' The last time they had seen each other Val had weighed in at an astounding twenty-six stone and had earned the nickname "Fat Val".

'Long story and not a pleasant one, I can assure you. Looks like you found what I lost,' Val said, casting an eye over Ella and wafting her cigarette between two fingers as if conducting an orchestra in two-four time.

'Yeah. I think I did. It's the bloody medication.'

'It suits you.'

'Don't be daft.'

'No, really. You used to be a tiny waif, trying to be invisible. Now look at you, all curves and flowing auburn locks. You look fucking gorgeous.'

They spent the rest of that evening imbibing copious amounts of alcohol and catching up with news of their lives.

IF VAL HADN'T PLACED one of her business cards in Ella's purse at the end of the evening, Ella's life, although it could never have been very ordinary, may perhaps have been less tragic, but not for the reasons you might expect.

3

THE FOLLOWING DAY

Examining herself in the bathroom mirror the next morning, Ella's shoulders drooped. 'What a beautiful sight,' she groaned with resentment as she lifted her breasts, one in each hand, before allowing them to fall and slap against her ribcage. Sticking a finger into her navel, she wiggled it making her rounded belly jiggle. She recalled Val's admiration of her figure, although she couldn't accept it as anything other than an old acquaintance trying to flatter her in sympathy. Either that or Val was making another admirable effort to lead her into homosexual temptation. Then she remembered the job offer.

At first, she hadn't known what to do about finding new employment and, during a fretful, sleepless night, had considered taking up regular waitressing again. Since her spectacular fall from normality seven years earlier, Ella had flitted from one job to another, bringing in money where she could to pay the rent on a ghastly bedsit. It wasn't all bad. She discovered that agency work enabled her to explore possibilities although she took great care to avoid too many split shifts as they were dangerously destabilising.

As far as mental stability was concerned, there had only been a hiccup or three in the last five years and it had to stay that way. Even the momentary lapse at the bingo club was nothing more than a ripple on a pond. She'd done so much worse than that, even before getting herself sectioned.

Prior to landing her regular weekend stint as a bingo caller, she had often worked with a waitress called Ada for an outside catering company. They became firm friends. Ada and Ella covered several conference events together and enjoyed each other's wry sense of humour and in particular Ella loved Ada's northern take on life.

'There's no need to run,' Ada had advised during her new friend's first conference catering experience. 'Carry plates t' table, put 'em down gently, smile at the buggers, then walk off and get some more plates. Not rocket science is it?'

After Ada bravely confessed to having had difficulties with depression, Ella relaxed enough around her to share her own experiences and the two began to exchange strategies for staying on top of their mental health challenges.

'I really have to watch out for my sleep pattern changing, so I'm regimented about exercise, relaxation and keeping to a routine,' Ella told her.

'What happens if you don't?'

'Nothing at first, I get a bit lively, but then all hell breaks loose. It hasn't happened for a while. There's no room for complacency. I learnt that the hard way with two disastrous relapses in the years just after my first mind-blowing, career-shattering, world-rocking meltdown.'

'Don't I know it … and we keep taking the bloody tablets, without fail, or else back off t' funny farm we go.'

Ada was open and endearing and, for Ella, acknowledge-ment of their newfound common ground was like finding another member of her special gang. Someone she didn't need to shy away from through fear of being exposed as a nutcase.

It had been Ada who dared Ella to accept the challenge of becoming an artist's model.

'You'd be ideal. I didn't think I could do it either, but let me tell you summat, I started about three years ago and it completely restored my confidence. You see, my little chicken, because it's art, it's not tacky at all, in fact it's very relaxing. You'd be amazed at how great you feel about your own body.'

Refusing to be persuaded by Ada's arguments, Ella pushed the suggestion to the back of her mind for some time. She continued to run herself ragged serving at tables to earn a few pounds, until she saw an advert in a local magazine several months later. Despite the fact that she'd never heard of such a specialist option, she went along for an audition as a hand model. She didn't get the job, but thanks to Ada's encouragement and the small modelling company in Crewsthorpe who insisted she was perfect, Ella could add an intriguing skill to her résumé - life modelling.

Once over the nerves of the first naked sitting, she enjoyed it immensely, and it was less physically demanding than waiting on tables.

It suited her.

She didn't fit in with the nine-to-fivers, the office skinny-Sarahs or the retail customer service sycophants. Instead she took what modelling contracts she could, served on tables at the odd conference or corporate event and covered her basic bills with the income from the bingo club. Ella would never be rich but she could manage her needs and not have to conform to the requirements of a real career.

Now, having lost the local bingo-calling job, finances would be dire. Ella considered her choices. To ward off the threat of eviction for non-payment of rent, she had toyed with the idea of offering her talents to the large bingo hall in Hollberry. But, in truth, the rumour mill about her unorthodox calling style would preclude her from other mainstream bingo franchises. Never mind an entry into the National Bingo Callers Competition!

On the other hand, Val's job offer had intrigued her.

'I know you used be a nightclub bouncer but what is it that you do now, exactly?' she had asked during her next meeting with Val, a sober affair held in a smoky, sparsely furnished office.

'Nightclub security, if you don't mind. And that was years ago.' Val's features softened as she recalled her time managing the main entrance of a local nightclub in Crewsthorpe. 'Me and Mal used to work the door of Frenzy. What a bloody dive that was back then. Mal was nothing but a wiry scrapper with a gift for talking his way out of trouble, but even then he had my back and I had his.'

'No wonder you two are still mates,'

'Yeah, it's handy having him around. Lots of family contacts in the Asian community too.'

Malik Khan covered many jobs for Val where a male was required, or where technological know-how had to be employed. He was good at that. Depending on circumstances, and when it suited, he could become too British to be Asian or too Asian to be British. In the main he tried hard to be both - a proper trifle of cultures.

Val sighed. 'I've expanded my repertoire into something altogether more reliable than nightclub security. The smell of vomit no longer appeals, so I gave myself a promotion. Besides, I don't 'ave the weight behind me for ejecting half-cut imbeciles onto pavements anymore.' She gave a short laugh which made her cough. 'These days I recover debts and occasionally pick up the odd bit of private investigation work. You know the sort of thing, "my husband's having an affair with his secretary, please help me to catch him out so as I can divorce the bastard and take him to the cleaners." It's quite lucrative as it goes.' She paused to scratch the end of her nose. 'Why don't you give it a try?' she asked. 'It has to be better than shouting numbers out to incontinent old duffers and brain dead council house scum.'

Val was never one for niceties. 'Try this course and see what you think,' she said handing Ella a leaflet, which she took, unfolded and read aloud.

'Become a private investigator. One day taster course for anyone considering a career change but who doesn't know what being a private detective may entail. Why not find out if you've got what it takes?'

WITH HER IMAGINATION running away with her, she decided it was a sensible way of approaching the question of whether or not she had the qualities and characteristics required. 'Ella Fitzwilliam, P.I.,' she said to her reflection in the bathroom mirror before she left her bedsit on the day of the course. 'After all, not just anyone can wear a mac.'

She would have enjoyed the adventure a whole lot more had it not been for the instructor; a chauvinistic old codger, ex-security services, who went by the name of Brian Watts. A grey, unprepossessing individual, he seemed to take pleasure in ridiculing Ella.

'Why on earth would you believe yourself to be suitable for covert surveillance? Look at you with your bright colours, all frocked up with shiny lipstick and fucking great tits sticking out a mile. You'd be no good for anything other than as H.T. material.'

It didn't take her long to discover that "H.T.", in the world of private investigation, stands for "honey trap".

He was probably right. She struggled with the need to

remain inconspicuous and had terrible difficulty in working some of the equipment they were shown; trackers, surveillance cameras, microphones and the like which required a rudimentary understanding of technology – a skill Ella lacked.

Brian Watts spent the day talking to her chest or making unnecessary comments about her weight. The fact that she had an uncanny ability to recognise faces and quickly identify a falsehood, seemed to pass him by. He delighted in belittling her and, in turn, she only tolerated him in order to claim her certificate at the end of the day. There was no way she would allow herself to fail. Val had paid for the course and Ella felt indebted to her for the second time in her life. It never occurred to her to wonder why Val would go to so much trouble to help an old acquaintance, especially one so inept and unsuitable for the job.

ONCE SEMI-QUALIFIED, her first official and unsupervised assignment had been easy. Spying on a man who was attending art classes. An infidelity case. With previous experience put to good use, she had been pleased at how well it had gone and felt a certain sense of pride on its successful completion.

On the final evening of that assignment she could entirely relax. She lay on the velvet chaise longue, one arm propping her trunk upright, the other draped across her accentuated waist allowing her hand and delicate fingers to rest on her uppermost thigh. A breeze had caused ripples of goose bumps to roll from her knees up her thigh and across the left hip, halting only where the folds of the crimson pashmina covered her pale skin. The shiver had brought Ella back from her daydream to the present of the oak panelled room she was in. The chill waft had passed, and the air became warm and still again. Only the scratching sounds of charcoal on paper and the breathing of the artists had gently broken into her consciousness.

Another forty quid in the bank. Cash. Not bad for sitting around semi-naked, she thought. It was relatively easy money. Two forty minute sessions with enough time to eat a banana in the interval and answer a question or two about how she had made the outrageous decision to become an artists' model. Usually the women asked, and the men hovered in the background, keen to understand but not daring to enquire.

'You're very brave.'

'Not really, I just have to sit still wearing no clothes. It's not technical or taxing. In fact, I find it allows me time to think; quiet contemplation if you like. I switch off from the fact that I'm being stared at.'

He was there again as he had been for the preceding seven weeks. Mr Alan Jenkins, a mouse of a man who rarely spoke. During the time that Ella had been contracted to pose for the art group he'd barely interacted with anyone other than the art teacher who encouraged and guided the students in their efforts to master drawing the human body.

'Alan, you have a real eye for this lady's curves and somehow you've managed to capture the glossiness of her hair. I'm impressed. This must be helping with that master-piece of yours.'

It hadn't taken long to confirm that Val would get her money from the client and Mr Alan Jenkins would be none-the-wiser he'd been under surveillance. His over-anxious wife would be reassured that he wasn't having an affair after nearly thirty years of marriage and he'd merely taken up an innocent hobby, just like he said. His change of habits, furtive telephone calls and the money missing from their account could all be explained away. His "masterpiece" turned out to be a painting of his wife, using a photograph he'd taken in their garden. A gift for their pearl wedding anniversary.

As Ella dressed and stuffed the cash into her purse from a gushingly grateful art teacher, she smiled, content. A happy ending for Mr and Mrs Jenkins, the successful completion of a case, and money. What a result!

If she'd known what Val had in store as her next assignment, Ella would have offered to remain as life-model in residence for the art group and lived like a pauper.

But she didn't know.

She couldn't know.

4

THE SEARCH

JANUARY

Lorna placed her bowl and mug into the dishwasher as Konrad continued to comment on the details of the article outlining the disappearance of Harry Drysdale.

'Do you want a lift to the station, Kon, or not?' she asked as she reached for the empty cafetière and her husband's drained coffee cup.

He looked up at her. The expression as he stared down the opening of her blouse changed from one of lecherousness to realisation. 'Shit. I'm running late - Bloody Barney's fault for dragging me into the pub again last night. What time is the next train?' Konrad leapt up from the table, chair screeching across the flagstone floor, and checked the kitchen clock. 'If we're lucky, I should just make the twelve minutes past. Give me two shakes.'

'Don't forget your eye-patch this time. I'm used to it, but I don't think the executives will ever forget that last meeting. You frightened the bejesus out of most of them.'

'Funny though.'

Lorna and Konrad had adapted to the sight of his scars and the loss of his right eye, but the pain of the attack that had caused them sometimes resurfaced and caught them unawares. Instead of dwelling on the events they used humour as a shield and never ventured to discuss in detail how his eye was lost.

Gliding across the room to the hallway, Lorna then pulled on robust leather boots and wrapped her favourite scarf around her neck before shrugging into her thick winter coat. She held Konrad's overcoat out for him as he stumbled towards the front door to their old stone cottage, forcing his feet into a pair of heavy leather brogues.

'Pass my "twat hat" there's a good girl. It keeps the wind out a bit,' Konrad said, ramming a tweed cap onto his head. He pulled the brim down against the icy blast that greeted them both when they stepped onto the driveway.

'Oh my, that's brisk!' Lorna exclaimed pulling on her gloves.

They were shuddering as Lorna started the engine. 'Hmmm. You may have to catch the next train. Grab the ice scraper from the glove box and do the front windscreen. I'll do the back with my Costco card.'

The journey to the station turned out to be a treacherous one. Frosty roads, frozen puddles, black ice. On a sharp bend the VW Golf they were in narrowly missed a car coming the other way. 'That was a tad close,' Lorna said, her quavering voice revealing the level of concern at the near miss.

'Good driving though,' Konrad conceded.

'Go on. Finish the sentence ... "not bad for a girl". I know that's what you were thinking, you old misogynist.' Lorna was teasing him again.

'Wrong word, my love. I may occasionally trivialise women, mostly the stupid ones, but I have nothing against you lot as a gender. Some of you are quite fetching.'

'I rest my case. You actually referred to women as "you lot". Good grief, man, no wonder the feminist hard-liners have it in for you on a regular basis.' Lorna was laughing, shaking her head, mocking. Konrad knew she accepted his old-fashioned attitudes and he in turn revelled in her chiding him for them.

He retaliated.

'See if you can manage to pretend to be productive today, there's a good wife. I'm not fooled. As far as I can tell, this working from home arrangement is a front so that you sneak off for coffee with Netty. I lay the blame firmly at her podgy little feet. You give the impression that you're researching for my next documentary series and she tells everyone that she's in her home studio editing my current one. Nice plan between the two of you.'

'Envy. It's not an attractive look on you. Now, get ready to leap out but don't slip on the pavement, at your age you'll break something.'

'Cheeky madam! Not so much of the old. The "forties" are the new "twenties" I'll have you know. '

'That makes you nearly thirty then, doesn't it?' Lorna brought the Golf to a steady standstill at the drop-off area outside Lensham station. Konrad leant over and kissed her before he swivelled in his seat to leave. He made as dignified an exit as he could manage wrapped in his large overcoat, carrying a leather document case and newspaper. Safely out of the car he waved at Lorna before closing the door.

'I'll phone you if I find anything out about Harry. You do the same. Okay?' He knew his wife well enough to be certain that she would return home, fire up the laptop and begin investigating Harry Drysdale's disappearance.

'Sure,' she replied. 'I owe that man my freedom, so the least we can do is help to find him. Do what you can, Kon. It sounds really odd. Not like Harry at all.' She blew a kiss as the door clunked shut. 'Oh and give my love to Eliza, and have a lovely lunch.' Although her voice was muffled, her words could still be heard. Her husband smiled.

Konrad had been swinging between excitement at seeing his daughter for the first time in months, and trepidation at the meeting scheduled for afternoon. A meeting that could make or break his TV career. He'd kept this matter of concern from Lorna, and the secrecy weighed on him heavily.

There had been rumblings that Channel 7 wanted to pull the plug on his documentary series, *The Truth Behind the Lies*, because it was too formulaic. His research team would identify a possible miscarriage of justice, or a perpetrator who was insistent of their innocence, and Konrad would interview them in prison, explore the story and expose the injustice or the devious nature of the guilty person he was interviewing. Other journalists and TV celebrity faces had done the same and a new slant was required to keep his career afloat.

Once on the train, Konrad had time to plan his defence and generate a counter-argument or at the very least some fresh ideas.

With little warning, the meeting of the executive board had also been called to review the contract, which was nearing its sell by date. Konrad suspected that his ex-wife Delia was behind this particular change of fortune.

It was Delia who had saved his stagnant career the first time round, and when his marriage went sour, she only remained as his business manager and agent because the money and kudos were important to her. She had cut the final strings eighteen months ago in favour of her new love, pretentious TV executive producer Robin De La Croix, who had infinitely more money and more influence than Konrad ever did. In Konrad's eyes the man was nothing more than a boring superficial plonker. So much of a supercilious berk in fact that he and Delia made a perfect match. No more than she deserved. But the question for Konrad was, could Delia be cruel enough to see him dispensed with? - Her ex-husband, father to her children? And the answer? Probably.

He stared around at the passengers on the train, he could usually tell if people recognised him. Being a regular on their television sets, he wasn't hard to miss. Silver haired, with an eye patch that matched the tie he wore, tall, with a deliberately piratical and confident air about him.

He always took a seat in the last carriage and placed himself so that he could see up the length of it without having to turn his head. All the end train carriages on that line had been decommissioned from their previous first-class status due to lack of use and overcrowding in second-class carriages. Fortunately most travellers were unaware of this change and often Konrad had the place to himself at off-peak times. On that day there was a sprinkling of other travellers probably heading for the last days of the January sales in London.

A curiously mismatched couple took his attention away from reading the Daily Albion. They had entered the carriage behind him at Lensham Station and made their way to seats with a table. The man was of athletic build and conventionally handsome, she too was striking, but for different reasons. Her long hair framed a round and radiant face. She reminded him of someone.

The woman on the train was animated, chatting to her companion as she tucked into a bag of Maltesers, popping them into her mouth one after the other as the slender man encouragingly looked on.

The beautiful woman - for without doubt she was stunning in her looks - wobbled with laughter at something the man had said. Her whole body bounced, with waves of flesh rolling and subsiding in gentle rhythm with her tuneful tittering. A Malteser had escaped and landed in her cleavage.

Konrad held his breath as the man aimed a finger and thumb toward his partner's breasts to retrieve the ball of chocolate before it melted.

'Eat up, Rhona,' said the young man, placing the Malteser on her tongue. 'We can't have you missing out on the calories. There's no fun without flesh.'

Those were the words that Harry Drysdale had used the last time Konrad had seen him. "There's no fun without flesh".

5

FOUR WEEKS BEFORE HARRY'S DISAPPEARANCE

Marcus Carver buzzed through to the phone in reception. 'Hello, Geeta. Is the surgery timetable for tomorrow still rammed? Or have I been reprieved of a late finish? I promised Lydia I wouldn't be late home for my birthday, not that I'm bothered, I'd rather forget how old I am. However, my wife has been planning something with the children, and until now it had totally slipped my mind. Could you check for me before Karen comes in with the next patient? Thank you kindly.'

The anticipation was starting to build. Wednesday morning clinic was well underway, filling his time and keeping his eager mind on the present. The rush of expectation usually came in the early afternoon as he prepared to leave the office with his overnight bag, a leather holdall, swinging him towards the door and the railway station.

There was a sharp salvo of knocks before Karen stepped into the stark and modern clinic room. She was willowy and efficient, dressed in a brilliant-white surgical tunic and trousers. 'Sorry, Marcus, Geeta says tomorrow's list is as it stands, but she has managed to preserve your late start time.

I hope that helps to reduce the travel stress. Shall I ask her to phone Lydia for you?'

'Thanks for the offer, Karen, but I'll break the news to my wife when I phone her later. Not to worry. It's nothing unusual. I'm always bloody late getting home on a Thursday.'

Karen smiled with implicit understanding. 'Your new client is ready - Rhona Charles. Here are the notes from the initial consultation if you need them, but the main electronic document file is up to date on the system. I've completed the baseline physical checks and explained the purpose of today's visit. Rhona's fiancé can't be here again today, so I'll chaperone.'

Holding out his hand for the folder, Marcus thanked his clinic nurse as she returned to the main waiting room to collect his patient. He hoped she hadn't seen his fingers trembling.

He stared at the name on the case notes and immediately summoned up the memory of the first time Rhona Charles had entered his consultation room, nervous, and slightly breathless. The younger ones often tugged at his sympathetic side. Without his help their self-esteem, and their long-term health could be in considerable jeopardy. Rhona was one of those. He couldn't be angry at her lack of self-control because he had heard the story before. When she sat before him in his plush office she had described herself as a survivor of bullying, but she wasn't. It was obvious to him that she was still a victim, and that made her vulnerable to flattery. Plain vulnerable.

Rhona Charles was as much a product of bullying as those who took to drugs and alcohol to cope with the psychological and emotional impacts from years of torment. She didn't self-harm, not in the usual sense of the term. She didn't cut herself to expunge the emotional pain and self-loathing. No. She chose a longer route to harm, a gratifying method of instant reward.

Food.

'It's a double-edged sword, Doctor. I was bullied for being the chubby child, but I derive such pleasure from eating.'

Rhona was articulate, intelligent, forthright, and incredibly overweight.

'Daddy was furious with the health spa in Hungary. He paid all that money, and I only lost half a stone, which I've put back on again. He says psychology is a waste of time and that's why I'm here; the last resort before the wedding. Surgery.'

Marcus counselled himself to maintain professional boundaries, to focus on the clinical issues and not allow his lustful desires to emerge. Even so, the consultation had been a delicate balance of diplomacy and truth. Marcus assumed that, like most of the rich women that entered his lair, Rhona was expecting him to be able to sculpt her into a slender version of herself. He could only guess at what she had imagined possible. Therefore, he started with a hit of reality. He asked her to stand and turn slowly on the spot.

'Rhona, you are a bright confident woman and for that reason I will be very direct with you. I can't make you into a model from a magazine. You will not have boyish hips and a flat stomach because that isn't how your frame or genetics have designed you to be.'

And you are already beautiful.

She was the archetypal jolly, bonny-faced, overweight young woman, hiding a frail soul. Despite the aching in his groin, he kept a steady tone of voice as he moved around her. All the while he made use of medical terminology to provide reassurance for his patient and to keep his own thoughts on track. Feeling her abdomen from behind, weighing her breasts in his upturned palms and then placing firm hands on her hips and buttocks he gauged the task ahead.

'What we will do first is to create a three-dimensional map of your body as it is now. From there we can explore your choices from straightforward liposuction to more radical surgery. In the meantime, I suggest you reconsider the use of exercise, diet and supplementary fat binding medication. Recovery from cosmetic surgery can take weeks, even months, so you could opt for a gastric band...'

Tears had started to tip over his patient's lower eyelids as he indicated for her to take a seat while he made notes.

'I can't,' she said. 'The thought of not being able to put forkful after forkful into my mouth is unimaginable. I need the taste sensations, the texture... of everything. I don't want to feel full and I definitely can't cope with those awful tablets again. The smell was revolting to say nothing of the ever-present fear of... what's that expression they use? Overflow.'

As a surgeon, Marcus could offer her salvation from type-two diabetes, reduce her future blood pressure problems, save her from a life of snoring and sleep apnoea, joint pain and premature death. Then again, this young lady had more money at her disposal than common sense and he could feel her determination to head straight for the cosmetic surgery solution. It saddened him.

'Take a couple of weeks to think it through,' Marcus said. 'And read this information thoroughly. It's a drastic step.' *And such a crying shame.*

Once she had been given time to apprise herself of the facts and the risks of surgery, he would need to see her again. It was important to thoroughly assess the best options, depending on the integrity of her skin and the distribution of body fat, before he took her cash.

Reputation and pride in positive outcomes meant as much to him as financial gain although in essence the very nature of his surgical skills ensured his income stream was more a thunderous torrent of wealth.

WHEN RHONA WAS ESCORTED into his clinic room that Wednesday, Marcus grinned to himself. Her make-up had been meticulously applied; she wore designer label clothes, which draped and swung over her midriff hiding the folds of fatty flesh beneath. She had accentuated her cleavage, her hair, her eyes and her shapely legs, making every effort to conceal her shame and boost her assets.

'Welcome, Rhona. Lovely to see you again. I understand Karen has explained what we need to discover about you today. You've done all the nasty blood tests and the rest of the physical examinations. Now it's decision time. There's no hurry but I do need you to undress behind the curtain leaving your briefs on. Make use of the robe if it helps you to remain more comfortable. Karen will stay with us at all times during the examination and I will be thorough and as thoughtful as possible. Please say if at any time you feel unable to tolerate the examination and I'll stop.'

This was a routine speech, one performed at each such appointment and one that Marcus used as a steadying professional mantra.

While his patient undressed and chatted to Karen, he brought up the computer-generated image of Rhona's body on the screen of his desktop. Apple shaped. Large breasts, oversized abdomen and buttocks; Rhona's arms and legs were relatively slim in comparison but there was an unsightly area of fat deposited on her inner thighs. Liposuction was a possibility for her legs, but the torso and her neck would, most likely, need the assistance of a knife. Everything hinged on the state of her skin. Elasticity and healthy skin would be the keys to a good result and to test that out he had to examine Rhona at intimately close range. He needed to palpate her flesh to feel the contours and lie of the adipose tissue beneath the skin. This was a potentially upsetting experience for patients without doubt, but for Marcus it was like putting a large vodka in front of an alcoholic.

The two ladies were exchanging thoughts on what Rhona had read in the leaflets and information booklets given to her.

'I understand the risks. He explained everything. Do you know, on one hand I'm almost relieved that he turned out not to be a crusty old man, but on the other he's a bit too good looking, really. Don't you think?'

Karen gave immediate reassurance. 'Don't worry. You're in safe hands. He's happily married with two children and a gorgeous wife. Living the dream.'

'Your staff here all seem to be stunning. A great advert for the practice I suppose. How does he cope surrounded by such attractive women each day?'

Marcus could hear every word and tuned in for Karen's answer. She laughed, dismissive of the inference. 'I don't think it ever crosses his mind. He's a professional, Miss Charles. We all are.'

By the way she spoke in short bursts, Marcus could hear Rhona's nervousness. 'He won't try to talk me out of it will he? I want to look my best for Tom on our wedding day. He doesn't want me too much smaller. He likes me as I am, but I need to look less like a whale, for me. My bum is fine, big but sturdy, as they say. My tits are my best feature by far, but my fat jelly belly has to go.'

'You'll be fine. Ultimately the decision is yours.' Karen was again the soothing voice of reason.

It sometimes amused Marcus that his patients, no matter how well educated, seemed to accept that a thin curtain pulled around them constituted total privacy. Rhona didn't whisper, she practically announced to the world her view on her body.

Marcus centred himself as he approached the examination couch, a bespoke item of equipment designed for the bariatric specialist. Heavy-duty hydraulics and wide upholstered reclining seat with an adjustable arm and footrests. The touch of a button helped to alter the angle and height.

Rhona was one of his more agile patients and he opted to begin by examining her back as she sat with her legs dangling towards the floor, facing away from him on the side of the couch. Karen knew the routine. What she didn't know was why he always chose to begin with the examination of the patient's back and shoulders.

'Marcus always makes sure he has warmed his hands and he'll talk you through everything as he goes along. If you're not certain, just ask.'

Suddenly Rhona was unnervingly mute as she allowed the robe to slip from her shoulders, exposing her back and the Dimples of Venus at top of her buttocks. Marcus stared in silent appreciation while she kept her head bowed.

Before placing his hands on her shoulders, he launched into his patter about the CGI information and what implications that had for the outcome of Rhona's proposed surgery. Then he began. The skin beneath his hands was soft and blemish free.

'Your shoulder area is fine, and, as I assess further, I see there is a well-defined waist, or there will be once we've tucked that tummy. I would suggest a little liposuction to reduce the underarm bulges in the area where your bra pushes them upwards. That way you won't have to worry about the line of your wedding dress.'

He felt her relax.

'Thank you.'

'Don't thank me quite so soon. Now when did you say the wedding date was set for?'

'Next June.'

'That's great,' Karen said, standing at the head of the couch. 'You'll have plenty of recovery time if we schedule surgery for the end of January and we won't spoil your Christmas. Now then, could you sit back on the couch, rest your legs for a while. Marcus needs to plan out your abdominoplasty.'

Taking care to look confidently into his patient's eyes, Marcus stood back as Karen helped Rhona to take position on the examination couch.

I am aiming for the umbilicus. I am palpating to keep my mind from wandering.

His hands moved confidently, pressing deeply, as he assessed. 'The skin is in very good condition. After some liposuction here, I think we will go for the tuck, but not too drastic. May I examine the areas on the inside of your thighs please, Rhona? I'm pretty certain that lipo will be beneficial, but I'd like to check. I don't need to touch for long.'

The agony of resisting the urge to probe deep inside her caused Marcus physical pain and the muscles in his right forearm cramped. He closed his eyes, moved his hand away from the edge of the briefs she wore and gave a final reassuring smile to Karen. 'That's all I need to see.'

'What about my chin?' asked Rhona as she sat up, not bothering to pull her robe around her; all embarrassment had seemingly melted away with the prospect of a miracle. 'Or should I say chins… can you do anything?' she asked as her hands cupped her lower jaw, fingers pushing the flesh into her neck.

Marcus, thinking the examination was complete had dropped his guard. He pirouetted on the balls of his feet and sucked in a short breath.

Look at her eyes. Stay professional. This is what you do. This is what you are. Keep your patients safe at all times. Maintain your defences.

He coughed. 'Gosh. I'd almost forgotten. We did say about a bit of a lift to rid you of those lady-jowls, if I remember rightly.' He prodded a few times to make the examination look authentic and meaningful, but it wasn't strictly necessary. His forearms brushed against her breasts and he backed away before his resistance failed him completely.

'Yes. We'll make a note of what we have agreed and book you in for surgery. Karen will take you through all the details. I'll leave you to get dressed.'

He was holding himself stiffly and his jaw was beginning to ache. If she hadn't been so confident and composed, his struggles would have been minimal, but she was, and for that reason the level of sexual tension resulted in a jabbing headache and an erection that needed to be hidden behind his office desk.

The water in the glass rippled as he lifted it to his lips. Not the steady hands of a surgeon, no, these were the tremors of a dreadful craving. Paracetamol may alleviate the thud in his temples, but the underlying condition could not be so easily remedied.

His desires were threatening to break free from their bonds and destroy him. He needed his fix.

6

NOVEMBER

'We've found him,' Val croaked as she threw paperwork across the desk for Ella to check. The pokey office was a place lingered in for as short a time as possible. It was far more helpful for anyone's future health to meet elsewhere because Val smoked like a chimney and cared little for Ella's irritation and complaints about the legal requirements for a smoke-free workplace. 'It's my office. I'll do what I bleedin' well like,' she reminded her whenever the subject of clean air arose.

'The main man?'

'No, the other one. The posh nob. Old-fashioned tracking and sleuthing was required. I asked Mal to keep him under close tabs and he's identified a particular place our mark regularly frequents. This man's private life isn't newsworthy and I doubt it will bother him too much if it was disclosed to the general public but his little peccadillo is a shared interest with—'

'But, Val,' Ella interrupted, 'if we keep spending time on this, you'll go bankrupt unless you have some mystery client who's loaded.'

Val shrugged. 'Might have, you never know.'

After taking a long drag and blowing air thoughtfully away from Ella's face, Val stubbed out her cigarette. 'Ideally, I want both of them to pay for what they've done, but most of all I want to be sure he's not still screwing up young people's lives. He's a fucking pervert and I know that lawyer of his is protecting him.'

'You didn't tell Mal what this is all about, did you?'

'What do you take me for? Some fucking moron? Of course I didn't. He thinks it's the usual unfaithful lover scenario. The less he knows, the better.'

'But if Malik's done all that surveillance then where do I come in?' Ella asked.

'We have a timescale to keep to and the next move requires your particular skills,' Val said.

'My skills? Are you sure? And a deadline?' Ella asked, keen to hear where her new career was taking her next.

Val fiddled with her pen and seemed to be searching for the right words. Hesitantly she said, 'Ella, I don't have the attributes for the next part of the case. You'll have to be the ears and the eyes on these two men from the inside.'

'For God's sake, Val. You don't need to sound like Sam Spade. Where am I going and why?'

Val wasn't prone to diplomacy but, for once, she chose with care how she broke the news to Ella about her next assignment. 'I'm too thin,' she said hoarsely.

'That's hardly my fault,' Ella replied. 'If you cut back on the fags and ate more, then you'd put on weight. The solution is simple.' She smiled at her employer, not knowing why she had begun her explanation with that phrase about body size. Not questioning why it was relevant.

Val sprang to her feet. 'Come on, it's easier if I show you. Grab your coat.'

They drove for nearly an hour before heading off the

motorway and into the town of Lensham, not twenty minutes away from where Ella had spent several weeks sitting naked in an evening art class each Wednesday.

'The station has direct fast trains to London. That's what makes it so convenient for our man. He stays overnight whenever he can, usually on a Wednesday. He travels alone, but Mal says he meets a male friend at the station and they either hop into a cab or walk together until they reach their destination. Mal has taken a couple of photos and I'm damned sure it's who we think it is, but *you* know what he looks like, beyond any doubt.'

'His face is firmly and regrettably etched in my mind, as well you know. Where's the hotel?'

Val parked up in the station car park. 'Twenty minutes free parking gives us enough time. Where they stay is within walking distance, come on you need the exercise.'

'Very funny…' Ella screwed up her eyes.

Contrasting in size and style, the two ladies walked the damp November streets where the smell of late autumn was in the air. Tree-lined avenues branched off a busy main road and from one of these, between houses, a narrow single-track roadway led to a handsome regency-style residence. Three stories high, with sash windows, and fronted by black cast-iron railings, it had a classic appeal. To the left of an imposing lacquered front door was a sign, rather like a plaque, the word *Buxham's* was painted in silver calligraphy on a black gloss board. *For the larger life …* was written beneath, as if from a quote. No phone number, no email, no website address.

'How classy,' Ella said.

Val released a series of rasping claggy coughs before being able to speak again. 'It's not on Trip-advisor nor Google ads but they do have a restaurant and bar licence and are a fully regulated premises with accommodation,' she informed Ella as they strolled past, nonchalantly. 'It is in fact a club, a private members' club.'

Withholding a vital piece of information, Val insisted that, as they walked by, they carefully scout what they could of the perimeter, which was nigh on impossible. An enormous solid oak sliding gate remained closed, preventing a view into the private car park. Either side of the main house were curved high walls, stately in their magnificence. The short roadway was wide enough for one vehicle to enter from the avenue but opened up to a sweeping turning circle in front of Buxham's main entrance; one-way in or out for any vehicle. For members arriving on foot, the main entrance or a discreet plain door through the high wall with a touchpad entry system were the two choices.

'Act as if we're lost.' Val pulled a pamphlet, advertising a local tattoo artist, from the inside pocket of her leather biker jacket, stopping to consult it. 'We can't hang around and there's nowhere to observe from without it being blatant what we're up to.'

She pointed back out the way they had come and they meandered to the avenue before speaking again.

'I take it you have a plan for me to become a member.'

The harsh laughter from Val answered that question. 'Very amusing.' She sighed. 'Look, Ella, I know you're not experienced enough for this but we've got no choice. I registered you with an agency that has been asked to send suitable candidates for interview at Buxham's. Here's your CV.'

7

FOUR WEEKS BEFORE HARRY'S DISAPPEARANCE

Ella smoothed the material of her pencil skirt, pushing the hem to her knees. Interviews used to petrify her but, since starting with agency work and joining Val in her peculiar world, they had become like acts of a play. She took on the persona of the candidate they most wanted to hire and on this occasion she had excelled herself. Ella had been invited back to Buxham's for a second interview.

'How would you feel about taking on the front of house management in our restaurant? Teresa is going on maternity leave and we have been struggling to find the right cover. Your CV and your references are excellent and more importantly you have the personality and style we need.'

It was irrelevant to Ella that she wasn't supposed to have been applying for a change of career and that Val had embellished quite a chunk of the employment history. When the offer was made Ella was flattered to have made such a positive impression, but within a matter of seconds the implications began to dawn.

'What an unexpected offer.' She smiled gamely. Beneath the neat suit and silky blouse her heart was hammering, pumping blood to her brain, which had put in an urgent request for supplies of oxygen to fuel the ideas department. She couldn't turn down the opportunity, but she'd have to try to strike a compromise if she were to avoid taking on unsettling shift patterns.

'That may depend on the package and the hours you expect me to work, but I'll certainly consider your offer with all seriousness.' She was stringing the interview panel along, winging it. The three managers looked to one another. The lady in the middle, whose name Ella had failed to register, took the lead.

'We quite understand. Before you commit to any contract, we need to ensure you have read and absorbed *all* the information we sent to you about the club. You should have a good basic knowledge of how it functions, to ensure you are aware of our ethos and expected standards. As you realise, our market is highly specialised.'

There was an intonation to her voice. Playing with Ella. Piquing her interest.

Maybe I should have read the information more thoroughly. It sounds like I might have missed something, Ella thought.

'We pay well for a forty-five hour week. You'll work late afternoon and evenings with an option for overtime especially at busy times of the year - only three weeks to go until Christmas,' she added with a chirpy inflection. 'We can offer you live-in accommodation and with regular days off you'll work five days out of seven. A three-month probationary period will apply during which either party can opt to withdraw from the contract with good reason. How does that sound to you?'

Ella was stunned. For a brief moment she believed she would have to decline on the basis that the hours would preclude her from undertaking such a role. Waitressing was what she had applied for, not a full-time management post, but the prospect of escape from the hellhole bedsit was most enticing and she felt her eagerness rise.

Talk slowly and don't gabble. Breathe.

Ella sought her internally memorised music playlist and pulled Nimrod into her head to keep the scales of her emotions in balance. Big changes were risky. 'That sounds very tempting, but perhaps I should take up your suggestion of a guided tour and full introduction to the club ethos, before I commit myself.'

'Very wise. Let's start with showing you the restaurant and kitchen. What did you think to the menu examples in your information pack?'

Ella couldn't help but grin. It was the descriptions of delicious meals and tasty temptations that had sidetracked her from reading the rest of the details about Buxham's club. Anywhere that made food sound that good was worth considering. When she thought she had been applying for a waitressing job she had dreamt about swiping tasty morsels each evening, stuffing them into her mouth and relishing the exquisite oral sensations.

The club's rooms and corridors were sumptuously decorated, somehow summoning more thoughts of food. Warm browns and creams, or strawberry and green shades dominated the themes. The restaurant area was subtle in its design. Tables in booths, gentle lighting where it was needed and a spacious layout to respect privacy without the area being stark. As she gazed about her, Ella approved of the tasteful Christmas decorations that served to enhance the amber of the woodwork, gold brocade of the upholstery and well-chosen artwork.

She was admiring the unusual lighting on the walls when, without warning, she stumbled to a halt.

'Oh God, that's me!' she exclaimed.

The words fell from her lips without bidding. There,

hanging in front of her, was a charcoal life drawing, in a plain frame, mounted in burgundy to accentuate the lines of grey on a cream background.

Carla Lewis, the manageress escorting her, flashed a knowing look. 'A local artist is a member here. He donated it only a few weeks ago. We recognised you at interview, even *with* your clothes on. I suppose it goes to show how honest you were on your application. You'll be a real asset to Buxham's. Don't you think?'

8

THE SEARCH

Konrad felt a tugging deep in his chest as he saw his daughter, Eliza, enter the Italian restaurant, heading straight for him. She always knew precisely where she would find her father; in the corner tucked away from prying eyes and guarded by the owner, Franco, who was vigilant and protective of his regular customers, especially ones as famous and generous as Konrad Neale.

As he stood to greet her, Eliza wrapped her arms around him and they embraced with equal force, happy to be reunited. It was a welcome treat, as far as her father was concerned, that Eliza did not have her boyfriend in tow. Mason was a nice enough chap but his American drawl lent a certain disinterested and patronising note to conversations that Konrad found tiresome. In truth, he wished for someone more dynamic for his lively and intelligent daughter. Mason wasn't up to the job. He could never reveal this to Eliza, nor the fact that he referred to boring Mason as *soppy-bollocks*, for if she ever found out he'd be ex-communicated and he couldn't bear the thought of that.

'You look more beautiful every time I see you,' he said,

holding his daughter at arm's length and getting the measure of her smart outfit and neatly plaited hair. 'The new job seems to be suiting you.'

Eliza effervesced with enthusiasm for her recent change of career. 'I'm absolutely loving it. No regrets at all. None. Well, apart from not seeing you as often as I'd like.' She wriggled out of her full-length coat. As if by magic Franco appeared to alleviate her of the burden of this and a couple of shopping bags which gave away the fact that she'd been spending her hard earned salary on books and clothes. When she sat opposite her father, she stared deep into his one working eye, examining every furrow on his scarred and pitted brow. 'What's up?'

Konrad shrugged. 'Nothing.'

'That's what teenagers say when they're trying to hide something. Please don't pretend with me, I'm too familiar with your facial expressions to be fobbed off with childish denials.'

He threw his red paper serviette onto the table. 'Bloody hell, Eliza. How do you do that?'

'A gift I learnt from my amazing father who can read body language like no other human being, that's how.' She grinned, taking her serviette from the wineglass and copying her father by launching it onto the placemat in front of her. They both laughed.

Franco approached to take their order before beating a hasty retreat to the kitchen to shout the order to Lucio, the chef. The chatter from the kitchen was a cheerful and energetic chorus of Italian banter and short bursts of song. The whole place had a charming, positive atmosphere, an escape for Konrad from the plastic world of media parasites that soured his enjoyment of life.

'Well?'

Eliza was waiting for an explanation and Konrad was

cornered. She was as determined to get to the truth as he would usually be when investigating a miscarriage of justice, or seeking out a story for his documentary series. His shoulders sagged as a long breath escaped from his nostrils. 'I think they are about to pull *The Truth Behind the Lies*, so I could be an unemployed celebrity, doomed to star in dodgy adverts for mobility scooters or pantos at Christmas next year. My only other projects are participating in the celebrity Bake Off thing and a guest spot on Countdown. Penury and obscurity are calling my name and laughing at me.'

Eliza was quiet. Too quiet. She fiddled with the tablecloth and reached for a glass of water. Konrad twigged why without having to question his daughter in depth. 'Your mother let slip then?'

'Not exactly. I overheard a little bird on the house phone when I popped in to see Mum on Monday. D. L. C. was plotting your downfall.'

D. L. C. was an accepted abbreviation for Robin De La Croix, used by all who knew him apart from Konrad's ex-wife, Delia. She hated the label.

'Channel 7 are looking for a more dynamic and interactive documentary series, more ...' Eliza paused, looking down at her cutlery, 'more ... Louis Theroux.'

Konrad puffed. 'God, I knew you were going to say that.'

'They want ideas and they want them quickly, but I'm pretty certain the other executives are determined to keep you as the front man, so if you can generate ideas of your own you can have control over the creative side.'

'Bloody marvellous. I've got approximately three hours to come up with a winning pitch. Couldn't you have warned me a few days ago?' The irritation in Konrad's voice pricked icy holes in Eliza's warmth towards her father.

'I shouldn't be telling you at all,' she countered. 'And shouting at me won't help.'

'Quite right. I'm sorry.' He was. His features softened, and he hung his head like a child would in response to a well-deserved admonishment.

Eliza continued. 'Anyway, I had to pretend I needed a wee so I could listen in on the upstairs extension. The upshot is that your big boss Dino Ledbetter remains a fan of yours, which without doubt irritates the hell out of D.L.C. And it goes without saying that mother is unimpressed by his loyalty to you. So, if you can keep the top man interested, then you can save your own skin.'

'Who was he talking to, did you hear?'

'D.L.C.? Some bloke by the name of Stuart.'

Konrad stared hard at his daughter. 'I can't quite believe you listened in to their conversation. I'm stunned at how downright devious you've become.'

'*Are* you stunned?'

'Not really...' Konrad put down his knife. 'Look, Eliza, thanks for going to all that trouble but please don't do it again. I don't want to drive a larger wedge between me and your mother than the giant sized one that already exists.' He knew that his daughter's motivation and determination were ingrained in her soul. She had his genetics, his sense of pride and he feared for her. However, he also respected her opinions.

'Stop worrying about me or Mum and listen for a minute, Dad. Here's my thinking. *The Truth Behind the Lies* could expand into underworlds. The lengths people go to hide the reality about their secret lives before they are exposed. Not just murderers, more than that. The bent copper, the fraudulent banker, the deceitful wife, the philandering husband; real cases, real lives.'

Konrad wore a strange far away expression. 'Disappearing barristers.'

'Pardon?'

9

WEDNESDAY 6TH DECEMBER

Val was waiting for Ella in the café around the corner from Lensham Station. Lack of creative inventiveness had resulted in it being known simply as The Old Station Café. Impatiently Val repeatedly picked up her mobile phone, checking for messages, each time replacing it on the table next to her coffee cup. The endless Christmas carols, blaring out from a radio in the kitchen, increased in volume every time a member of staff launched themselves through the swing door carrying a tray. A brief smile changed the general direction of the wrinkles on Val's face as Ella bounced through the café entrance sending a brass bell jingling above the closing door.

'You could have called to put me out of my misery. Well? What happened? Are we on?'

Unwrapping her coat and shuffling herself free, Ella was beaming. 'We are on. I got the senior hostess job, live in, plus a wage. I can take Gordon the goldfish with me and I recommended Ada for the job as a waitress. If she gets it, I'll have her there to keep an eye on me. Oh, and there's an extremely useful three-month probationary period. I'm hoping that will be long enough.'

'I hear a 'but' coming.'

'But… I need to pay rent on my bedsit if I take the live-in job, and it's too far for me to travel if I don't.'

'I'll cover that cost as your payment. Will that do you?'

With relief Ella sat back. 'Yes. That's great. I've told them I can start next week, but they suggested I might like to bring a friend for dinner this evening to get the feel of the place. Fancy a slap-up meal? You look like you could use it and it could be handy, being a Wednesday. There's a fair probability our targets will show up.'

Val hesitated. 'I'm not sure if that's a wise move for either of us. You are already buzzing, which is a bad sign, and I don't want to be seen by either of those conniving bastards. On the other hand… Give me the insider's gen on the place. What are we dealing with?'

She waved to the waitress who took their order without cracking her make-up or achieving any degree of eye contact.

Ella found the scene amusing. 'Enjoy your job, do you?' she asked, dipping her head in an effort to force the waitress to meet her gaze.

The girl of indeterminate age, dark-rooted straggly platinum-coloured hair tied back in a loose bun, shrugged as she cleared away Val's empties. 'It's aw'right. Want anyfing t'w'eat?'

'No, thank you. We're eating out later at Buxham's. Do you know it?'

Finally, the waitress crossed the line from ignorance to vaguely sociable. She raised one heavily sculpted eyebrow and reluctantly looked at the faces of the two ladies sitting at the corner table. 'I know of it. Private place for posh twats who can afford it.' She scoured Val with her panda-black eyeliner eyes and gave a derisory snarl. 'They won't let you in looking like that.'

Ella swallowed hard and waited for the riposte from Val that arrived right on cue. 'Is that right Miss Queen of the Undead? And since when did you become the judge and jury on dress etiquette for private clubs?'

The girl was unfazed. 'I'm just sayin' you should neaten up a bit, even diesel dykes should 'ave standards.'

As Val's lower jaw headed for the table, the girl sauntered off in the direction of the service area where she slapped the paper order on the counter.

Ella, with eyes wide and an impish grin, held back, stifling the belly laugh that threatened to escape. She bit her lips together and opened her eyes wide.

Val blinked, leant forward and whispered, 'That cheeky fuckin' little madam thinks I'm scruffy.'

'Well she does have a point, Val. A dear friend you may be, but if we're heading out for dinner with the well-to-do, you'll have to snazz up. Emo-waitress got the diesel dyke bit bang on.'

'I don't know what you're laughing at; diesel dykes are usually fat so that counts me out these days. She obviously assumed we are a couple, just like they all do. Such a soddin' shame you never fancied me.'

Ella reached across the table and patted her friend's hand. 'You're my boss, a friend and that is all. Anything else would completely ruin our working relationship. Let's have this and go shopping for a frilly frock… just kidding. Trouser suit?'

Despite how well Ella described the luxurious interior of Buxham's restaurant and encouraged her friend to join her there for dinner, Val would not even consider a change of style. It would take more than that to ever persuade her to change from her usual black jeans, Doc Marten boots, roll-neck sweater and leather jacket.

'Gender or sexuality are pretty much irrelevant from what I've gathered, but smart dress *is* required.' Ella tapped her fingers on a large manila envelope that she had placed carefully on the table. She frowned. 'I really should have done my bloody homework before agreeing to this. The general manager, Carla Lewis, was a funny sort, attractive but not. One of those people that, no matter how hard they try, they never look sexy. Do you ever watch re-runs of the Carry On films?'

Val nodded. 'Yeah, 'course I do. Doesn't everyone?'

'Well Carla Lewis reminded me of Hattie Jacques. Welcoming, courteous and highly informative: the polar opposite to Emo-girl over there. She was easy enough to cope with, but the clientele have very particular requirements and I'm not confident I can manage to pull off what you're asking me to do. Do you recall the sign outside the front of the club? "For the larger life…", well that is what the club specialises in. Some parts of the country boast a local naturist club, some clubs are men only, and some are for liberated sexual beings. This one is for individuals who love big food and big flesh, if you get my drift. Carla used words like - gastronomic glorification, foodies, Rubenesque beauties, lovers of curves—' Ella stopped.

Guilt waved hello to her from Val's every pore.

'You knew! That's why you sent me. You used my big fat arse to—'

The volume and extent of Ella's accusations were tempered by the return of the waitress who materialised carrying their drinks on a tray. On this occasion there was an exchange of glances between Emo-girl and Val who produced one of her infrequent grins. This blossomed into a wide stained-teeth leer when the waitress winked at her.

Ella was dumbfounded. Folding her arms, she sat silently back in her seat until the girl moved away to deal with a stroppy man at a table nearby who was demanding a refill of coffee.

'Oh, for fuck's sake. I've been so stupid. You've used me to get what you want, and now you're hitting on Emo-girl. What do you want *her* for?' Ella asked, then without pausing answered her own question. 'Have you just pulled? No, no, no... you've been coming here for quite a while now, so it's been planned. Working your way into her knickers. What an unscrupulous cow you are, Valerie Royal! Isn't she too young for you?'

'Take a closer look. She's older than you think.' The hunger on her companion's face was not for want of food and Ella surrendered to the inevitable truth. Val was not going to be swayed from the chase although when she did finally drag her eyes away from the wretched joyless wait-ress, she answered Ella's query. 'And no I didn't know exactly what or who Buxham's caters for, but I did have a pretty good idea. It doesn't take a genius.' She paused, craning to catch a glimpse of Emo-girl's backside. 'I think I'll give dinner a miss.'

'Great. Who am I supposed to go to Buxham's with if you don't come with me? Ada's already covering my old art class so that I can help you instead. That's another forty quid you owe me, by the way.'

Val picked up her phone and, after a short delay, snapped her orders. 'Mal. Get your glad rags on and use one of those flashy cars of yours, you're taking Ella out to dinner. I'll text you the details. Yes, tonight. Naturally it's work, you moron. I'd hardly ask you to do this if it wasn't. No, you're not a babysitter; she needs your experience and advice. You can pretend to be Ella's brother. Adopted brother. You'll think of something.'

Ella was relieved. Having Malik with her would be so much more comforting than coping with Val. He would fit in, be well dressed enough to be unobtrusive, be observant and with his cocky attitude, invaluable.

'Is he picking me up from home? Tell him seven o'clock. I don't want to miss too much. Evidently, they hold a gourmet pudding club on a Wednesday once a month. It could be that our two men are regular attenders. I didn't have a chance to see the table bookings for tonight.'

Val coughed, crackling catarrh making an abrasive sound. 'Don't be too nosy too soon. Enjoy the evening; absorb what you can. Let Mal seek out the CCTV and security issues. You behave like a nervous new staff member.'

ELLA HAD no need to pretend, she was already playing host to nervous anticipation as she examined her appearance in the full-length hallway mirror in her bedsit. Her glamorously curled hair tumbled over her right shoulder, laying on the exposed neckline of her 1950s retro swing dress. Red and black. Striking.

She grinned to herself. A clandestine club for lovers of full figures, flesh and food, how brilliant. She would fit right in. As the doorbell rang she experienced a rush of long-dormant excitatory neurochemicals, but she failed to properly register their arrival.

'Mal. Don't you look every inch the James Bond! Handsome, dashing and smelling divine. Does my carriage await me?'

There stood Malik, exhaling a long 'wow!' at the sight of his date for the evening. Malik Khan, Mal to his friends, or sometimes Magic Mal when he was on top form, had the whitest, broadest smile Ella had seen outside of advertisements for toothpaste. Other than his smile there was nothing unusual of note about Mal. His accent was South London; his presence registered as a tall solid Indian man with an air of self-confidence and a sprinkling of unpre-dictability.

'Makes a change from being *The Invisible Asian Taxi Driver* when I'm scouting for Val. Like the whistle?' he asked, flashing his jacket open to reveal an iridescent purple lining.

'Lovely,' Ella replied, giving him an assuring grin, before she closed the flat door behind her. She didn't want him to see inside her lowly home.

Once she had calmed down from the initial thrill of being driven in a brand new Porsche 911, they had enough time to agree a strategy for the evening.

'As I said on the phone, I had to ring ahead with our details and the car reg. I hope you don't mind what I chose for you as a name,' she said.

'I love it. Phil-the-print was mightily impressed.' He passed her a plastic wallet containing several business cards. 'I think the ink is about dry.' Mal was to be Ella's busi-nessman stepbrother, giving him the honour of becoming a Fitzwilliam for the duration of her time at Buxham's.

'I bet everyone calls you Ella Fitzgerald.'

'Yes. They do. It gets on your wick after a while. Espe-cially when they think it's the first time you've ever heard the joke.'

Mal whistled as they approached the entrance gate of Buxham's. 'Clock those cameras. No one goes in and out of here without being seen.' Leaning through the opened window he pressed the intercom. 'Ella and Mallory Fitzwilliam. We are expected.'

'Welcome. Carla Lewis has approved your admission. Once through the gate, please park in the bays on the left.'

Ella's mouth was dry as she clung to the clutch bag on her knee, looking intently through the windscreen while the car moved through the opening gate. The engine of the Porsche made a comforting low throb.

'Well, *Mallory Fitzwilliam*, let's go and see if we can convince anyone you are my rich protective stepbrother.' She passed him back the small wallet containing his bespoke business cards. 'Very professional.'

'Yep. What's more, I didn't even have to lie. I *am* a security specialist. Hang on I'll come round to your side and help you out, these cars are a bit low. Amita always used to moan about how unladylike it is. Then again, she disapproved of my passion for high end sports cars altogether.'

'I could get used to it. Are you and Amita a thing of the past then?'

'Yeah, thank Allah. Apparently I'm a disgrace as a Muslim because of my loose morals, so within twelve months of our hideously pricey arranged marriage ceremony she made a case for divorce. My parents have accused me of bringing shame on the family name but at least she's pissed back off to Bradford and I'm free of her incessant bleedin' nagging in that stupid northern accent of hers.' He gently closed the door to the Porsche with a clunk. 'It's on loan. Don't get any ideas.'

'On loan?'

'One of the family businesses. Executive sports car hire. Some of my fellow Asian brothers like to look the part even if they can't afford it.'

'Oh, I see,' Ella said, swallowing a smile. She couldn't fail to notice the designer watch that poked from beneath Mal's pricey-looking shirt and the sleeve of his tailor-made suit. *Probably snide.*

'This makes for a pleasant change from being your minder, doesn't it?'

'Minder? Have I been that bad as a pupil? I thought you were supposed to be my mentor, showing me the ropes, honing my skills.'

He was teasing.

She let the matter drop. 'Yes. It does make a lovely change from sitting with you in a car for hours.' Ella was trying to appear relaxed in Mal's company and, on the whole, he was on his best behaviour, being unusually attentive to help manage her nerves. They entered the building through a set of elegant glass doors and into the main reception where they were greeted by neatly attired staff keen to help.

'Good evening and welcome as our guests to Buxham's. We hope you enjoy your first experience with us. As non-members, we need to inform you that, like smoking, use of mobile phones is not allowed inside the club. We ask you to switch them off, or if you prefer, we can take them into safe-keeping. We know how tempting it is to sneak a peek at your messages, but the privacy of our guests is paramount. This rule must never be breeched. Phones can be used on the veranda at the rear of the bar by our gourmet members and for our full members they can use them in their accom-modation.'

Mal didn't react negatively. 'What a refreshing idea, luv. Yes, that's no problem.' He pulled a smartphone from his pocket, switched it off and handed it over, giving the recep-tionist the benefit of his dazzling smile. Ella did the same.

The lady they handed their phones to grinned back. 'I'm Caroline and this is my colleague Nula. We're looking forward to working with you, Ella. I hope your husband likes his food.' She risked an admiring glance at Mal.

'He's my big brother, actually. But he is married, in case you were wondering.' Ella touched Mal on his sleeve before taking the receipts for their phones that had been placed in individual locked metal boxes and stored in numbered pigeonholes behind the reception area. The lie about him being married had fallen merrily from her mouth without her having to think why. He was handsome, single, and he was with her, working. Minding her. He was not there to be interfered with by lecherous women he'd never met before.

'Thanks for the lovely welcome, I'm sure I'll be very happy here,' Ella said, saying a secret prayer to herself that she didn't become too happy. Too happy meant excited, elated and inappropriate. Too happy meant hypomanic, unstoppably chatty and overconfident. It could lead to disaster.

She and Mal were directed to the restaurant and met by a heavily pregnant lady who Ella rightly assumed to be Teresa, the incumbent hostess whose job she was to cover.

'Welcome. How would you prefer to be addressed?'

Ella and Mal looked at each other, slightly bemused by the question. Teresa continued. 'Confidentiality dictates that we avoid using full names in public. The privacy of members is very important, so we mostly stick to sir or madam, but if you prefer we'll go with Ella and …?' Teresa was smiling. She too seemed more interested in Mal than in meeting her replacement, but, nevertheless, was warm and polite.

They were shown to table number sixty-six in a luxurious booth and sat down opposite each other, not quite side-on to the rest of the room. 'Table sixty-six. Interesting,' commented Ella as she took a menu from Teresa. 'There can't be that many tables in here.' She was given an unexpected thumbs-up from the glowing hostess. 'You pass your first test. Very observant. Buxham's prides itself on its generosity. Portions of food fit for Roman banquets, wide comfortable seats, and huge bedrooms. Indeed everything has ample proportions to meet the needs of our clients, and for that reason the table numbers reflect the ethos of the club itself. Bigger is better. Therefore, table one becomes eleven, two becomes twenty-two and so forth.'

Ella couldn't help thinking about bingo calls. *Legs, eleven.*

Two little ducks, quack, quack, twenty-two. Clickety-click, sixty-six.

She and Mal scoured around taking in the sumptuous surroundings and humming their approval. 'Will tonight be busy?' Ella enquired, keen to glean as much information as possible from Teresa, while she had the opportunity.

'Wednesdays are brilliant. I shall miss them. The first Wednesday of the month, today, we host The Lensham and District Pudding Club, who are a noisy bunch of delightful individuals. The chef prepares four courses for them. Each one is a dessert and the pudding club members discuss and vote for their favourite. Simple pleasures, devoured with much enthusiasm. We have our regulars and, without fail, table number eighty-eight will be in use as it is every Wednesday. You'll get to know them very well.' Teresa popped her eyebrows skyward. 'We'll meet in private to discuss our regular clientele. I'm afraid, as your husband is here, I can't divulge confidential information.'

Mal stepped in. 'I'm her brother. Stepbrother actually.' He handed over a business card as Ella again reiterated his marital status, untrue though that was. She hadn't predicted how irresistible the female staff members at Buxham's would find her colleague. *Bloody flirt,* she thought, as she watched him with Teresa.

'I find pregnant women incredibly appealing, as it happens,' he said casting his eyes towards Teresa's firm, rounded pregnancy. 'I've never been able to work out whether it's because they seem to radiate health or whether it is to do with the signs of miraculous fertility.' Ella cringed as Teresa melted and let out a girlish titter, whispering the words printed on his business card.

'Oh, I see, Mal is short for Mallory, what a lovely name.' She held the card aloft. 'Security advisor. Can I pass this on to the general manager? He's looking for someone in your line of work.'

Seconds after Teresa had turned to head back to the meet, greet and seat area, Ella coughed, putting Mal on alert. She had spotted Harry Drysdale the lawyer, and his friend. The men were accompanied by two over-endowed, alluring women in their late thirties and the group were aiming rapidly towards a booth in the corner of the room where they could hide from enquiring eyes. The ice in their drinks tinkled as they passed by.

The woman with her arm through that of Harry Drysdale's was fair-haired, bouncy and blue-eyed, dressed in a flowing skirt and blouse. In sharp contrast, the tall lady with Harry's male companion was tastefully attired in a cream two-piece suit that served to accentuate her curvaceous figure and contrasted most strikingly with her coffee coloured skin. The black buttons and collar detail hinted at how up-market she was dressed and she looked every inch a powerful businesswoman, her style speaking of her intelligence. The tight-fitting skirt reached modestly to her knees and yet the apparent lack of shirt beneath the jacket signalled a deeper intention. Sleek black long hair lay flat against her back, waving gently with the rhythm of her strides as she walked confidently by, hips swinging.

They took their seats at table eighty-eight. The number was on a small brass plaque neatly screwed to an ornate wooden upright at the entrance to the private booth.

Two fat ladies, eighty-eight.

THAT SAME EVENING

Marcus Carver could barely contain himself. Leonora had become his chosen favourite. Pressing his right thigh against her left, he slid his hand around her waist. He rested it on the shelf of flesh there, savouring the feel of her, pushing his fingertips gently downwards to experience the resistance. His heart rate increased alarmingly. He could hear the beats in his head and noted the pressure in his chest. She turned to him, an understanding pity in her eyes.

'We eat first. Then, and only then, do you earn your reward, Mr C,' she whispered, touching him softly on his right cheek.

Marcus smiled and passed her the menu.

His friend and companion, Harry Drysdale, was less restrained. Orchestrating a fumble as if he had dropped his serviette, he rocked forward and, pretending not to be able to locate it, buried his head deep in Ciara's lap as he scrabbled about. He breathed in loudly.

'Oh God, that is so warm and welcoming,' he declared when his head popped up from beneath the table, shaking his cheeks like a dog. 'I must apologise again for keeping you both waiting in the bar. My dear friend, Mr C here, got his knickers in a twist about his birthday tomorrow and had to have a long phone chat with his wife to placate the scatty woman.'

Marcus shifted uncomfortably and shot a warning look at his friend. He disliked any reference to his family life. Not on a Wednesday that was the rule. Home life, real life and his secret life had to be compartmentalised for his own sanity and his professional reputation. The lines were becoming blurred between his work and his desires, and this was a dangerous time, a battle with himself.

Harry shouldn't have mentioned Lydia, and he apologised immediately before changing the subject to a more accept-able one. 'Ladies, shall we explore the menu?'

This part of the ritual was more than titillation; it was an excruciating form of foreplay for Marcus. He took every opportune moment to touch Leonora's hands, thighs, and waist. Occasionally he ventured to place his thumb against her upper ribs allowing his fingers to find the curve of her right breast as she sat leaning against him. His eyes swept from the line of her jaw, down to her collarbone and thence to her cleavage. The most magnificent heaving chest beck-oned to him, but which was not to be accessed until later that evening in the privacy of his room.

The conversation ranged from current affairs to film and entertainment until the food arrived. When it did, silence fell broken only by low hums of gratification at the flavours and textures of the irresistible dishes placed before them.

When Harry had first introduced him to the pleasures of Buxham's restaurant, Marcus had been amazed by the effi-ciency of the club's employees. The hostess was always the height of discretion and never announced their full names in public. The waiting staff appeared only when required and didn't linger or disturb the flow of the conversations. None of them passed comment about the female guests that were signed in each Wednesday and who left in the early hours by taxi. If Harry weren't due in court the following day, his female companion would sometimes stay the entire night.

Harry liked variety.

Marcus preferred the familiarity of Leonora. She had an uncanny knack of identifying his weaknesses, playing games with her eyes. She was demonstrating her ability at that very moment by sucking on a straw, holding it daintily, then wiping a stray splash from her chin and intentionally, slowly, licking her finger. In any other context this would go unnoticed but for Marcus this was heaven and she capitalised on his reaction with a brief shimmy. The resultant rippling undulations in her breasts forced him to close his eyes and chastise himself for his reaction. If it weren't for the tablecloth hiding his groin, he would have been mortified at his lack of control in public.

'Not eating, Mr C?' Harry asked, noticing how quiet his friend had become.

'Yes. Saving myself for pudding.'

'Indeed.' Harry was laughing at him. They'd had an in depth discussion during their walk from the station and Marcus had confessed to his dread of Christmas putting a barrier in the way of his weekly indulgences. He'd also disclosed his crumbling defences and the risks he had begun to take in his professional life. It hadn't been the phone call to Lydia that had made them both late for dinner with Ciara and Leonora; it had been an emergency meeting in Harry's room.

MARCUS HAD CONVINCED himself that he was heading for a meltdown of biblical proportions. He'd paced back and forth while Harry lazed on the bed watching him.

'If Lydia hadn't contrived to take herself to the verge of starvation in the misguided belief that she had to look like a trophy wife, then I wouldn't be in this mess,' Marcus announced. 'I can barely get it up these days she's so scrawny. I miss the proper Lydia, the whole person I moulded, the breasts I could fall into, the belly I could knead and her magnificent buttocks that rolled and swayed with divine rhythm. The only way things could improve is if she could, by immaculate conception, fall pregnant. The trouble is I no longer find her sexually attractive, not for months – not even if I fantasise my heart out – and now, for Christ's sake, she's insisted we get counselling. What the fuck am I going to do?'

'What's so wrong with this as an alternative?' Harry asked. 'It's not the same as being unfaithful in my book.'

Marcus wasn't sure whether to laugh at that outrageous comment. 'Your book is vastly different to mine. For one thing, I'm married with children. I know they're not mine, but it's the principle. You, however, are the oldest playboy in town. No one will judge you too harshly if the truth came out. On the other hand, I would be in deep and smelly stuff right up to my neck. I am a fucking bariatric surgeon with a client base rammed full of wonderful rounded women all wanting to be thinner and I can't – mustn't indulge myself. It would be career suicide.

'Lydia used to be my safety net. There when I got home to do with as I pleased and now she's screwed it all up. I cannot believe what she's done. Do you know, I've even begun to consider confining my surgical skills to men only, to reduce the temptation.' Marcus looked up at the ceiling. 'Yes! That's the answer. I'll deal with it on Friday,' he said, waving his arms in the air, his words coming in staccato bursts as he searched for solutions. 'Harry, I'm in real trouble. It's all I think about and if I carry on like this I'll lose everything, my practice, my reputation, my registration - the lot. The whole fucking lot.'

'Then you will have to remain secretive, just as you are, Marcus. You must hide your desires from public scrutiny. Unless, of course you force Lydia into changing her mind...'

Marcus ran his fingers through his hair as he sat heavily into the bedroom chair next to an oak dressing table. 'It's like a drug. I can't change.' He sighed long and low. 'You're right. Until I can get my own wife back under control, I'll have to get my kicks here. Maybe I could stay more often and that way I'll be less of a risk professionally. If anyone who knows me sees me in the restaurant, I look like I'm entertaining clients, so that's no big deal. Lydia knows I stay here every Wednesday to make travel manageable for Thursday surgery, so it's all covered.' He paused in his excitement. 'God, you see, even the thought of it makes me as horny as hell. I'm dribbling.'

Harry bounced from the bed. 'Come on then. No time to waste. Food, then flesh, lots of it. Sins of the flesh. Big sins.' He rubbed his hands together.

FROM ACROSS THE ROOM …

Ella was staring at the back of the man's head, waiting for him to turn to the left again so that she could catch sight of his features. She wasn't watching Harry Drysdale. She was transfixed by the possibility that she could confirm the identity of his companion. The angle was awkward. Could it be him?

'You okay?' Mal asked her, raising his voice slightly. The noise level in the restaurant had increased with the arrival of several couples that had made their way to the bar for a drink.

'I'm not sure.' Ella was having the most disconcerting flashbacks to her student nursing days and began to worry that the man may recognise her thus putting an end to Val's carefully planned caper. She took a sip from her wineglass, anxiety drawn across her face.

'The mark?'

'No. His oppo.'

'Mr Suave?'

'*Dr* Suave, I suspect.'

'You know him?'

'Once upon a time, a long time ago when I was toned and willowy, I came across him.'

Each of the booths in the restaurant at Buxham's was offset, affording more privacy to the occupiers and intentionally preventing an open view from other tables. The upholstery and panelling dulled the sounds, making it virtually impossible to listen in to the conversation unless it became raucous. Most chatter was coming from a large round table at the far end of the room. The Pudding Club meeting was in full swing. Chair of the club announced the menu for the evening accompanied by cries of joy from the club members, some of whom banged a spoon on the table for emphasis.

Ella couldn't concentrate. Seeing a face from years ago in her former life perturbed her, a man who may remember her. She had certainly never forgotten him.

'So much for sitting back and enjoying the evening, absorbing the feel of the place and letting you suss out the security issues.'

'Would it matter if he recognised you?'

Ella thought about Mal's question for a few moments. She had to keep reminding herself that as far as he was concerned, they were following Harry Drysdale because of an infidelity issue. She patted the linen serviette onto her lap giving a wry smile to Mal.

'Clever man. Good question. I don't think it would make any difference at all. My CV detailed my nursing career and anyone can end up in the hospitality trade, can't they? It shouldn't matter to him.'

'So it could even be an advantage?'

'Yes. I believe it could.' Anticipation. Excitement. A chill of the thrills to come made Ella shudder and shift in her seat. 'It could even mean a—'

She stopped mid-sentence as Harry Drysdale slid from

the curved banquette seating of table eighty-eight. He was laughing with his companions. 'Back in a moment and you …', he said, aiming a finger at his male friend, 'don't touch what you can't afford. You have your own to play with.'

The slight man, no taller than Ella herself, strode past her, strutting like a peacock. Self-assured, almost arrogant, he stopped briefly to talk with Teresa who had been allowed use of a cushioned bar stool with back and arms, to rest herself. Heavily pregnant she exuded gentle contentment. Mal had the best view of the exchange and gave Ella a running commentary between mouthfuls of his seafood starter.

'They must know each other well. He's walked up, kissed her and laid both hands straight on her baby hump.'

'Do you mean, "bump"?'

'Call it what you like, it's a bit soddin' forward, for a customer. Blimey. She's put her hands on top of his and is helping him to feel the baby. At least I think that's the general idea. Right, he's off again. Striding over to the bar… no he's carrying on to the gents' toilets. I'll give him a few minutes then I'll check them out myself.' Mal stabbed another king prawn, scooped some pea shoots onto the fork and stared at the mouthful before eating. 'This tastes bleedin' amazing.'

Ella was distracted. She was able to see Harry Drysdale's date and was trying to work out if they were a stable pairing or whether this was a one off of some sort. The woman was spilling from the top of her low-cut, ruffled blouse. Her right wrist shone and glittered with silver bracelets, her hands finely manicured and smooth skinned. She had shiny blonde hair, cut in a long bob, and was immaculately made-up, smiling with moist full lips. No matter that she was beautiful, there was no getting away from the fact that Harry Drysdale's lady friend was rotund, probably verging on the clinically obese.

She's the reason he's here. He likes them that way. Ella

thought. *They both do. Bingo.* Val had been correct.

Mal had been watching her spying on the occupants of table eighty-eight and had seemingly read her mind. 'My old mum calls it being short for your weight.'

Ella grinned at him. 'I was expecting him to be caught with an escort girl or two, but not one of plus size vital statistics. Maybe I do stand a chance of landing a sugar daddy.'

Then it struck her; she needed to play along with Mal's belief that they were on an infidelity assignment. 'Mal? Why are we trying to provide evidence of the mark's habits if he's not married? What does it matter to anyone if he likes his dates on the large side? This mystery client, is it a prospective wife?'

Mal stuck out his bottom lip and sat back. 'There's a thought. I hadn't really wondered. I s'pose Val may have the answer to that one. All I know is that we have to provide indisputable photographic evidence of his bedroom antics before we get paid. So first you will have to find out what those antics are because so far all he's done is to have dinner with two fat ladies.'

'Eighty-eight.'

'Exactly. Two fat ladies - eighty-eight. I'm off for a pee and to check out the place.' He rose and stepped from the table, passing Harry Drysdale within a few paces. The two men nodded at each other. Ella looked carefully at Harry as he marched by. He didn't register her existence, not noticing her as she sat in the booth of table sixty-six.

Clickety-click. That is what the camera will do when I catch you at it.

Ella smirked to herself, but again wondered what the driving force was behind Val's request for photographic evidence. Was she planning to blackmail both men?

Who was Harry Drysdale? A barrister. A respected

barrister who was divorced and therefore free to do as he pleased unless it was illegal in which case his career and reputation would be sullied. Was the revenge worth the effort and the expense? Ella debated this with herself. Did he look like a pervert? Not at all.

As the spruce lawyer returned to table eighty-eight, the other man – the man from her past and the subject of Val's hatred – turned to greet him with hands spread wide. 'Never touched her,' he joked.

'Is that so, Mr C?' Harry mocked.

That's enlightening.

Mr C was altogether stockier in build, like a chisel-jawed rugby flanker, with a quiet air about him, less confident than Harry Drysdale. Twitchy. He swivelled his head to his left and caught Ella looking over at them.

She smiled, an automatic response. He turned away again preventing Ella from reading his reaction but she guessed it hadn't been favourable. He shuffled to his right, hiding from view, but as he did so she was able to confirm her suspicions.

It *was* him.

Older, but it was definitely him.

Marcus Carver.

She tensed at the bitter recall of when she had first met Marcus Carver. His tastes hadn't changed.

Harry glanced across at her as if directed to do so by his friend Mr C. Ella, caught out again, held his gaze determined to appear innocent of prying or nosiness. She flashed her eyes as she beamed a bright inviting smile and saw him acknowledge her greeting. He had the temerity to wink.

A player. A pocket-sized player. What games do you play I wonder?

Ella's thoughts were gate-crashed by Mal's return to the table, followed shortly by a chatty waitress who cleared their starters and offered more drinks. Before Mal could share his findings, their main courses arrived and all thoughts of investigations went on hold.

'Oh, this looks so delicious.'

They tucked into their plates of food with joyful noises, and within minutes Teresa approached to check on their level of satisfaction with the dining experience. As she was about to retreat, having received overwhelmingly positive responses from Mal and Ella, a request for attention came from behind her. Harry was calling.

'I think he's asking who we are,' Ella guessed, trying to warn Mal that she had perhaps aroused unnecessary curiosity from the table diagonally opposite. She tried to eat and chat nonchalantly with Mal, acting as normally as she could, but with one eye on the interactions between Teresa and Harry. Teresa unfurled an arm in Ella's direction and was explaining to the guests on table eighty-eight who their fellow diners were. There was a muffled 'Aaaahhh,' which arose above the booth confirming that all was well.

Ella forced a grin while muttering updates and manoeuvring food onto her fork. 'The lawyer's nodding a lot. He's looking over. Shit.'

'What?' asked Mal, through gritted teeth, as he reached for a glass of water.

'Mr C.' The man she recognised from her past had shuffled across toward the edge of the upholstered leather seating and turned his head to his shoulder again. This time he caught Ella's eye and kept it, raising an eyebrow. He regarded her with an intense stare.

'Fuck me,' she murmured.

'What?' Mal asked again, exasperated at not being given the reason behind Ella's responses.

'He licked his lips. The bloody lecherous bastard,' she whispered.

But he didn't recognise me.

THE SEARCH

JANUARY 25TH

Konrad felt queasy. His stomach churned endlessly as he waited for the Channel 7 executives to call him in to answer their questions, propose new ideas and to provide a sound rationale for his vast salary.

He sat on the leather chairs in an open plan office area beyond the glass-walled meeting room. He could hear raised voices behind the closed blinds. With his palms sticky from nervous sweat, gluing his hands to the leather document case on his lap, he struggled to find his usual composure. There was too much at stake and the level of tension threatened to undo his efforts to save his own career. Requiring a confident pitch to the top men, if his anxieties got the better of him, he would stumble over his words and that would never do.

Around the smoked glass oval table, the suits sat with laptops in front of them and, as Konrad entered the room, a hush descended. Even mild paranoia was hard to control.

What did they know to make them react in this way? he wondered. Was this the end of his career? Was he destined to cope with being a third rate media has-been?

His guts lurched, and he braced for the bad news.

The salt and pepper-haired man, his beaked nose resembling that of a bird of prey, motioned to a chair opposite. Dino Ledbetter was the man with the power and the budget, keen to present the production forecasts for *The Truth Behind the Lies.*

'Konrad. Welcome. Take a seat,' he purred, placing his elbows in front of him and intertwining his fingers. 'Viewing figures remain high for *The Truth*, however, after some discussion, we are of the opinion that a shift in emphasis may go a long way to revitalising the original concept. We would very much like to hear your views while we consider whether to renew your contract with us.'

Expecting the worst and then hearing it, Konrad wracked his brain to find the right response and, as a result, Dino, who stared intently with his closely set, predatory eyes, prompted him, misunderstanding his delay. 'Konrad. You are well respected and hard working. Please consider what we have to say very carefully before making a decision you'll regret.'

Konrad glanced swiftly around the table and caught the eye of Robin De La Croix, - D.L.C. himself - who immediately shifted his eyes towards his laptop screen. His raised brow and haughty look alluded to an argument won while Konrad was not even on the battlefield.

'There was a minority view that it was time to call an end to the series. A tiny minority, let me add,' Dino said.

Konrad smiled to himself as Dino's body language confirmed D.L.C. as one of the culprits. Stuart Barnfield, the co-conspirator to D.L.C.'s right, shifted awkwardly and rubbed the side of his nose with one forefinger. Dino continued. 'We need something from you Konrad. What would you suggest?'

Konrad drew a deep cleansing breath. 'I would consider it

foolhardy for Channel 7 to undermine the faith of the viewing public by shelving a popular show, but I agree there does need to be a reinvigoration of the format. Can I point out that I've been very much put on the spot here. I would have thought, out of respect, that any discussion about contracts should have been preceded by a less formal consultation, but as I'm here—' Dino Ledbetter was about to speak again, but Konrad cut him short by raising a hand, not wanting to stem the flow of ideas that he and Eliza had developed earlier. His speech, although appearing spontaneous, was well rehearsed.

'Let me pitch this to you: Hidden lives, ladies and gentlemen, those lies that people tell to cover up sordid secrets, not necessarily the tricksters, the scammers and the downright deceitful, but the opposite. You know the sort of thing. Our viewers are interested in real-life stories that explore the little known facets of human behaviours, quirky ones, kinky ones, obscure fascinations, socially unacceptable pastimes for those in authority or positions of trust.' Konrad turned to bore into Dino's eyes. 'It is possible to broaden our horizons from straightforward miscarriages of justice without losing the central theme of seeking the truth. May I also say that we should maintain the same production standards or we risk losing the interest of the public. My team and I are the right people for the job. We live and breathe documentary.'

He swept the room with his remaining eye, ensuring he caught the return gaze of each man and woman who sat in judgement of him. 'You could choose a new more handsome face, if you so wish... but if I wanted solid returns on my investment, then I'd bet on the sure thing.'

Konrad managed to disguise his despair at being made to fight for his position. Only just. Seeing a chance to gain the advantage over his detractors, he calmly inhaled deeply before making his final argument and leaving them to debate his future.

HE HAD PREDICTED that by this time of the proceedings he would be humming a repetitive melody on the way back downstairs to reception. He visualised himself skipping from the lift and stepping lightly towards the main desk at Marriot and Weston's, the office block where Channel 7 housed its headquarters. However, his brush with the executive board had not gone well. He hadn't lost the fight, but he was waiting for the judges' decision on whether he had won on points. The alternative scenario was that dastardly D.L.C. and his sidekick, Muttley – Stuart Barnfield – had swayed the consensus in their own favour. Delia's favour.

Konrad's greatest fan, concierge George, was manning the front desk and squeaked with unbridled anticipation when Konrad leant over the polished desk surface to have a private word.

Gorgeous George was known to every member of staff in the building. His genuine optimism for life was infectious and his hilarious campiness made for delightful entertainment. George's co-worker, the simpering Lillian, had become desensitised to this behaviour. She loved George's outrageous mannerisms and he in turn appreciated her quiet enthusiasm for meeting and greeting. They made a fabulous contribution to the first impressions of visitors to the soulless building. Lillian approached as Konrad whispered the news. He couldn't face causing upset, so he put a positive slant on the outcome of the meeting in the hope that it would come true.

'You'll have to put up with me for a while longer by the looks of things.'

George almost sank to his knees, he had an unerring

crush on Konrad and fawned over him at every given moment, thus, with dramatic flair, he clutched at his heart. 'Oh thank God for that. I've been worried sick. Haven't I, Lillian?'

She nodded as George interrupted any attempt she may have made to speak. 'Sick to the core, Mr Neale. I couldn't have imagined coming to work and not seeing you again. It doesn't bear thinking about, does it Lillian?'

George's longsuffering co-worker shook her head slowly, smiled and said, 'He's been in a terrible state since you arrived for the meeting.'

Konrad stifled a laugh, managing to keep a straight face as he patted George on the shoulder. 'Everything is fine, George. As you were.'

Lillian handed over a large brown envelope. 'A courier delivered this for you, Mr Neale. Private and Confidential. I assumed it was the one you'd been waiting for.'

Konrad thanked her for her diligence and tucked the envelope into his document folder as he walked through the revolving glass door. Once outside on the noisy London streets he frowned and uttered an expletive aimed towards the snow-laden sky. He pulled his tweed cap from his over-coat pocket and headed to the park. It was the best way to march off his adrenalin and find the nerve to call Lorna and speak to her as if nothing in the world were wrong.

It didn't work.

'When were you going to tell me it was under threat of being cut?'

He'd been blown. His daughter Eliza must have been in touch with Lorna, or vice versa.

'I didn't want to worry you. Anyway, I made a strong case, and I even managed to negotiate a change of executive management, should I be reinstated, on the grounds that D.L.C. and I have a conflict of interest. That way Delia, the unprincipled bitch, can't put the kybosh on my future. Our future. If I win, then we can safely say that the rebellion has been well and truly quashed.'

'I do hope your confidence is well founded. When will they decide?'

'I have to make another pitch with a fully formed concept for the new series by the second week in February. I'll think of something.'

He wasn't at all certain that he could develop a workable proposal by then, let alone sell it convincingly. A cold sweat sprang from his forehead as a wave of nausea hit.

'Can we make Harry Drysdale's disappearance our first programme of the new series?' Lorna said without hesitation. Konrad lifted the phone from his ear and stared at it before speaking again.

'What?' he asked.

'Seriously, Kon. I've been digging, and I have tidings, tantalising tidings but not of great joy. Of mystery and puzzlement. Do you think you can get back on the train before they stop running because of the wrong type of snow on the tracks? Come home. We're meeting Barney and Netty in The Valiant for dinner and a preliminary facts discussion about Harry and his secret lifestyle choices. They are what you would call big and juicy.'

'Yes.' He sighed loudly with relief, not needing any more of a clue from his wife. 'Yes, you bloody marvellous woman, I'm on my way right now.' Konrad tapped his leather document pouch. Hopefully he would have something valuable to contribute later that evening and with any luck he may drag a miracle from misfortune and save his pride before the public witnessed his fall from grace.

13

THE MORNING AFTER DINNER AT BUXHAM'S

Marcus Carver stretched and yawned. A contented sigh escaped as he surveyed the evidence of a satisfying evening with Leonora. She was long gone, sometime around midnight. Dessert had been served in his room, as usual, and they had eaten together savouring each mouthful: he a small dainty portion, she an amount worthy of a banquet for the gluttonous.

There the trolley stood by the door, laden with dirty crockery and cutlery waiting to be collected later by the housekeeping staff. They would also have the unenviable job of dealing with the soiled sheets and towels; the ones covered in essential oils and bodily fluids.

He drew a deep breath through his nostrils, filling his senses with the recollections of his hands on Leonora's rolling folds. Recalling the feel of her sweat on his forefinger as he played with her deep naval cavity, his eyes closed with the pleasure of the memory. Those moments would have to serve him for a whole week until he could return for another helping. Then he smiled at the thought of the new restaurant hostess, the one he had been introduced to the previous evening as he and Harry were heading for their rooms with Leonora and Ciara in tow.

He had spied her earlier in the evening and been shaken by a distinct feeling of déjà vu. Mild panic had set in as he wracked his brain trying to place where he had seen her before. It was only when Teresa directed them to the charcoal life drawing by the entrance to the bar area that he made the connection. That drawing had been the talking point of the previous three weeks with both he and Harry taking turns to name the mysterious beauty.

Now she had a real name: Ella. She also had an enticing coquettishness that deserved attention and Marcus found himself fantasising that he could persuade Ella to be his personal life model. She could pose for him in his room. Couldn't she? Yes, she could if Harry didn't beat him to it.

Their rivalry was part of the game.

His mobile phone rang, jarring him upright from his early morning daydream pose on the edge of the bed. It was Lydia. His wife didn't usually bother him at the club. She seemed to sense that it was better to leave him to his male only, old-fashioned antics. He had never lied to her about the club. As far as he knew, she'd made the assumption that he stayed at a gentlemen's club and sat around with a bunch of professional cronies. No doubt she thought they discussed articles in The Lancet while sipping brandy, just like his father used to do.

'Morning. Sorry to disturb you but I just wanted to remind you not to be late if you can help it. The children are planning to trash the kitchen after school and are determined to make a birthday dinner for you. Marcus? Are you there?'

Whenever Lydia spoke to him on the phone, he had a picture of her in his mind of how she used to be; fulsome, a proper shape for a woman. A size befitting a lady who gave generously of her time to charity and doted on her offspring, the homemaker, the housewife. He wanted that woman back and his heart gave a short flutter of extra beats in recognition of the fact. He'd worked hard to win her in the first place.

'Yes. I'm here. I'm listening. I'll try not to be late, but I can't promise.'

'Thanks. The girls are so keen to cook for you. Good night with the rest of the stuffed shirts was it?'

Their conversation was false. 'The food was excellent as usual, but I went to bed early. Surgery's turning into a slog on a Thursday at the moment.' Marcus stared at the mess surrounding him and smirked to himself at the contrast between his night of pleasure and the banal communication he was having with his wife.

'Pre-Christmas panic?'

'What? Oh, I see what you mean. Surgery being busy because of a last minute panic? God, no. It's far too late for anyone to have surgery in time for Christmas. No. This is the summer holiday and wedding panic. Six months recovery and healing time.'

'I should have realised. How stupid of me. Listen, Marcus, while you're on the phone. I've been in contact with a counsellor, he's highly recommended and he's got space to see us in January, but–'

'You can go if you like, I'm not stopping you.'

'Marcus, please. It's for both of us but it will have to be on a Wednesday evening near your London clinic.'

Briefly Marcus held the phone to his chest. His hands began to shake as he returned it to the side of his head. 'No. That's impossible. I have surgery on Thursdays and I need to be nearby the previous night. It's too long a journey otherwise. You'll have to ask him to rearrange.'

There was a pause. 'This is about our marriage, Marcus. Can't you make an exception for a few weeks? He's a highly sought after counsellor and won't have space for another six or eight months after that.'

Irritation arose in Marcus's voice. How dare she? Did she think she was in control here?

'Then find someone else, or, better still, forget the whole idea. We'll work it out between us. How hard can it be?' There was a bitter edge in his tone. He heard it but couldn't smooth it out.

Lydia's response was equally barbed. 'I wouldn't know. Yours hasn't been hard for over a year… unless it has been for someone else.' She paused. 'Marcus, if you're having an affair then I think you should have the good grace to tell me.'

Marcus was stunned. 'Shit, Lydia, this is a physical problem not a marriage problem.' As the words bumbled out he knew they were wrong.

'You're a doctor, aren't you? If it's impotence, then speak to one of your medical buddies and get it sorted.' He could hear defiance, or was it mockery?

'You know bloody-well that it's not about me.' He stabbed at the phone ending the call, his heart racing, his eyes burning into the phone screen. Seething.

As the months of pretence and denial had dragged by, he and Lydia had resorted to telephone calls as a safe way of discussing his alleged lack of sex drive. She had blamed his high levels of work stress at first and he had played along only dropping the odd hint about her weight loss being counterproductive. Then he began to beg her not to diet any more. She ignored his pleas and countered by reminding him how her self-esteem had improved, how much more fun she was having with her children and how healthy she felt.

Those were his lines, the ones he used to persuade his overweight patients to proceed with exorbitant surgery.

One night as they were preparing for bed he held her by

the shoulders and confessed. 'I find you more attractive the way you were. I love the curves.'

'I know you do, but you should love me however I look. I'm happy. Don't take that away from me, Marcus.' He didn't. Not then. Instead he went looking elsewhere for pleasure.

14

THE SECOND WEEKEND OF
DECEMBER

Thanks to a release of tension during his evening with Leonora, Thursday's surgery list had been uneventful. Later that day, his evening birthday treat at home with Lydia and the children had been bearable, but only because he had a weekend medical conference in York to look forward to. With Friday and Saturday accounted for, he wouldn't have to face Lydia's bony prominences again until some time on Sunday afternoon.

The lectures had been informative and inspiring but his world shook as a personal earthquake hit at about nine o'clock on the Saturday evening.

Standing with his nose over a gin and tonic, he had been privy to a general discussion between colleagues in the bar of the hotel. The lively debate had been about the ethics of offering surgery to friends and relatives of colleagues. During the exchange of views, his old mentor and one of his business rivals, Charles Broughton, approached him and took him to one side.

'I noticed you were rather quiet. I suppose it's a subject painfully too close to home. Can I ask how Lydia is doing?'

'Lydia is doing fine thanks. Why do you ask?'

'She certainly seems to have benefitted. Wouldn't you say?' Charles was speaking in his usual pompous manner, but it was the nature of his enquiry that threw Marcus. Why was Charles Broughton asking about Lydia? Then Charles revealed himself. 'I'm always interested in how well my patients are faring after surgery. Aren't you? Gastric bands can be so effective for—'

There had been a burst of raucous laughter from the nearby gathering of fellow surgeons, amused at an anecdote. Charles had turned towards the noise but looked back at Marcus in time to see him reel back in shock at the dawning realisation. He placed his drink on the nearest coffee table and, with a thunderous look in Charles' direction, he turned to leave without engaging in any form of reply.

Not far away the gaggle of doctors had picked up on the tense interaction. What followed was a palpable silence broken by low sounds of 'Oh-oh' from a young intern. After a few long seconds, a stammering apology came from Charles Broughton who raced after Marcus down the wide carpeted hotel lobby.

'Marcus. Marcus, wait. Christ, old chap, I do apologise, that was insensitive of me. I thought you knew.' Charles Broughton had paled, suddenly aware that he had committed professional transgressions that could place him in the line of fire for accusations of misconduct.

Marcus wasn't even thinking in the same vein. He aimed one shoulder at Charles Broughton, avoiding a face-to-face confrontation and a withering, contemptuous look shot from his slitted eyes. He said, 'Do the words professional courtesy mean nothing to you?' Marcus could barely manage to finish the sentence. Confidentiality be damned, this was deliberate professional sabotage designed to inflict lasting damage. What would people think if this ever got out? The internal rage he felt at that disclosure and that open declaration and breach of confidentiality never left him. It festered.

Worse than anything was discovering that Lydia had deceived him, battering the last of his personal defences, decimating any trust between them. He knew nothing of her gastric band, but he did recall her words as she announced her intentions to change. 'You have to stop feeding me. I can barely get up the stairs without puffing. We don't go out together, which is hardly surprising, and I know you say you want me like this but I have to think of the children.'

Lydia had tried dieting, tablets, exercise, and he honestly thought it was her self-determination that had finally helped her to succeed in spite of his forceful assurances that it was unnecessary. He was emphatic that dieting was not the answer, even so and despite the harm she was causing, she had disobeyed him. She hadn't found a miracle diet; she hadn't become Weight Watchers' success story of the year because, unbelievably, she had secretively sought the services of his competitor, his adversary, Charles Broughton of all people.

Back stabbing bitch that she had become, she didn't even have the common sense to ask one of his practice colleagues. How could she be so much more self-assured? Where had this inner strength to defy him come from?

He thought back to the time when she would have contrived to undergo the surgery. She had travelled with her mother to South Wales with the children to recuperate from some minor surgery to remove a problematical polyp in her uterus. That's what she had told him and he hadn't been interested enough to ask details. Being honest with himself, he had been glad of the respite their departure had brought. They had gone to Lydia's parents' holiday cottage in Tenby, and stayed for over three weeks, but, when he phoned her there, he was too distracted to enquire beyond everyday happenings.

'Hello, darling. Having a good time? Feeling better? How are your parents? The children? Good. Nice weather there I notice from the reports...'

Her health problems, fictitious ones as it turned out, had prevented her from carrying out her wifely duties for several months prior to her surgery and thus she was unavailable to satisfy his sexual appetites. He was irritated by her excuses, and with his hunger increasing, had sought to indulge himself elsewhere, desperately skirting the obvious availability of his trusting but sexually magnetic obese patients.

Flicking through health magazines for tantalizing "before and after" weight loss pictures failed to supply the necessary release. Public transport merely provided him with seedy fleshy encounters that did nothing more than drive his need; he brushed against plump women on the London Underground rather than take a cab. He once stood in a queue at a fast-food restaurant and accidentally reversed into a large lady standing behind him. With fear of exposure impeding him, he could do no more than make a grab for her enormous arm as he apologised to her cleavage.

In desperation he resorted to use of a plus sized prostitute by the name of Wanda. However, her cheap perfume, lack of intelligent conversation, sordid rental room and disrespect for his particular requests left him feeling dirty. She rushed him. He hated that.

Spectacular relief came in the shape of a call to Harry Drysdale.

'Harry, it's Marcus. That offer you once made me... I'd like to take you up on it if I may?'

The Wednesday of his wife's first week on so-called holiday, Harry had taken him to Buxham's as his guest. That initial foray into the expensive but utterly gratifying world of indulgences led him down a path he could not resist. The very next week he signed up for full membership and his inner demons escaped from their box permanently.

Packing his bag to leave the hotel in York on the Sunday after the medical conference had finished, he planned to leave without having to face his esteemed surgical colleagues and their inevitable questions over breakfast. He was angry. Bitter.

His wife's actions had completely sideswiped him. Was it a spiteful act of revenge for *sexual bullying* - as she had called it? If it was, he couldn't understand what had brought about such change. She should have been grateful to him. After all, he'd taken her on with two children in tow and all she had to do was satisfy him. She had always been his release, his safety valve to protect him from himself until she deliberately removed herself from his playground.

Armed with the knowledge that her weight loss had been the result of surgery, Lydia could be forced to change her mind. He would remove the gastric band himself if he only he could. But that wasn't possible.

Without her cooperation he would be left making use of a three hundred pound woman, who cost him over three hundred pounds sterling an hour, each week, in food and services rendered. On top of that he was dabbling at work. Lydia had to be made to gain weight again, to meet his requirements. What were wives for if not that?

Christmas was coming and geese were getting fat. It was time that Lydia did the same.

Marcus checked the calendar on his phone to reassure himself that the yuletide holidays did not fall on a Wednesday. He knew he wouldn't make it through the charade of jovial happy families without his next top up. He would find the right time to confront Lydia and in the meantime he would let her believe what she liked about his impotence.

After all, the most vivid of imaginations could not help him pretend his deflated wife was an adequate substitute for Leonora. Or better still, the new hostess, Ella.

Now there was another viable option, he thought. Ella. He could hire her as a housekeeper perhaps, or lure her with promises and make her his mistress.

He picked up his suitcase and headed for the door of the hotel room. Harry was right. Wednesdays were sacrosanct. Nothing should be allowed to change them. His other life should remain hidden for now and so he vowed to placate Lydia until he could find the best way to fuel his increasing obsessions. After that, perhaps he would have no need for his wife, her extra skin and her sweet daughters. She had become too different and he could not reconcile himself with her objectionable behaviour.

15

THE SEARCH

JANUARY 25TH

'Late on parade, Cyclops. You're two pints behind, pal.'
Barney announced. Konrad meandered past him to disrobe
and hang his overcoat on the stand in the corner of the
public bar, gloves stuffed into one pocket. Lorna was
greeting Annette, Barney's wife, with a mid-air kiss aimed
towards one cheek as Konrad replied to his best friend. 'Must
be my round then, old buddy, old chum. Make room.' Barney
stepped to one side allowing Konrad to elbow his way nearer
the beer pumps to inspect the choice on offer.

Rob, the landlord of The Valiant Soldier, was on
standby with a straight pint glass in one hand, a wineglass
in the other, awaiting instructions from Konrad. 'The
lovely Mrs Lorna Neale will have her usual glass of red
wine, a large one if you please. No holding back on the
alcohol tonight, we are walking home this evening. Well, to
be fair, I think skating would be a more accurate description. We resembled a couple of pissed penguins on the
journey here. The roads are bad enough, but the damned
pavements are lethal. Leaving the house is a risk to human
life in the village at the moment. We barely made it back

from the station in the Golf without crashing, purely because my wife is an expert driver. So she tells me anyway.'

Barney drained his glass and plonked it down in front of Konrad. 'I'll have another pint of your fine Hophead please, landlord.'

'You can wait your turn,' Konrad said. 'Rob, I would like an... umm, now then what beer shall I have this evening?' he asked, making a great show of examining the badges on each of the brass beer pumps. 'What a difficult decision. I'll be with you in a minute. Netty, what would you like? Another cider, is it?'

Barney fidgeted, knowing the wind-up would get worse if he reacted. The sausage-like fingers of his right hand were still wrapped around his empty pint glass and he tapped one foot impatiently as Konrad built the tension. 'Is this one an amber ale?' Konrad asked, indicating to the pump on his far left. 'No, Kon, that is an IPA, India Pale Ale like it says.' Rob was being most helpful, playing along.

'Could I try a taster of the Red Kite? I don't think I've had that one before.' He had, and Barney knew he had. While his thirsty friend looked on, Konrad picked up the glass of wine and pint of still cider. He delivered them in slow motion to Lorna and Annette who sat at a table near the fireplace. They had a front row view of the scene being enacted for their benefit and Annette was timing the event.

Konrad waved cheerily at an elderly gentleman who sat alone at the far end of the bar. 'Good evening, Duncan. Cold enough for you?'

'Arrr,' came the muffled reply. The man had a handkerchief to his large hooked nose.

When he returned to the bar Konrad leant across to Rob, a concerned expression on his face. 'Is he alright?'

'Not really. The dew-drop that lives permanently

attached to his hooter - you know the one - froze solid. Quite painful by all accounts.'

Konrad pursed his lips and nodded his understanding as Barney huffed with impatience.

'Do you have steak and kidney pudding on the menu this evening, Rob?' Konrad asked. 'I have a real yearning for winter food.'

Barney took the bait. 'Bollocks. There is no way you will eat suet pudding, you poncey git. You're too worried about your precious waistline to go near proper food like that. Now stop piss-arsing about and get me a beer.'

Annette was rocking with laughter. 'Pathetic. You didn't last much more than three minutes.'

'What's wrong with three minutes? You don't usually complain, missus. Three minutes is good going for me.' Barney was grinning madly. Rob shook his head and pulled Konrad's favourite pint. The joviality was honest and familiar, and a fitting beginning to an evening of lively discussion.

'Don't they ever get sick of that game?' Lorna asked.

'No, it's been the same for years, apparently. They've known each other far too long, I reckon.'

'Look at them. They're so different, most people would never imagine they were as close as brothers, but Kon would be lost without you and Barney. He thinks that pretty much everyone else who pretends to be his friend turns out to be the opposite.'

The pub was unusually quiet, mostly due to the disheartening weather conditions, allowing the four friends to make use of two large tables pushed together. They spread themselves out, to eat, drink and examine certain documents and photographs that Lorna and Konrad had brought along.

'Right, gang. Here's the gist of the article in this morning's papers,' Konrad announced as Barney approached the table with a full pint in his meaty hand. He oversaw proceedings from behind his wife's left shoulder as he rested his back against an old oak upright beam, preferring to stand for a while.

'When we went to the Pudding Club do, we all saw Harry at Buxham's on the night before he apparently disappeared, Wednesday January the third. He left the restaurant with his male friend and two marvellously dressed, well-endowed women, at about nine thirty. He bade us goodnight and inferred that he was about to receive more than pudding served in his room.'

'Maybe he got his just desserts then,' offered Barney.

'Perhaps he did.' Konrad frowned, recalling events. 'I didn't enjoy myself much that night. It was torture watching everyone stuff themselves stupid. I can't tell you how bloody relieved I am that the festive season has finally finished and I don't have to attend any more damn parties.'

'Yes, you certainly were more of a miserable bastard than usual that night. God knows why you can't give in once a year. I'm sure your adoring public wouldn't have noticed a few pounds going on. It's winter; wear a jumper,' Lorna said as she ruffled Konrad's silver hair in response to a low growling noise he made, conceding to her argument. She then poked a finger at the newspaper article.

'It says here that Harry stayed the night at Buxham's and checked out early in the morning but hasn't been seen since he boarded a train at Lensham.'

'Come on then, Lorna, you're famous for sniffing out a good story - what have you discovered so far? Who was he with?' Konrad asked, keen to get on with things.

Lorna pulled out her iPad and placed it on top of the Daily Albion article. 'The handsome chap with our little Harry on the night we met them, was this man.' She brought up an image on the screen showing a gentleman standing at a lectern. 'This well-groomed individual in a bespoke dinner suit is Marcus Carver, son of the famous Sir William Carver, surgeon and pioneer of specialist reconstructive facial surgery. If you'll pardon the pun, Marcus has carved out a name for himself as a bariatric surgeon and cosmetic surgery is his stock in trade. It was his duty to follow in his father's not inconsiderable footsteps. With a surname like that he had little choice.'

Konrad smirked. 'Nominative determinism it's called. There are loads of examples. I once met a man called Mr Mike Churn who used to work for the milk marketing board. When I was in hospital in Manchester I was told of a Sister Cartilage who worked in osteopathy, Lorna's old GP was called Dr Bone, and when we were in Bangor there was actually an undertaker by the name of Hugo Stiff, do you remember?' he asked Lorna.

She chortled, 'Oh yes! I'd forgotten that one. Anyway, as I was saying, the sign on the cosmetic medical group's Harley Street door reads, Marcus Carver, BSc. MBBS. FRSC (plast).'

Annette was immediately enthralled by this information. 'How ironic. A bariatric surgeon as a member of Buxham's club; does he go there to tout for business?'

Lorna gave her friend a wicked grin. 'My guess would be even more ironic than yours. Unless he has an eating disorder, like bulimia, then I would suggest that Marcus Carver and Harry Drysdale don't go to stuff themselves stupid with delicious highly calorific food and drink. The way they were behaving towards their lady-friends and the extremely attractive restaurant hostess would suggest a more carnal motive.'

Annette wobbled with anticipation at what was to be revealed next.

'This makes no odds for Harry,' Lorna said in a matter-of-fact voice. 'He's divorced and reckless, cares little for tabloid opinion about his private life but *is* dedicated to his income.

He wouldn't have done anything so rash as to run away with his latest floozy and miss an important court case. So therein lies the mystery.' She waved her hand and poked at the screen. 'However, this man, Marcus Carver, with a wife and two children - hers not his - and a massively successful business in the private cosmetic surgery field, has a lot to lose if his personal playtime antics were revealed as being...'

'Fat?' suggested Annette, looking round at Barney who shrugged.

Lorna caught the exchange and pushed for confirmation. 'Come on. You two have been trotting along to The Lensham and District Pudding Club nearly every month for the past year. You know more. Spill.'

Konrad put his beer down and folded his arms, waiting. 'Yeah. Spill,' he echoed.

The sheepish expression on the faces of Barney and Annette prophesied confessions still to be imagined. Spotting this, Konrad and Lorna made themselves comfortable and ordered more drinks from Rob who was attending to the fireplace, poking at the burning embers and adding a couple more logs. He was nosily tuned in to the conversation, eager to learn what secrets were to be told.

Suet pudding secrets with jam and custard.

'We didn't know it was him. Buxham's is obsessive about privacy and although we all use our first names in the pudding club, the full members of Buxham's are anonymous. Your friend Harry didn't react too badly when you recognised and called out to him, but the staff never refer to the guests by anything other than sir or madam. Or an initial. Harry was always Mr D, his mate was Mr C, but it's more customary for a simple table number to be used. They always sit at table number eighty-eight. The whole pudding club knew it. *Two fat ladies, eighty-eight.* It was a standing joke.'

Konrad listened intently to every word. His radar was on

and whirring madly. 'You think Harry was there every Wednesday with the same man and at least one woman. You said two fat ladies, but are they always the same two fat ladies or does it change? Is Harry with Marcus Carver each time or is he joined by anyone else and how come neither of you mentioned this to us previously?'

Barney wore a look of confusion. 'We didn't know it was Harry Drysdale. Neither of us. Did we Netty? Remember, it's been a few years since we've seen him and even then he was wafting about in a wig and a gown.'

'It feels a bit peculiar to think we never recognised him at all,' Annette said, 'but honestly even though he was smartly dressed for dinner he was relaxed, full of cheerful banter and just another customer as far as we knew. You can't really see what goes on in those booths anyway. It's a place for private members to relax and not to have to worry about being recognised.'

'Yes, but why?' Lorna asked.

'We reckon the two fat ladies are ordered in,' Barney said. 'We've seen at least four different ones pass by, heading to or from table eighty-eight and a couple of other tables, if I'm right.'

'Yes, that's true and Barney checked each one of them out as they wiggled their buttocks in his direction,' Annette said, thrusting her head playfully backwards into Barney's rounded beer belly.

'It's free to look.'

'Is it? Maybe it's a pound an ogle, and you were lucky not to get caught.' Barney squeezed his wife's shoulders and bent forward to kiss the top of her head. 'Only one woman for me, oh-chunky-one. I could never imagine losing my head in anyone else's breasts.'

Konrad heaved a sigh. 'Thanks for leaving me with that picture in my mind. Now can we please get back to the matter in hand? What connection do we have regarding these larger women and Harry's disappearance?' He looked at each of them. 'We don't. Do we, Lorna?'

Wearing a serious face, his wife concurred. 'There is nothing to suggest anything illegal or untoward in Harry's case. However, I went on an exploration of Marcus Carver's past and first, I stumbled across something that may have a bearing and, secondly, an astounding discovery about his wife that will raise your eyebrows. If we zero in on Marcus Carver, we may find out what has happened to Harry.'

16

THE WEEK BEFORE CHRISTMAS

Ella was settling into the demands of the festive season at Buxham's to such a degree that she occasionally forgot she was there to gather vital information and set up the two men that were now firmly in her crosshairs, Harry Drysdale and Marcus Carver.

Nothing about her new role had been beyond her capabilities so far. Although her aching feet often complained by the end of the evening, she was revelling in the challenges of the frantic restaurant service on each shift.

Much to Ella's relief, Ada had taken up the job offer and, despite being a part-timer, was now accepted as a hard-working member of the front of house team in Buxham's restaurant. The rest of the club staff had been friendly and helpful enough, with the exception of the cantankerous head chef Schubert. That was his surname. Everyone referred to him as Schubert or more simply as Chef.

Yes, Chef, No, Chef, three bags full, Chef. Ella would say to herself when he began his daily criticism of the waiting staff.

He was a pernickety Austrian shouting machine with a

vocabulary made up mostly of volcanic expletives. He reminded Ella of a furious bulbous Arnold Schwarzenegger. Ada was so upset by the man that she'd threatened to hand her notice in within the first two weeks of commencing her new job.

'He's a bastard. I'll not 'ave him talk to me like that. Once more and I'll stick his hollandaise sauce where t' sun don't shine.'

His hypercritical approach made most of the waiting staff jittery. When Flora, one of Buxham's best waitresses, had burst into tears the previous evening, Ella was forced to make her case to Schubert for him to ease up on his ranting before there was a front of house mutiny.

There was little opportunity to resolve matters during that busy evening service, other than to lodge her complaint with Schubert over the pass.

'Chef, will you please refrain from addressing staff in such a hurtful manner. I think we should speak about this again tomorrow when you have calmed down.'

Schubert was sweating over several plates that lay under the heat lamps awaiting his final tweaks of presentation. He rounded on Ella, eyes narrowing. 'Fuck off back to the restaurant. I don't need your advice, new girl.' A waft of garlic accompanied his words.

When she emerged from his small office the following morning she pasted a smile on her face for the benefit of the kitchen brigade. The chefs were putting on a good show of concentrating on their preparations, their *mise en place*, but she caught their veiled signs of approval and admiration.

The heated exchange between Ella and Schubert could easily have been heard from several feet beyond the office. His initial onslaught was booming to the degree that the glass panels in the door shook, but Ella had stood firm. She blasted him for his appalling man-management and with her final suggestion, about how to control his temper Schubert rocked back in his creaking chair and howled with sarcastic laughter.

'You are seriously suggesting that if I want to swear, that I go to the walk-in freezer and shout in *there*? Are you mad?'

'That's a distinct possibility, Chef, but mad or not, it's my duty to tell you that your behaviour constitutes bullying and harassment. It's unnecessary and undermines the efficiency of the restaurant team, which, I hasten to add, includes your brigade.'

'How I manage my fucking team is up to me, Bella,' he roared.

'My name is Ella, and you are mistaken. I do not allow myself to get bullied. Not anymore. I don't bully anyone else and it is unacceptable in the workplace. Encouragement and constructive criticism are welcome and the odd swear word is fine as long as it is not aimed at individuals. Do I make myself clear?' Ella had stood with her hands on her hips, staring defiantly at Schubert, not faltering, not flinching.

I do not get bullied.

'Who the fuck do you think you are, talking to me like this?' Schubert stood from his seat and leant over his paper-strewn desk, both sets of knuckles resting on draft menu cards. His ears reddened.

Ella declined to be intimidated and in her head she truly believed her own charade. Her part was to play a confident restaurant manager. '*I* am the person tasked with ensuring that the magnificent food served in your kitchen is delivered to our customers efficiently, effectively and competently by cheerful conscientious waiting staff. *I* am the person who manages the timing of the orders for your brigade to avoid overwhelming them. *I* am the person who represents *you* in that restaurant.' She took a step forward and opened both hands towards Schubert. 'That is who the fuck I think I am. Over to you, Chef.'

Chef straightened and folded his arms. *Oh, dear. That's a bad sign,* thought Ella. However, for once, she was wrong. Schubert's face mellowed, as did his tone of voice.

'Well said, young lady. You have balls of steel and I admire you for having the guts to stand up for your staff and yourself. You have a valid reason and I apologise, unreservedly. I am a perfectionist, you understand.' He angled his head to one side.

'I do indeed, which is why I knew you would appreciate hearing the truth. We should work together.'

'Agreed, young lady.' Schubert pumped Ella's hand and then in an unexpected manoeuvre he raised it to his lips and kissed gently. 'I thank you for your observations. Together we shall achieve perfection.'

Moving through the kitchen, swelling with pride and a sense of immense satisfaction, Ella could feel a dozen pairs of eyes watching her.

'Have a good service tonight, team. It's going to be another busy one, so let me know if you need changes in the running order as we go. See you later.'

She stepped onto the carpet of the restaurant, exhaling loudly and checking her hands for tremors. Spiros, the maddest Greek barman Ella had ever come across, was giving her a silent round of applause from behind the bar. 'If you do not cry, then you have done a wonderful thing.' His specific meaning wasn't clear to Ella, but the sentiment was positive enough.

Her third Wednesday evening service was looming, the one just before Christmas, and she had arranged to meet with Val at the Old Station Café at three o'clock.

Approaching the glass door she could see Mal slumped in a corner, huddled into a black puffer jacket, reading a daily newspaper, but no sign of her boss, her old friend. He dropped the edge of the paper peering towards the door as she entered. He beamed, allowed the paper to complete its journey to the table and stood to greet her. 'Hi, sis. How's the new job going?'

'Great thanks. It's a bit busy with the Christmas festivities so I can't stay long.' She sat down alongside Mal to ask quietly, 'What's making you grin?'

'These adverts.'

He poked a well-manicured finger toward some small advertisements in the personal section of the newspaper.

'Getting lonely, are you?'

'I'm not that bleedin' desperate, luv. Not quite.'

Ella shuffled closer to read. 'Usual stuff… massage, home visits… oh dear, why would anyone want to have an exciting intimate time with someone old enough to be my granny? And what is a BBW when it's at home?'

'You are.'

'Am I?' Ella asked, somewhat astounded.

'Big beautiful woman. BBW. There's a few in here.'

'Hang on a minute,' Ella said, affronted at the insinuation, 'are you putting me in the same bracket as an oversized escort girl? Thanks a bloody bunch. I used to like you. Anyway,' she said, moving back to her own personal space on the bench seat, 'where's Val?'

In avoiding the question, Mal drew attention to himself. Ella noticed a sorrowful look in his eyes, a grey tinge to his skin and he seemed anxious, his face pinched. Before she had a chance to challenge him, Emo-waitress appeared at the corner of the table.

'Where's Val, your scruffy mate? I've left her a couple of

messages.' A puzzled look strayed across her black eyebrows. 'Swinging both ways now are ya?' she said to Ella chewing on gum while sliding her eyes in Mal's direction. If anything her make-up was more heavily applied than the last time Ella had seen her. The girl was so morose that instead of hair piled on her head it should have been a gloomy cloud.

Mal responded with a sardonic smile. 'Val's been a bit poorly the last day or so, luv. She might not be in to see you for a while. You hang on in there, darlin'. I'm sure she'll be sniffing round again before too long.'

'What the fuck would you know?' Emo-girl snubbed Mal and returned her enquiries to Ella. 'Drink? Summing t'w'eat?' Her sloppy diction was a source of fascination to Ella who made the waitress repeat the question purely to delight in hearing her pronounce the Queen's English so badly.

'Hot Chocolate, if you have it please.'

There was a tut and a sigh. Emo-waitress then tipped her pen towards Mal. 'E want anyfing?'

'A smile? Some cheerful witty banter to make my day complete, luv. What d' you say?'

'I say, do you want anyfing or not? If not, then fuck off.'

'Another cup of your finest coffee would be great, luv, ta.'

Emo-waitress didn't reply other than to roll her eyes. Then she skulked off in the direction of the service area where she set about providing two drinks accompanied by unbridled swearing, crashing of crockery and clanking of utensils.

Ella turned to Mal who was continuing to shake his head at the entertaining misery displayed by their waitress.

'What a foul specimen. Does Val really fancy that?' he said.

'I think it's already gone beyond the chatting up stage. Let's not dwell for now. Tell me about Val,' Ella demanded.

'She's in hospital having a few more tests done.'

'A few *more*? What bloody tests? Hang on, Mal, she never mentioned this two days ago when I saw her. What's going on?'

'It's not brilliant news, I'm afraid. That cough has turned out to be a bit of a bastard and she's got something up with her guts as well.'

'Like what?' Ella asked, drilling into his eyes. He avoided her scrutiny by peering at the newspaper again.

'Oi! Stop dribbling over the escort ads and try to be honest with me,' she insisted.

'You know what she's like. She hates admitting to any sort of weakness, but she sends her best and asks you to carry on as planned,' he said, glancing up. 'Waste of time being over sentimental. She's as tough as old boots and she wants you to get on with the job she sent you to do. Besides, we both need the money and I've got a reputation to uphold. Mal always gets his man. Know what you've got to do?'

'Yes, but the agency have cancelled our lawyer friend's choice of companion for this week, and it's such short notice they can't re-supply. I spoke to the duty manager and offered to make myself available for a life-drawing session by way of compensation. I only hope one of them takes the bait and that I haven't fed myself to the wolves.'

'Couldn't you try one of these adverts instead? Get another escort girl in?'

'You have to be kidding me. The agency they use at the club is high class, top notch, and they charge a fortune. You saw them on table eighty-eight. Fragrant, educated, articulate, expensively dressed and gorgeous. I'd be sacked on the spot for ordering in a fat minger from Scumsville as a substitute.'

'Sorry. Just trying to help. Well done anyway. You did good.'

Ella fidgeted. 'I have no problem posing in the altogether,

but Mal, I'm a bit crap with surveillance equipment. I'm not permitted to use my mobile phone and I'll have to set up a camera in the room, if I manage to get that far. How the hell am I supposed to do that with the poxy things you've given me?'

Mal rested his hands on top of the paper. 'You'll have to do your best. I had a meeting with the general manager at Buxham's and they are tighter than a duck's arse when it comes to sweeping for hidden cameras and bugs in that place. The equipment they have is first class. I'm told there was nearly an international incident involving a rich Arab and an undercover reporter some years ago and since then they are obsessive. They check for bugs in air fresheners, USB chargers, remote controls, you name it they scrutinize it. Our secret services couldn't do better.' He sighed before continuing.

'The only suggestion I made, to justify my bill, was for them to make confiscation of all mobile phones compulsory for anyone who uses the restaurant. So, young lady, you will have to do what you can. Get some pictures and then wait for instructions. After that we plan your resignation. Mind you, if Val's going to be out of action you might have to stay on. You may have no other income and I could be left short myself.'

'So we have to finish this job. We can't let Val down. Not now.'

'Yep. That's about the size of it. Here is a list and lay out of the CCTV cameras. If you need anything else you have my number and I'll come to your rescue like any big brother would. No questions will be asked, just don't get caught.'

Ella had considered telling Mal about her history with Marcus Carver but decided against it. She would do as she thought fit. Val had a plan for setting up Harry Drysdale and she would do the same for Marcus Carver. Two for the price of one. How best to go about manufacturing their undoing would depend entirely on what happened in the following three weeks. It was up to Ella to find out the details, to prove Val's hypothesis. But how?

17

THE WEDNESDAY BEFORE CHRISTMAS

December the twentieth had not worked out as planned. The XL Agency had cancelled Mr D's date for the evening and there had been a peculiar competitive feel to the dynamics on table eighty-eight as a result. It wasn't long before Ella had determined that she was the subject of desire to fill the gap left by Harry's escort but that both men were vying for her.

She made a show of caving in to a special Christmas request, agreeing to sit as an artist's model for Harry Drysdale after dinner service. This was despite the fact that the idea had been hers in the first place.

'Mr C has the curvaceous Leonora to keep him company and so it's only fair that I should take up the club's generous offer of another companion for the late evening hours. Art for art's sake,' Harry said.

Ella felt the pit of her stomach lurch as the reality of her offer sank in. She was dubious and uncertain as to what she was about to undertake. All the staff at Buxham's assumed that both men's appetites were left of normal. However, in reality, they had no evidence to suggest exactly what went on between their members and the ladies of the XL Agency.

The staff team signed binding contracts and were well paid for their silence; even tittle-tattle between the club's employees did not stray far beyond innuendo, euphemism and brief offensive references. The phrase "to lick the bowl clean" took on a whole new meaning at Buxham's on a Wednesday.

The restaurant emptied much sooner than was usual, with many gourmet members forced into catching earlier trains home due to disruption from industrial action on the railway lines. This played into Ella's hands. She had time to shower, reapply her make up, and take her much need medication. The nervous anticipation had begun to excite her and knowing that she was required to sit motionless she made judicial use of a small blue pill. Lorazepam. It would take the edge off her hypomania and allow her to carry out her investigative duties calmly. After consulting her goldfish, Gordon, about the need for underwear, she changed into a long-line cashmere V-neck jumper and leggings. Satisfied, she then presented herself, pashmina at the ready, at the door of Harry Drysdale's suite a few minutes after nine-thirty that evening.

Not knowing what risks she may be about to take, she had made sure to inform the duty manager and get a message to Mal. The text that came back from her colleague made her laugh aloud.

Any trouble, just kick him in the nuts and cry rape.

The advice from the duty manager was much more customer focussed. He was impressed that Ella's talents were being put to such good use in providing a range of services at Buxham's that had not been previously available. What's more, he'd shared words along those lines with Ella while he calculated how much additional charge to add to Mr D's monthly bill. 'A nice boost to your earnings, Ella. A Christmas bonus. You'll have no trouble as long as you set your boundaries and keep to them. You decide the limits of the agreement. I will be charging for three hours in total. Any more than that please let me know.'

Ella stared at him, unsure what advice to ask. Was he condoning personal services of an intimate nature?

She found out within minutes of entering Harry Drysdale's lavish suite. He had changed from smart clothes worn for dinner, into extremely casual linen trousers and a T-shirt, and signalled for her to enter. She stood a couple of inches taller than he did until, shaking slightly, she slipped off her shoes and padded towards the sofa. Prodding at the upholstery, she tried to work out where she could place her large handbag so that the camera within would pick up what she was to be confronted with.

'No. I'd prefer it if you could pose on the bed for me,' Harry said.

Ella froze. She stammered as she forced the words from her mouth. 'I, I need to make it abundantly clear, Mr D... I'm not here for sex. This booking is for life modelling.'

Through a strong sense of foreboding her bladder was playing tricks, and she felt a sudden urgency to urinate. It was fear. Her confidence and self-assurance had deserted the moment her eyes moved from the sofa to the bed and the calming effect of the lorazepam had not so far been felt. She fidgeted, rocking from one leg to the other.

Harry bent over and from the coffee table he picked up a sketchpad.

'I know. I believe that was my request. If I had wanted anything more, I would have negotiated harder. Please, feel free to make use of the bathroom to undress and come out when you are ready.'

For a while, she couldn't regain control over her imagination but she did at least manage to reduce the nervous quivering of her limbs. For Ella self-soothing involved talking through difficult times, usually aiming her words towards Gordon, her goldfish, in the privacy of her own room. In the bathroom of Harry Drysdale' s suite, as she stripped off her clothes, she had a full-on internal monologue.

Right you stupid biddy. This is where you need to be. Build trust with the man then you can use him to get to Marcus fucking Carver. Be elusive, make him want you and work for the privilege. She looked in the mirror and looped the pashmina around her back and over her arms. *Off we go. Sit still and silently. Let him do the talking.*

He was as good as his word. Harry gave instructions on how he wished her to lie on the bed and checked that she was comfortable. Sitting in a chair across the room he began to draw using pencil, not charcoal. The air was warm and gentle music was playing in the background, Spanish guitar music. Harry seemed to be concentrating hard on the artistic task and there was a distinct lack of conversation, putting Ella in an unusual position as far as developing a trusting relationship was concerned. With her breathing under control, her thoughts slowed, and her focus regained, she became aware of her own vulnerability, not because of her nakedness, but because she couldn't fathom out what was to come next.

How on earth was she going to wheedle information out of him if there was no meaningful verbal interaction? Her great scheme to offer this as exclusive entertainment for VIP club members had not been so brilliant after all. A basic novice's error on her part, she realised.

Ella could now see that the man drawing her was in

charge, silently managing the whole situation and revelling in that certainty. After several long minutes, he ran his tongue across his lower lip and a frown appeared. 'This is a little delicate, but there are lines where your lingerie has marked your skin. I wonder would you mind taking a break and perhaps we could place the pashmina in such a way that those creases are covered. It's such a shame to ruin the sweep of your torso.'

He approached as Ella sat up. She was embarrassed for failing to take this into consideration as she used to do for the art classes when she prepared well ahead of time, removing soft underwear and rubbing moisturiser into her skin. That evening, however, she didn't have the luxury of wearing such unsupportive bra and briefs. In the restaurant she routinely wore large sturdy knickers to hold herself under control and her bras were specifically designed to lift and restrain her breasts from swinging about and causing backache. Looking down she quickly realised how unsightly those marks were. 'I'm so sorry. I didn't have time to moisturise. I sometimes use bio oil to—'

'Good idea. Let's try that. Here, feel free.' Harry handed her a tall cylindrical plastic bottle from the nearest bedside cabinet. She undid the cap and sniffed warily, checking his eyes for giveaway signs of deceptive intent. The smell was familiar. She rubbed a little on her fingertips and inhaled once more. Lavender, bergamot, and patchouli - a light perfumed oil that absorbed into the skin in seconds. Ideal. She didn't take time to question why he should have it in his possession, she was more relieved to know that it would be suitable for her immediate needs. Without thinking, Ella began to shuffle to the edge of the bed aiming for the bathroom. Harry stopped her. 'Please, carry on where you are, that way we can chat.'

Her breath caught in her throat. Stay and play, or hide

and lose the opportunity to work her magic by befriending Harry Drysdale. She had no real alternative. 'I might make a mess on the lovely bedspread,' she said looking around for a way of improving her plight.

'Quite right young lady. How very considerate of you. I'll fetch a bath towel.' Ella sat transfixed, watching him. How cunning of him to use the hiatus in proceedings to get to the bathroom, perhaps to access her bag for information about her, to gain advantage. Convinced that her naivety was going to be her downfall, she berated herself silently for lack of a plan, a workable, practical plan. She was winging it.

Harry took his seat again as Ella began to rub her skin with oil.

'So when did you begin life-modelling?' A standard question from Harry. Nothing untoward. Safe subject matter about her life, but not at all useful in exploring his life story, habits and secrets, or his friendship with Marcus Carver.

'I only started a year or so ago, to earn a little extra cash between jobs.' Ella had spoken herself into trouble. Her preoccupation with the indentations on her skin had resulted in a rash lack of concentration.

'Have you always been in the hospitality trade?' A peculiar emphasis on the word *hospitality* made Ella stop stroking her skin and look into Harry's eyes. He averted his gaze and looked down at the sketchpad on his knees. 'I only ask because you seem so confident out there in the restaurant, I assume you've had a few years to hone your skills.'

Ella didn't get a chance to answer. The bottle of oil slipped through her fingers and she scrabbled to retrieve it from the towel as its precious contents glugged out. Harry was suddenly beside her holding the container and chuckling. 'Clumsy. Here... let me.'

Holy shit. He's touching me.

Nothing untoward happened. Ella accepted the free

massage. Another five minutes passed during which she tried to steer the conversation towards information about Marcus Carver. 'How long have you and Mr C been coming to Buxham's?'

'A while.'

'You must be quite good friends. How do you know each other?' Harry would not be drawn on detail and Ella had to back off before she was rumbled.

'There, your skin looks lovely now,' Harry said, twisting the cap back on to the bottle of oil. 'There's a special sheen to it. Lay back as you were. Just relax and take a break while I draw.'

She did as she was asked and valiantly fought the fatigue that threatened to overwhelm her. It had been a hard few days and the long hours, extra concentration of learning a new job, a dose of Lorazepam and being undercover were beginning to sap her usual boundless energy levels. The daily battle with her brain chemistry was exhausting enough.

WHEN ELLA AWOKE, she was covered by a towelling bathrobe and Harry was gathering her clothes and belongings from the bathroom. The scene made its way slowly into her conscious mind, and only then did the consequences of her error dawn on her. Falling asleep had been unforgivable. When she eventually made sense of the world around her, she saw that Harry had been looking at the contents of her substantial handbag. He had one hand inside the bag, the other holding it open by the loop of leather handle as he crouched on the bathroom floor.

She spoke up, croaking.

'Oh God, I'm so, so, so sorry. How rude of me. I can't apologise enough.'

Unexpectedly Harry laughed. Releasing his grip on something inside her handbag he looked at her as he stood upright. 'Please don't apologise. I've drawn my best ever work. Look at this.' He dropped Ella's clothes onto the bedspread where she could reach them and left her bag on the floor beside the bed. He then rushed over to the table, eager to show her his sketch.

Having hurriedly put on her bra and pulled the cashmere sweater over her head, she remained sitting on the edge of the bed, her lower half covered by the bathrobe. Ella stared in disbelief at what she saw. Holding the sketchpad in both hands, nausea ascended her throat to the degree that saliva predicted she would vomit. She held on. Cold. Empty. He must have moved her hand while she'd been asleep because the drawing showed her fingers placed strategically between her legs.

Had he?

She couldn't be sure. Maybe she'd moved in her sleep. How could she know?

He seemed to read her expression. 'Don't be embarrassed. This is beautiful. So natural, so incredibly erotic, and it's mine to keep and gaze upon. I'm ecstatic, Ella. Can we do this again sometime?'

With no way of knowing precisely what had happened, Ella simply nodded, and gathered up the rest of her clothes before skedaddling into the bathroom. Once there with the door locked behind her, she stood at the sink to steady herself. Breathing rapidly, she scanned up and down in the mirror yet she found no unusual marks. She checked her most intimate places and could find no evidence of interference. Nothing.

Pull yourself together, woman. Get back out there and smile, for God's sake. Your mistake. You sort it.

What had his facial expressions told her? Had he lied? Was he teasing her? She didn't know. For once she could not work it out. All she could reasonably do was to apologise once more before she left to return to her own small room on the upper floor, in the eaves of the main house. Once there, heart thumping like a maniacal drummer boy, she removed every item of her handbag contents and placed them on her bed. Ella then reviewed what each could reveal about her to anyone who may be interested. To Harry Drysdale. Fortunately, obeying the rules of the house, her mobile phone had remained in her room. It lay on her bedside table. She reached for it, desperate for advice and reassurance.

A second before she pressed the favourites button on the phone to contact Mal, she glanced at the time. Holding herself back from making such a call in the middle of the night she sent a placatory text instead.

Two words.

ALL FINE

The smallest of big lies.

It was too late at night to phone Ada; Ada needed her sleep. She didn't even entertain the idea of contacting Val because she could only imagine the fury with which her confession would be met. Ella could almost hear Val's words 'You fell asleep? You stupid fucking moron…'

Calculating the hour or so she had lost, Ella was horrified. There was no way she could have slept for that long, she thought, and checked the clock in her room again. A whole hour fast asleep on the bed of the man she was employed to find out about. Sixty long exposed minutes with the person she was assigned to spy on.

She knew no more now about Harry Drysdale than when she had first met him. He, however, probably knew her full name, that she had a dentist's appointment the following week and that she was on medication. Which, if he cared to look it up, would tell him that she was under treatment for a serious mental health condition. Apart from that, he would have scavenged little in the way of personal information from the contents of her bag. On her bed lay the usual culprits: hairbrush, tissues, lip-gloss, alcohol hand rub, a small pharmacy of pills, some for headaches, and two pens. She also carried with her two torches, or what looked like torches, but which were in fact small digital cameras. *No barrister would have any clue as to their true use,* she convinced herself.

Wait.

Where was her tiny notepad? And more importantly what had she written in it?

Without her phone to hand while she was on shift at Buxham's, Ella had taken to scribbling ideas and observations into a handy-sized note pad that lived in her pocket when she was working, or in her bag. She hadn't been so stupid as to write names down but to someone astute and intelligent like Harry it would be a gift.

In a state of abject panic she thrust her hands back into her handbag to double check and with an overwhelming release of tension finally located it wedged into an inside zip. She stared at the small book, flicked through the pages and put a hand to her mouth. 'How incredibly fucking thick am I?' she whispered bitterly.

There was one question that persisted throughout the restless night; did Harry Drysdale read anything written in that notebook while she had slept?

19

THE SEARCH

JANUARY 25TH - THE VALIANT SOLDIER

'Shall we start with Marcus Carver's wife? What's the scandal there?' Annette asked as she picked up her fourth giant deep-fried onion ring of the evening. She had polished off a four-teen-ounce T-bone steak with hand-cut chips and peas and was grazing on the remnants of the side orders.

Konrad had scraped clean his bowl of carrot and coriander soup, reluctantly donating the second slice of farmhouse bread-and-butter to Barney to mop up gravy from his plate of steak and kidney pudding.

Lorna wiped her fingers on a paper serviette and from her bag she took out a spiral-bound reporter's notebook, flipping the cover and the first three or four pages. Having found the page she was looking for, she began to list a number of facts about Lydia Carver.

'Thirty-two-years-old, so a fair few years younger than her husband. Nothing wrong with that, obviously,' she said looking over at Konrad. 'Her two children, eight and six are from a previous relationship. Her first husband skedaddled off with his accountant, his male accountant, by the name of Jordan Wallasey, who has a notoriously filthy drag act as a side-line to book-keeping. This outrageous turn of events understandably left Lydia feeling devastated, especially as she was pregnant at the time.'

'This sounds reminiscent of a cheap drama series,' Annette said licking at her fingertips. 'Does this mean that she and Marcus haven't been married for too long?'

Konrad chuckled to himself. 'Right on cue, Miss Marple.'

Lorna smiled gratefully at Annette. 'Spot on, Netty. She and Marcus had been married for over four years during which time she put on an enormous amount of weight. She was never svelte, but the few photos I managed to find demonstrate a dangerous upward trend in dress size from the moment she met him.' Lorna pulled up images of Lydia Carver on to the screen of her iPad and swung it round for all to see.

'Fine looking woman,' Barney said.

'She was *then* but let me show you how she looked just before Christmas.'

'Bloody Nora! She must have lost a whole person's worth of weight,' Annette exclaimed, examining the photographs on screen more closely. 'I thought it was a different woman for a mo.'

'Quite a radical turnaround,' Lorna confirmed. 'In the ten months leading up to this Christmas the weight dropped off, revealing a woman who had shrunk down to a size fourteen from a size twenty-six. Too good to be true of course.'

'Definitely,' said Annette. 'He must have made her lose weight, put her under the knife or sucked the fat out.'

'No. That's where you're wrong. I assumed the same, but Konrad's sources in the world of plastic surgery tell a very different story indeed.'

Konrad subconsciously touched the scarring on his face, stopping only because Lorna had become silent. This was an uncomfortable subject for them but Barney cut through the

short awkward pause with his usual unsubtle humour. 'So
the man who rebuilt Cyclop's face has something to do with
fat Mrs Carver becoming thin Mrs Carver.'

Lorna grinned with gratitude. 'Not quite, Barney, but
neatly put. An eminent bariatric surgeon by the name of
Charles Broughton fitted a gastric band at Lydia Carver's
request, without her husband's knowledge. Rumour has it
that Marcus was furious when he eventually found out.'

There was a chortle. It came from Barney. 'I'd be bloody
livid if Netty did that. Cor, bugger me. What would *I* do with
a skinny bird? No. That's a shocker. What was she thinking?'

Annette wiped grease from her lips and kissed her
husband on the cheek.

'That's almost exactly how we thought you'd react,' Lorna
said. 'But you see, Kon and I didn't respond in the same way.
We initially assumed that she wanted to lose weight for her
own reasons, perhaps to improve her health or feel better
about herself, and that his practice had simply declined to do
the surgery because she was his wife.' She paused.

'But to go ahead without her plastic surgery husband's
knowledge tells a different story. So I tried to explore in
more depth the reasons why, because not only did she have
surgery behind his back but she chose his rival.' Lorna looked
around her. The faces were blank.

'Lydia met Marcus when she went for a consultation as a
patient. He never performed any surgery, he chased her,
metaphorically speaking of course, and pursued her roman-
tically until she submitted. That's the story. He wanted her to
stay fat, at least that's how it looks.'

Annette clapped with excitement. 'Superb. What's
the catch?'

'I planned to interview her for an article in a health magazine to get a bit more of an idea about their relationship and
as I'm freelance, there were no lies on my part but—'

'She declined your offer?'

Lorna shook her head. 'Worse than that, Netty.'

'She ran away?'

'No. She's dead. Ostensibly – so the story goes – her gastric band ruptured and killed her just after the New Year celebrations.'

'Ruptured! Oh dear, those poor children. Do they know what happened? Was there a post mortem?'

'Yes, there was. The Coroner has yet to set a date for a hearing but there's an ongoing inquest. I tried to find out the details by bribing Katie at Wakeman's Funeral Services but the Chinese whispers had resulted in a ridiculous story about Lydia over-indulging. Falling off the food waggon while she was staying with her parents after Christmas.'

'That's preposterous,' Annette agreed, 'a gastric band is supposed to reduce your ability to eat too much. There has to be more to the story than that.'

Barney stretched, scratching his belly through layers of shirt and jumper. 'How is this going to help us find Harry? I'm sorry that surgeon's wife died and all that, but what *is* the connection between Marcus Carver and Harry, apart from having dinner with two decent sized women on a Wednesday?'

Konrad had been biding his time, waiting to disclose the spicy information he had been given earlier that day. While his wife - consumed in her mission to find Harry - had been on the case of Lydia Carver, he had been putting feelers out to answer the question Barney had so eloquently raised. 'You may well ask, old pal.'

'I did ask.'

'Yes. Well done. I may have part of an answer for you. Now then, what does Harry do for a living? ... so I started there. My first call was to Rupert Van Dahl who I managed to catch in a semi sober state. He'd had the right amount of alcohol to loosen his tongue, but not too much to be unreliable as a grass. His chambers were involved in the same case.'

'What case?' Annette asked.

Konrad took great satisfaction in stringing out the story of how Harry met Marcus because of allegations that sexually inappropriate examinations had been carried out by him in the course of his consultations.

'Not only that, but he was charged with sexual assaults carried out shortly after surgery at a time when patients were sedated and or semi-conscious. According to Rupert Van Dahl QC, Harry Drysdale had been spectacular in his defence of his client.'

'He must have been,' Lorna said. 'If the CPS felt there was a good enough case to go to court, then surely the evidence was solid enough to charge him and to expect a conviction.'

Barney appeared to be fascinated by the corner of an old oak beam. He looked up to the ceiling with a smirk. 'Hang on a minute. I don't get this. Marcus Carvery ...'

'Carver.'

'Yes 'im. He is a surgeon. His job is to cut fat bits off people. How would he do that unless he had a good old feel about? You know, prodding and kneading to work out where to cut and how much. Checking his handiwork after surgery and all that. I've seen them on the telly.'

Konrad leant back in his chair. 'You, my oldest and dearest fat friend, have hidden intellectual talents that are wasted in that workshop of yours. Wasted.' He clapped his hands, slowly and deliberately as he took to his feet. 'Ladies, this man has the mind of a barrister. That is the exact argument that Harry Drysdale used to defend Marcus Carver in court.'

With his hands either side of his shoulders, palms upwards, Barney beamed. 'It's a gift. My amazing intelligence is what attracted Netty to me in the first place. Not only am I an engineering wizard, but I'm an intellectual brain-box in disguise. This caveman outer shell is a clever ruse designed to fool the public.'

'Alright, Barney, don't overdo it.' Annette prodded him with her fork, making him flinch.

Lorna leant in. 'Surely the prosecution would have been prepared for that as an argument. It's so predictable, even Barney raised it.'

Barney deflated like a pricked balloon. 'Thanks, Lorna. There I was thinking I might actually be clever.'

'No offence intended. You are clever, just not conventionally.'

'None taken.'

'Can you two please stop making my husband out to be the village idiot, and Barney, stop interrupting, let Kon answer Lorna's question.' Annette had rested her fork against her plate and was poised for Konrad's response.

Konrad cleared his throat. 'Harry made use of a team of investigators to examine the lives of the three women who made the accusations. But, despite some damning evidence from the prosecuting lawyers, he undermined their credibility to the degree that the case collapsed. Not only did Marcus Carver walk away with his reputation intact but he was exonerated, leading to his skills being in greater demand than ever. Magnanimously he declined to sue for damages against the women. Incidentally, they were then charged with making false statements and perverting the course of justice with the aim of financial gain. It was a dog's breakfast for the CPS.'

'When was this?' Lorna asked, looking again at the notebook she held in one hand.

Konrad tapped the page she had open. 'Would you believe, the most recent charges were made in 2013 but the case took over nine months to reach court. In that time what did Marcus do?'

'Don't tell me… he married Lydia,' Barney said, nodding sagely.

'Bloody hell. You are on fire, old pal.'

20

THE WEDNESDAY AFTER
CHRISTMAS

Marcus hadn't bothered convincing Lydia of a fictitious surgery list for the week between Christmas and New Year. He told her and the children that he was to attend a black-tie event at his gentleman's club and staying over as he usually would on a Wednesday night. As he packed his bag, checked his suit, and gave a final buff to his shoes, he was closely watched by Lydia.

'Don't forget cufflinks,' she reminded him, curtly.

'Thanks.' He gave a sideways glance. She sat on the corner of the double bed following him with her eyes as he moved between the wardrobes, the chest of drawers, and the leather holdall open on the vast underused bed.

'I need an answer by the first week of the New Year,' he said, his voice commanding. 'There's a theatre slot the following week reserved for you. Nigel Macklin will perform the adjustment. I can't make you do this, but if you don't, then we are pretty much over, Lydia.' He stood at the end of the bed. 'Do you want your selfishness to be the cause of a divorce? For your children to be deprived of the stability of a fine home and education? Honestly?'

There was something in the way she held her chin high that was niggling at Marcus. Why was she continuing to oppose him? She hadn't even denied her treachery when he had confronted her about her secret gastric band the day before, in fact Lydia had been dismissive.

That same pattern continued today.

'I start my new job on the third of January. I won't be needing the adjustment to my gastric band.'

Marcus stalled. Where was her usual timidity?

'A job? What job? I never said you could get a job.' His jaw extended towards her. 'You haven't been employed for years, what would you know about working for a living?'

'What do you care?' Lydia slid to her feet. 'And I've set up my own bank account, by the way. The money I earn will be mine and I won't have to request any from you in future. Sorry, I meant to say *beg*. I can't exchange sex for money anymore, can I? I'm too thin to earn my keep from you.'

Marcus was confounded. She wasn't raising her voice; she wasn't spitting vicious words and accusations at him. Lydia was merely stating the facts.

'Actually,' she said with a lilt, 'divorce sounds preferable to me. I can book my tummy tuck with Charles Broughton with the proceeds.'

A derisory laugh emanated from Marcus, his disdain at the mention of Charles Broughton only served to increase his anger. 'Divorce. You wouldn't know where to start. You can't live without me. I manage your life for you, Lydia. I always have done. This… betrayal… this wicked betrayal has to end now. You will have the gastric band removed, you will go back to being the woman that turns me on and you will do as I say.' There was a cold hard knot forming in his gut. Bitter gall burned there. 'On what grounds are you divorcing me anyway? Thought of that, have you? "Oh, Your Worship, I'd like a divorce please. My husband makes me live in a fabulous house with my two lovely children from a previously doomed relationship - who go to costly public schools. I have an allowance and can go shopping and meet the girls for coffee every day if I want to. It's such a fucking terrible existence that I can't take any more, Your Worship".'

Marcus strode over to the doorway, preventing Lydia from leaving. He pulled her roughly back into the bedroom before closing the door. 'I married you for who you used to be and you will either return to being that woman or you can leave.'

Still Lydia didn't resist, she chose to remain impassive as she replied, 'That suits me fine. I'm not the person I once was, Marcus. It's taken me a while to find my strength but don't take me for an idiot. You have systematically abused me for years and you used me like a sex facility. I fulfilled your needs at the expense of my own freedom. I used to be your necessary but embarrassing secret in a society that will not forgive you for the way you treat women. How stupid I was to think that doing your bidding would ensure a happy marriage. No more, Marcus. No more. When the children get back we are going to stay at my parents.'

'What?' He grabbed her by her shoulders and shook her, hard. 'I decide. Not you.'

She stared. Daring him. 'Okay then. Come with us. We leave this afternoon and we're staying until New Year's Day.' A steely glare convinced him that she was not making idle threats. 'There's a dilemma for you.' She threw down her challenge. 'If you are serious about maintaining this pathetic marriage to protect yourself, then you will sacrifice your night at the club to put on a pretence of happy families. The price for your decision will be that we stay married in name but not in the bedroom. You get to keep your money and your precious reputation. What do you say to that proposition?'

'And if I don't agree?' Marcus asked.

'Then I tell all and you are ruined.'

'Tell all? Just what is it that you think you are going to tell?' Dilemma was not a strong enough word. Marcus didn't know if Lydia was putting on a brave show, trying to dupe him. What did she know? This was make or break time, shit or bust. He could have his professional reputation, his unenviable private life, his financial security and still feed his addiction, but only if he played along with Lydia.

He had to at least give the impression that he was willing to relinquish control. There was far too much to lose. He allowed tears to well up. To his perplexed wife these were tears of shame and hurt, but in reality they were born of fury.

The pitch and tone of her voice changed. It became higher and less assured.

'What? What is it, Marcus? Don't tell me you're surprised. I've known for years that you prefer a woman with meat on her bones. That aside, I managed to convince myself that you loved me for my personality and that my size was irrelevant, but that was not the case. You fed me. You controlled me and you created Mrs Roly-Poly. Me. Fat me. For your pleasure. It took hours of counselling to work that out for myself. I thought you cared but you couldn't give a shit about my health or my happiness. It was about you. But what you forget is, I have the girls to consider—'

Marcus dramatically staggered to the edge of the bed, his knees collapsed as he dropped, twisting his backside onto the mattress holding his head in his hands.

Another approach was called for in order for him to regain the upper hand.

Counselling? Fucking counselling? So that was the impetus behind the change. How? How did she sneak around doing these underhand things behind his back without him knowing? And why? Who put her up to it?

Lydia had out-foxed him, and for a few minutes she had called the shots, blackmailing him.

His thoughts raced as he sought to find a strategy to manage the implosion of his world. Marcus needed a stronger, more meaningful emotional manipulation. He had been fooling himself that Lydia would continue to comply with his demands, now instead, she would have to be moulded by her own willingness for harmony. Mothering instincts were her weakness and one he could easily exploit.

He sobbed into his upturned palms. 'No, you've got it all wrong. I didn't want anyone else to have you, so I took control. I'm a monster, Lydia. What have I become? This is killing me.' He grabbed onto her waist as she went to him and she held his head against her stomach, gently stroking his hair.

'I'll call the club and cancel tonight,' he gasped. 'Let's go to your parents' for the weekend and try to patch up our differences. I'll make a proper psychiatry appointment. Counselling won't cut it, Lydia. I'm in much more trouble than that. What have I done to you? I'm so sorry.'

She squeezed him to her, pity in her eyes. 'Thank you, Marcus. You'll see. It'll be worth it. You just need to understand where this problem stems from. You don't need to control me, just work with me to help you.'

Marcus invented a snivel and sighed, eventually releasing her. 'We should have talked about this properly instead of bickering and carrying on as if nothing was wrong. I do have a problem, Lydia, and admitting it to myself has been hard enough, but admitting it to you has been the most painful confession of all.'

Speaking those words out loud was a matter of performance. He was regrouping, consolidating his position and reassessing the obstacles placed in his way by his errant wife. She was risking an unhappy ending.

21

THAT SAME EVENING

Ella's disappointment was genuine. Her carefully laid plans for the Wednesday after Christmas had been undermined. 'I'm so sorry to hear you can't make it this week, Mr C. I do hope you feel better soon and that we see you as usual next Wednesday, in the New Year.'

Everything had gone to pot.

Marcus Carver was supposed to be at Buxham's and she had been painstaking in her efforts to capture his tawdry secret life on film at the same time as providing evidence for Val about Harry Drysdale. She knew which rooms they were booked into and Leonora would already be on her way expecting to entertain Mr C as she had done seven days previously. Trudy had been booked for Mr D, so now, like it or not, there would be two fat ladies on table eighty-eight, both available for use by one Harry Drysdale. Ella had to find a way of getting to the room Harry would be using and setting up the tiny camera in the best possible place. If only she knew what that would be or the details of what went on behind closed doors at Buxham's between Harry Drysdale and the ladies from the XL Agency.

When Harry strutted in to the restaurant, he seemed genuinely pleased to see Ella, and he already knew that his friend Mr C had cancelled at very short notice.

'Family pressures. It's the same every year for men like Mr C. I don't have such unnecessary encumbrances and am therefore at liberty to enjoy the excesses of Christmas in whichever way I choose, Ella.' Harry's warm manner was a tonic, and assured her that he couldn't have read anything contained in her handbag the previous week. He was simply too relaxed and engaging. She had misjudged him in that respect, perhaps. But even so, Ella was left wrestling with how she was going to spy on Harry as he indulged in dessert with either or both of the escort ladies at his disposal. How was she going to gather the photographs that Val needed?

Leonora was waiting in the bar, and the other escort, Trudy, was heading from the ladies toilet in Ella's direction. She looked stunning.

With no possibility of capturing evidence on film of Marcus Carver's exploits, Ella knew she had another shot at uncovering Harry's guilty pleasures. It was a reprieve of sorts, but just how she was going to set about being invited to his room was eluding her. The competition was too great.

Reception had sent a message that popped up on her terminal screen.

Table No. 88 lady guest #2 'Trudy' has arrived for Mr D.

'Welcome back to Buxham's.' Ella greeted Trudy with a charming smile and personally escorted her to where Mr D was indulging in pre-dinner drinks with Leonora. Once there, Harry had caught Ella's elbow and whispered, 'Don't tell her I said so, but she's my favourite. I do so enjoy her company. Good. Merry Christmas to me and a most indulgent New Year.' He raised his glass and winked.

Ella's job was to discover what he meant by that. What

was involved in getting to know the two fat ladies on table eighty-eight and what was it that Val needed to find out about Harry Drysdale in particular? More frustrating was the uncertainty surrounding the late cancellation by Marcus Carver. Teresa had said he never missed a week. Never.

The atmosphere in the kitchen had been tense all evening. Schubert was in a peculiarly sarcastic mood and, instead of swearing he chose to ridicule anyone who came within range.

Ada had grown tired of his mercurial moods. 'I think we may have to take him aside and force-feed him some of your quetiapine. He's an insufferable wazzock tonight.' Ada was correct; Ella caught a broadside the moment she appeared at the pass.

'Ah, here she comes, like Mary-fucking-Poppins, she's almost perfect in every way.'

'What's got your goat this evening, may I ask?' Ella enquired. There was an odd feel to the conversation as if she had missed some vital information. Gossip perhaps.

'Don't act so sweet and innocent. I thought you were better than that.'

Ella scoured the sweaty faces of the chefs and the kitchen porter for clues but they remained resolutely deadpan. Only Schubert spoke. Orders were coming in slowly and the pace was dramatically less frantic than on a usual Wednesday night service. The festive slump of the week between Christmas and New Year was as evident as Schubert's contempt.

'We have had a special request, as if you didn't know, to provide a trolley of desserts. This you are to deliver person- ally to the room of a certain gentleman who reserves table number eighty-eight every week. We all know what he expects of you in return…'

Ella must have appeared shocked, forcing Schubert to examine the facts with her. 'You deny this?'

'I don't know anything about it,' Ella replied, eyes wide. 'Who made the request?' Her beseeching eyes met Schubert's, and he left the pass in the hands of his sous chef in order to meet her by the door to his office. 'Come in, take a seat.'

LATER THAT EVENING

'I will escort you,' Schubert announced.

'What?'

'When you take the trolley to Mr D's room, I will escort you. That way you are fulfilling his request but not placing yourself in a compromising position.' Schubert placed a fatherly hand on Ella's shoulder. That one simple gesture meant so much. He was trying to protect her, like her own father used to before she disgraced herself. 'Now get back to the restaurant and don't worry.'

Ella's plans were unravelling. Lacking the usual number of club members because of the Christmas holidays, the place was quiet; too quiet, and Ella had no choice other than to allow Ada and Flora to go home early, leaving herself alone to clear the last few tables. She couldn't leave the restaurant to access Harry's room to place a camera, her absence would be glaringly apparent. She couldn't get to her phone to alert Mal, and she would have to manage by herself.

Her mind was racing, exploring possible solutions and madcap schemes to fulfil her brief, but she was becoming muddled and her behaviour reflected this. She was usually so ordered and organised. *Stay in control by being controlled* that was her personal mission statement. However, as the restaurant emptied, and the time ticked by, Ella rushed around, failing to complete tasks, distracting herself with her random thoughts because there was little else to take her away from her own dilemmas.

Even table eighty-eight was less jovial than usual and Harry's request for dessert to be served in his room came much sooner than Ella had anticipated. He waved her over with a smile.

'Ella, both my lovely lady guests will be joining me for dessert in my room this evening. Chef has the order and I've asked if you would deliver the trolley personally. We'll take our drinks with us, but could you make sure there is a jug of water on the trolley? It was missing last time.'

'Of course.' Ella stared into his eyes seeking a pointer as to his expectations on this occasion. Any level of planning for covert surveillance had been eradicated by Schubert's insistence on escorting Ella to Harry's room. She couldn't hide a camera on the trolley; there would be no opportunity to do so.

'But why me? Why do you wish me to deliver the trolley?'

'I'd like to take your photo to send to Mr C, to make him jealous. I want him to think that you are joining us for the best part of our evening. He'll be livid.'

Leonora let slip a throaty chuckle, her eyes sparkling with amusement. 'The competition,' she said.

Ella wasn't sure what was meant. 'The competition?'

'You are my competition,' Leonora explained. 'Mr C would do anything to spend an evening with you. Since you started working here, I have become a poor substitute.'

'Come along now Ella, you must know how gorgeous you are,' Harry said. 'Mr C and I have been competing for your affections and my little plan to present him with my drawing of you for his Christmas present has been horribly delayed. I was so looking forward to seeing his face. He'll be beyond envious.'

Ella looked from Harry to Leonora, and then to Trudy. The two ladies giggled and hugged each other. Trudy stopped laughing to give Ella reassurances. 'Don't look so perturbed, sweetie. We get paid huge wads of money to keep these gentlemen company but there's no envy of each other involved. If you want to join us, you could earn yourself a mint. Just saying...' Trudy had a very slight lisp, although barely noticeable it added a childlike charm to her encouraging words.

Taking a moment to compose herself, Ella stepped into the unknown. 'I don't know what to say because...' she looked around to check privacy. 'Because I don't really know what it is that you provide, as a service, if you see what I mean?'

Harry breathed her in. 'Oh Ella. Bring that trolley and we shall show you.'

SCHUBERT COULD NOT BE DISSUADED. He followed her along the corridor to room fifteen and on arrival he stood like a panting Buddha. Wheezing noisily, he waited for the door to be answered, his chef's hat leaning to one side, a clean apron tied about his ample waist. Ella could feel the heat from his body and the ruddy glowing complexion of his enormous jowls.

When the door opened inwards, she watched as Harry's face fell with disappointment, although he quickly recovered and invited Ella and Schubert to enter the large suite. Leonora and Trudy were seated at a round walnut veneered table, holding cut glass champagne flutes, chatting amicably.

They greeted the arrival of the trolley with glee as it was wheeled towards them.

'My favourite dessert, Charlotte Russe just like my grandmother used to make and, Trudy, look at the caramel sauce to go with these choux buns.' Leonora dipped a fingertip into the jug containing the warm sweet liquid. Placing it on her tongue she hummed with rapture at the taste.

'Chef, this looks amazing,' Harry announced. 'Thank you so much for taking the trouble to deliver these in person and thank you, Ella.' Having surveyed the trolley Harry frowned. 'Just one thing. The jug of water?'

'Oh dear, that's my fault,' Ella gasped. 'I'm so sorry. I'll fetch it straight away.' She finished ironing out a tablecloth with the flat of her hands, laying the table with protective placemats and several sets of cutlery.

Harry winked at Ella as she pulled the door to.

Schubert began to wheeze as they cantered down the corridor towards the stairs. 'I'll take it. You rest, Schubert. It'll take me two minutes to deliver a jug of iced water then I'm off to soak my feet and have a shower. All these silly rumours were clearly a load of old nonsense, they just want to eat and drink in the privacy of their room. No need to worry, just like you said.' Her words gushed forth like a fast flowing waterfall.

Schubert didn't argue. He couldn't muster enough breath to speak. Ella moved off, leaving him, arm braced against the wall. His cheeks blew in and out like a set of pink bellows as he waited for the lift. It would take him to the ground floor where he could make his way home for the night.

'Thank you, Schubert, it was very gallant of you,' Ella said.

Still unable to speak, he mimed the doffing of a cap in recognition of her words.

Racing back to room number fifteen with a large cut-glass jug balanced on a silver server, Ella swore to herself. 'This is so fucking wrong.'

She hadn't informed Mal by text, she hadn't any way of smuggling a camera into the room, she had no way of predicting what she was about to let herself in for. Despite all the warnings from her inner conscience, she knocked on the door and entered.

'Stay where you are for a second,' Leonora called out. She held a mobile phone in her hand and lined up a photo shot of Ella in the doorway. The door was held open by a smiling Harry who said, 'Great, that should do the trick. Mr C will be royally pissed off. Let's have my phone back and I'll send him that one for starters.'

Four chairs were placed at the table in Harry's room and he motioned towards an empty one. 'Ella, please join us.'

'Thanks but I'm not really supposed to fraternise with guests. Besides, I'm not at my best after a shift. What I need most is a shower.'

'How long will you need? We'll wait for you. Please accept our invitation, there's pudding enough for all.' Harry had a face every aunty would want to squeeze and his invitation was incredibly tempting. Ella was hungry and the trolley groaned with delicious appeal. 'I'll be offended if you don't. I might even complain to the management...'

'Twenty minutes max.'

'See you in fifteen.'

'Okay, fifteen it is. Don't eat it all before I get back.'

Ella ran to her room and was unbuttoning her blouse as she stepped through the door. She greeted Gordon with a cheerful hello, as she sprinkled a few flakes of fish food into his tank, standing in her underwear.

'I'm off to a late supper with the Napoleon of Buxham's and two of his wenches. Wish me luck.' Standing in the shower, sponging soapy shower gel across her body, she searched for inspiration. How on earth was she going to plant a small camera into that room without getting caught? If she took her handbag, it would look contrived. She needed to take her room key, a couple of tissues, and lip-gloss, so perhaps she could take a small clutch bag.

At top speed, she applied minimal make-up, lipstick, mascara, eyeliner, and then released her hair from the shower cap, brushing the long thick locks into reasonable shape. She abandoned the idea of court shoes in favour of comfortable flat ones and slipped into her favourite acid-green wrap dress. Easy to wear, didn't crease, and the colours made her feel confident. Squirt of perfume, a final check in the mirror.

'How do I look, Gordon? Good? Now I must go.'

The goldfish let one small bubble escape and rise to the surface of the water in his round bowl. She took that as affirmation. In her haste and rising excitement she failed to make contact with the outside world and didn't register her rising euphoria.

Harry was wearing the same linen trousers and T-shirt that he had when he had drawn her the week previous. He smiled. When she entered further into the room Ella was astounded to see Trudy and Leonora lying on the bed, in each other's arms, naked. Only when Harry strolled to a chair to collect his drawing pad, did Ella understand.

'What do you think?' he asked, showing her his outline sketch. Not waiting for her to answer, he placed his hand in the small of her back and directed her to the table where a selection of desserts had been laid out. 'Yours. Pile up a bowlful then come over and lie on the sofa next to me. You must be tired. Put your feet up. You eat. I'll draw - but first, another teaser for dear Mr C to dribble over. Pick up your spoon, dip it in the cream then lick it slowly.' Harry used his mobile phone to take the short video clip. 'Here we are in my room. Ella has such a gentle tongue. Merry Christmas, Mr C.'

Cackling laughter could be heard from the bed. 'Trudy ate my strawberry!' Leonora announced.

Ella found the food to be mouth-wateringly moreish. Every so often Harry would glance sideways, watching her eat and when her plate was empty, he stopped drawing to refill it. 'Eat up; don't be embarrassed, we left you plenty. Girls do you want thirds?'

They didn't need encouragement. Leonora and Trudy rolled to opposite edges of the bed and raced each other to the dining table, surging flesh undulating, breasts swinging. There was a complete absence of self-consciousness. They were stripped bare, holding bowls of creamy dessert facing each other and grinning between mouthfuls.

'Magnificent creatures, aren't they?' Harry stated.

'Is this what they get paid for?'

'Sometimes. It depends what mood I'm in. Other times I dive right on in, but this evening I'm tormenting myself by drawing their beauty before I behave like a beast.' He didn't smile. 'Would you pose with them? For a photo? I don't wish to keep you. You must be tired. But I could draw from a photo instead. Naturally, I'd pay.'

Ella's head was buzzing. She had managed to place her clutch bag, flap open, on the table. With no idea what was being filmed or recorded on the surveillance camera disguised as a protruding torch, she had to decide whether to take the next risky step or not.

'Naked?'

'You're a life model aren't you?'

'Yes, you know I am.'

'Then what is the problem?'

'Nothing. I'll get undressed.' Her heart beat faster than she could imagine possible and Harry watched as she undid the ties on her dress. Nervously she kicked off her shoes, and she heard him catch his breath when she let her bra fall.

As they bounced back onto the bed, Trudy and Leonora seemed intent on recruiting her. 'With a figure like that you could make a grand a night. Depends on how far you are prepared to go, mind you. What shall we do, Mr D? The three wise monkeys? The three graces? What about the three little pigs?'

Harry jumped up. 'Great. The three wise monkeys. We'll draw lots.'

Trudy posed on the edge of the bed; legs crossed at the ankle, arms extended, locked at the elbow and placed as props behind her. Finally, with a sugar coated choux bun wedged into her mouth, she sat still, her eyes wide with mirth. In an unsteady kneeling position to Trudy's left, Leonora had her hands raised to her ears, her breasts resting against Trudy's shoulder. Ella was asked to lie with her head in Trudy's lap, facing upwards. She placed her hands on her eyes, as instructed, and bent both legs, but there wasn't much space between the aprons of fatty flesh and Trudy's knees on which to lie. The whole set up was a precarious one.

'No, that's no good. Ella's boobs disappear under her armpits and I keep losing my balance,' Leonora said.

Ella almost slithered from the end of the mattress as she sat up.

Harry reappraised the tableau as the girls discussed alternatives. For Ella the fun had overridden any nerves, and she had begun to enjoy the experience. It was the liveliest art class she had ever posed for.

'I could use those two pudding bowls,' Leonora said, pointing to the table. Once she had gathered the necessary equipment and returned to the bed, Harry carried on giving instructions. 'Ella, let's make use of a linen serviette as a blindfold, that way you can use your arms to brace yourself the other side of Trudy. One hand on her thigh, the other on her shoulder. Good, now hold still.' Harry tied the blindfold.

'Leonora, hold the bowls up to your ears. Rest your back against Trudy's left side. Gently. Now turn your head towards me. Great. Ella. Aim your chin towards your right shoulder. Lick your lips. Yes. Good. Trudy, give me that surprised look again. Superb, my lovely girls, really top class. Worth every bloody penny. Leonora look at the lens and flash those lashes at me. Excellent.'

At the moment he said this there was a squeal from Trudy as the girls lost their balance. Leaning into Ella who toppled backwards, Trudy grabbed at her. Leonora dropped both bowls but couldn't prevent herself from falling onto Trudy's lap. She in turn coughed out the oversized profiterole, spraying cream into the air like a wet fart.

Ella could hear the sound of Harry snapping away, taking photos of the chaos and having landed in an undignified heap upon the carpeted bedroom floor, she removed her blindfold.

There stood Harry Drysdale grinning as he checked the small review screen on an expensive-looking digital camera. Ella glanced across to where her clutch bag had been left. It was no longer there.

'Fuck,' Ella said.

'Fuck indeed, Miss Ella Fitzwilliam.'

THE SEARCH

FRIDAY 26TH JANUARY

'Mr Neale, we are thrilled to consider your application for full membership of Buxham's,' Carla Lewis said, as she pushed her office door open for Konrad to enter. She stood with her back against the architrave not leaving him much room. 'I take it your recent visit to our restaurant has persuaded you.' She was somewhat breathless and flighty, and her panting could be felt as warm puffs of air on his neck as he squeezed himself past her. He took great care to aim his pelvis away from her.

He could tell how much her exuberance was fuelled by his presence from the way she pandered to him. Konrad was familiar with the effect he could have on others. He knew it would pass.

'Mrs Lewis, I understand that your discretion is assured.' Here he was, a celebrity, who she would believe had a secret fat fetish, a man who would bring increased revenue as well as the need for tighter security. So eager was she to please that he played on her willingness to meet his every requirement. 'I'm sure I don't need to exaggerate how important it is that absolute confidentiality is applied to the discussion we are about to have.'

'You have my word on that,' she said, clasping her hands to her chest as she moved towards the far side of her desk. 'The reputation of this club relies wholly upon total discretion.'

Konrad took a seat, his one twinkling eye never leaving her face. 'Before signing on the dotted line, there are a few things bothering me that require addressing.'

Carla stood to attention behind her desk. 'Oh? Such as?'

'The number of CCTV cameras for a start. If the popular press were ever to lay their grubby hands on your security records then my visits would have been recorded, would they not?'

'Indeed, Mr Neale, but there are no cameras inside the building. We are meticulous in our efforts and housekeeping do a daily sweep of all rooms for any devices. I know that you of all people will understand why we would go to such extreme lengths to ensure the privacy and security of our members.' Carla raised an eyebrow in Konrad's direction. 'All CCTV cameras face outward above entrances or perimeter walls where access could be gained. Apart from that there is never a chance of filming occurring in the building or the grounds, which is why we insist on mobile phones being handed in. We used to rely on goodwill but these days it is an absolute rule. No mobile phones are permitted anywhere other than in the privacy of accommodation. The same rules apply to staff.'

Konrad probed a little further. 'Talking of staff, what vetting procedures are carried out and what detail is there in the employment contract regarding confidentiality?'

Carla Lewis didn't hesitate to give full and frank replies to Konrad's questions. He knew she would expect him to ask them, and when he had exhausted his list of queries about privacy, he asked to see the facilities that would be available to him as a full member. Carla paused and picked up the membership form that Konrad had completed, buying time.

'Ordinarily I would show you around, but I'm afraid we have several police officers in the building today and you may wish to avoid being seen?'

Konrad smiled to himself as he answered. 'That's very thoughtful of you. Why are they here, may I ask?'

'I'm sorry, I can't divulge that information.'

'Good answer. I applaud your standards. That is what I hoped you'd say, however, I confess to knowing why the police are here. Harry Drysdale was my wife's barrister, and we last saw him here in your restaurant the Wednesday after the New Year celebrations. I had a friendly chat with him.'

Carla Lewis flopped into her leather office chair with such force that the adjusting mechanism couldn't tolerate the downward load and the chair sank without warning. Buxham's duty manager for the day let out a cry of alarm, before apologising. 'Please forgive me. I didn't realise it was you who breached the rules that evening.'

Having recovered her composure, Carla leant across the desk. 'Mr Neale, if you had read the information given to guests you would have known that we have a strict code of conduct. That should have prevented you from disclosing that Mr Drysdale is - was - is a member here.'

'Yes, it was rather unfortunate that I hadn't understood quite how stringent you are. It was my fault. It was a natural reaction to call out to him. I spied him across the floor of the restaurant as he was heading back from the gents' toilets. I was with my wife and two friends who are members of The Lensham and District Pudding Club. Harry didn't seem to object at the time.'

Carla's reaction was one of incredulity. 'He most definitely would have minded! That man and his companion have scrupulously protected their privacy as have we.'

'You mean Marcus Carver.'

Konrad waited for Carla to reveal her secrets. This she did through unmissable body language. She pushed her chair back from the edge of the desk that separated them, subconsciously further distancing herself from him. Once the back of the chair met the wall, she folded her arms and her eyes narrowed. 'You're not here to complete your application for membership, are you, Mr Neale? I may be a little slow on the uptake, but I'm not so naïve as to think that you have suddenly developed an interest in gastronomy. Or that you harbour a penchant for women of more than adequate proportions. I can only assume you are after a story.'

He liked Carla. She spoke his language. No nonsense, straight to the crux of the matter. She made as if to stand, so he motioned for her to remain seated. 'Hear me out.' He rested his hands on his knees. 'Harry Drysdale is a hell of a barrister and without him my wife would have been languishing in prison and my life would have been flushed down the proverbial. If he is in trouble, then I want to help him. I'm not here to cause difficulties for you or any of your members, unless they deserve it.'

He tipped his head to one side. Listening intently she mirrored his actions as he continued.

'My friends and I were some of the last people to see Harry before he mysteriously vanished and the news reports say he hasn't been seen since leaving Lensham on Thursday the fourth of January. He would have been here at Buxham's because he came here every Wednesday and he sat at table eighty-eight with two fat ladies and Marcus Carver. He did that week in week out, without fail, unless he had a trip abroad or he was unable to get here during a high profile court case out of the area. Am I right?'

He knew his information was accurate. Carla Lewis remained impassive as he continued. 'The question is, Mrs Lewis, do the police know that he was here or are they simply grasping at possibilities?'

With her hands cupping her face, Carla let out a despairing sigh. 'They think he left the club the next morning. The CCTV camera picked him up walking through the pedestrian side entrance with his friend Marcus Carver.'

'And did he?'

'It certainly looks that way. The touch pad registered the time of the exit at six twenty-seven.'

'You said "the police *think* he left the club the next morning". What do *you* think?'

Her silence spoke volumes.

Konrad tried again. 'If they think he left on the Thursday morning, then why are the police here today?'

Before Carla had time to generate an answer, there was a firm knock. The person opening the door hadn't waited for permission to enter. 'Sorry to interrupt but I need access to your—'

The man, in a grey suit that required the attention of dry cleaners, stopped short. 'Well bugger my boots. Konrad Neale, what brings you here? As if I didn't know.' He winked.

'DS Quinn. What an unexpected pleasure. DC McArthur not with you today?'

'Yeah, he's interviewing staff. If I'm not mistaken, you are on my list of customers to question in relation to a missing person's enquiry. You may well have saved me a journey.'

'Always happy to assist the police.' A note of derision could be heard in his reply.

Carla sat with her mouth slightly open.

Feeling sorry for her, Konrad stood to shake her hand. 'Sorry Carla, it would never have worked. I can't accept your kind offer of full membership here at Buxham's. I'm afraid there would always be a chance that I would be recognised, discretion notwithstanding.' Konrad couldn't help the sarcasm contained within his next request to Carla. He and DS Quinn had met before and Konrad hadn't been impressed by the detective's acumen. That opinion remained unchanged. 'Is it alright for DS Quinn to make use of this office to ask me a string of unrelated questions in the vain hope that I might have the answer he's looking for?'

THE THURSDAY AFTER CHRISTMAS

Val looked dreadful. Her skin was more sallow than usual and, as she sat down opposite her in the café by the station, Ella immediately noticed a slight yellowish tinge to the whites of her boss's eyes. Jaundice.

'Jesus, Val, your liver must be in a shocking state.'

'I have an obstructed bile duct. Gallstones, if you must know. They operate tomorrow if it's not cancelled again. Either way, this had better be important, young lady, because I'm in pain and I feel like a pile of warm shit. What is so fucking urgent that you and Mal have dragged me out of my pit?'

Ella didn't have time to answer; Val's new girlfriend strutted towards the table, order pad in one hand pulling a pen from her hair with the other. She was scowling at Ella. 'What d'ya want?'

'Good morning...' Ella left a pause hoping that the girl would finally disclose her name.

'Her name is Saskia,' Val volunteered.

'Is it?' Ella whispered. She cupped her hands to avoid

being overheard. 'She doesn't look much like a Saskia. Slightly lacking the sass if you ask me.'

'Nobody did. Now answer the girl.'

The waitress had reached the edge of the table.

'Hi, Saskia. I'd love a mug of hot chocolate, whipped cream on top and could I have some extra sugar in it today?'

The sulky waitress aimed her pen at a glass sugar dispenser. 'Sugar's there. Anyfing else?'

'A smile?'

Saskia sneered. 'I'll bring your drink.'

Ella watched as the ghostly girl approached an ancient coffee machine behind the counter; the sort used in Italian restaurants the world over. Having poured milk into a metal jug she placed it beneath a steam jet pipe and waited for the noise to subside before removing it. She took a mug from a shelf and placed it on a battered metal tea tray. Once she had produced a frothing hot chocolate, she squirted cream from a white pressurised canister and carelessly shook a flour sifter over the top, dusting the creation with fine chocolate powder. Order complete, Saskia made her way back to the table where Val and Ella sat in silence while the waitress unceremoniously slid the tray in front of Ella. Saskia took time to stop and place one hand on Val's shoulder. A twisted smile appeared as she then released it and walked away.

'Touching,' Ella said with sickly sarcasm.

Val shot her a warning glare. 'Mind your own bloody business. Now start blabbing. What is this about? What happened last night?'

After taking in a deep breath Ella tried to explain. 'I've screwed up. Not a bit. A lot. I have committed a huge monstrous cock-up to put all other cock-ups in the shade and Mal will probably wash his hands of the whole thing.' Ella was gabbling, and to stop her hands from shaking she clasped the handbag perched on her knees as if it were a shield to protect her from the wrath she was bound to encounter.

Val didn't disappoint. 'Before I rip your pretty head off and shit down your neck, you tell me what happened. Exactly what happened.' The grating of Val's voice had a ruthless edge to it, a prediction of more vicious tongue-lashings to come.

Ella listed the chronology of events leading up to the moment when she lifted her blindfold to see Harry Drysdale. In doing so she noticed that her clutch bag was not on the table where she had left it.

'I was pathetic. The first thing I did was to ask where my bag had been moved to. It was on the floor as if someone had knocked it off the table. This made him horribly suspicious, and he demanded to know why I was so worried about it. He examined the contents as he put them back in the bag, but as there was nothing of interest, in the end, he seemed to accept that I was some sort of irritating neurotic type. I wondered whether that was an act for the benefit of Trudy and Leonora. He didn't want them to know what was going on, so before he sat me down to answer his questions he sent them into the bathroom to dress, after which he sent them packing. You should have seen the looks they gave me; as if I were an unpleasant smell.' Ella screwed up her face. 'Once they'd left, Mr D asked me loads of questions, quizzing everything I said. It wasn't so much an interrogation, he... mind-raped me.'

Val put down the coffee cup she was holding. It clattered onto the Formica table. 'He did what?'

'He's a barrister, so he did his lawyer thing and questioned me over and over about why I was working at Buxham's. He asked about my past employment and then about the notebook he'd seen in my handbag the previous week.'

A look of utter disbelief crossed Val's already tortured face. 'What fucking notebook?' She didn't wait for an answer. 'You idiotic, moronic, half-wit, doorknob, fucking little twat-face. You made notes? Written notes?'

Ella had nowhere to hide her inadequacy. 'Yes, but it's not as bad as it sounds.'

As Val's hand slapped down on the table, the resounding thwack made Ella jump and hold on tighter to the bag in her lap. An old man in a grubby beige trench coat turned from the newspaper he was reading to check where the noise had come from, and Emo-waitress, the permanently petulant Saskia, emerged from behind the counter. Val waved her away before holding two fists up to her own chin like a boxer would and she hissed her response through gritted teeth.

'Not as bad as it sounds! You may have screwed up months of work. Where the hell does this leave us?'

'In a different position, that's all. There's a possibility that a complete disaster can be averted.'

'Oh yes? You honestly think so?' Despair had replaced the anger in Val's demeanour. She held her palms to her face as Ella continued to dig herself out of trouble.

'When he tipped out the remaining contents of my clutch bag, the torch, the camera torch, wasn't there. It must have rolled out. So you see it's not as bad as you think. He never found anything incriminating. Nothing. I've asked house-keeping to look for it.'

'And that's good news, how? You were supposed to supply me with evidence of what exactly Marcus Carver and his side-kick lawyer get up to. But for some bizarre reason you decide to reveal yourself as a tu'penny ha'penny snoop after a cheap thrill. If you were party to a pathetic nude romp for the sake of art then why in God's name did you feel it necessary to film anything? Why?'

Ella bit her bottom lip as she replied. 'I was acting in

anticipation that it might be something more substantive. More lascivious.'

A series of hacking coughs prevented Val from speaking again for several seconds. 'Are you quite mad? You don't understand. If he's sussed you out then we are as good as finished. Next week is our deadline. I can't afford to drag it out any longer than that.' She blinked twice as if desperate to reason her way through the problem.

'Look Val, I know I've been an idiot and I'm out of my depth but it's all a bit odd. I mean, Marcus may be a sex pest but his lawyer just draws or takes pictures of oversized, beautiful women and occasionally has a bit of hanky-panky with them, from what I know. Where is the big deal?'

Val bent over and groaned. 'Oh Christ! This hurts.' She pressed against her lower right abdomen, huffing. 'Ella, ask Saskia to call me a cab, I need to go home and dose myself up with everything I can lay my hands on.' She stared up at Ella. 'You have no bloody choice other than to carry on. We need to know what Marcus-bloody-Carver gets up to otherwise... if it gets risky then—'

'I know, kick him in the nuts and cry rape.' Ella was getting up from the table when Val grabbed her arm and there was uneasiness about the way she asked her next question.

'How much does he know about me?'

'Mr D? About you? Nothing. I kept to the same details as on my CV, the one you invented for me. It's not too wide of the truth but he's not an idiot. If he chose to he could have me checked out and the flaws would soon show. Having said that, he appeared to accept what I told him as being legitimate. It seemed to help.'

'Oh you'd love to think so, but I doubt it,' Val snarled. 'Now get Saskia for me and piss off. Keep me informed by text and don't do anything else stupid.' Val was talking in short bursts, wincing with pain if she drew too deep a breath.

Saskia did as she was asked and called a mini-cab before hurrying to Val's side. Watching them together, Ella was taken aback at the show of affection between the two women and felt an unexpected pang of guilt for being so harsh towards Saskia that morning.

25

MOMENTS LATER

Turning the corner of the avenue leading back to Buxham's driveway, with her head full of thoughts, Ella almost ran into two women in long overcoats barring her way. One wore a navy blue full-length wool coat topped off with a red beret, and the other, a camel coat matched with a knitted beige beany hat pulled over long straight dark hair. They took up most of the pavement, leaving Ella no choice other than to step into the road. It was only when the woman in the woolly hat took hold of her elbow, did Ella realise who it was she was trying to avoid.

'Leonora? What are you doing here?' She took a better look at the shorter of the two ladies, the one in the classic blue overcoat. 'Trudy? Is something wrong?'

There was hardly any need to have asked that question. Both women had their chins jutted forward and Leonora's nostrils flared as she breathed out her undisguised anger. 'Walk with us a while,' she said, her voice deep and doom-laden. 'We have matters to discuss with you in private.' Ella found herself being frogmarched between them, back in the direction she had come from, but before reaching the railway station the trio made a left turn. Through the grey of the winter morning the lights of MacDonald's beckoned, and sure enough Ella was directed to sit at a table in the corner with Trudy, while Leonora ordered drinks and muffins.

With steamed-up windows and a noise level to rival a departure lounge at an international airport during silly season, the place was heaving. Parties of exhausted parents and their irritable offspring took up almost every seat. Some families were accompanied by pasty-looking grandparents at the end of their polite patience. At other tables were groups of foul-mouthed youths escaping the niceties of spending the festive season incarcerated with ancient relatives and over-bearing adults.

To any onlooker, Ella, Leonora and Trudy were just three overweight ladies having a morning coffee together. At the table, however, Ella was feeling decidedly apprehensive. Trudy reached into her handbag and when she produced the camera torch that Ella had lost the previous evening, the nerves became worse. She wasn't certain how to react and her words came hesitantly.

'Oh, brilliant. You found my torch.'

Trudy gave a half-smile, the sort that never reaches the eyes, and pressed the button causing the torch to shine at Ella. 'Yes. A nice little torch with five LED bulbs.' She switched it off again, holding Ella's gaze. 'But what, we have to ask ourselves, is the pinhole for? The one in the middle of the ring of LED bulbs.' The long glittery fingernail of Trudy's left index finger revealed a minute hole in the centre of the torch head.

'Well … I …' Ella had no answer to give, and she noticed that Trudy's slight lisp, previously so appealing, had disappeared. The woman had looked so angelic until that moment and now she harboured a dark menace that Ella couldn't understand.

Leonora returned laden with warm drinks and a selection of muffins, which she placed in the centre of the table. 'Leo, would you credit it, our chatty flirt of a hostess doesn't have an answer to my question about this most unusual torch, or is it a torch?' Trudy said. 'Isn't that peculiar? She normally won't shut up. A most endearing quality being friendly, isn't it? She gets a job at Buxham's and within a matter of weeks she lands an invite to Mr D's room for a nude drawing session. Then yesterday he asks her to stay for dessert and we see *this* poking out of her clutch bag.' Trudy's voice had suddenly developed a caustic quality. 'You are some fucking stupid amateur.' She shook her head, tutting as Leonora took the torch from her and played with the buttons.

'If we hadn't distracted him and rescued this from your bag, then you would have been caught, and that is a major problem for us. Do you understand, little girl?' Leonora's tone was low, threatening.

'No. I don't understand. Are you the police?' Ella asked. The two women who had been so friendly and inclusive only the previous day, had for some reason become intimidating.

'Oh, you really *are* stupid. No we're not plod, far from it in fact. Now tell us who you are, what you are up to and what Mr D spoke to you about once we'd left last night. Everything. Don't leave a single thing out,' Leonora said, her gravelly voice vibrating the air.

Ella wasn't prepared for this confrontation and she floundered. 'Why should I? What's it to you?'

'If you don't, then we hand the torch to Mr D and any deal is off.'

'What deal?'

'That depends on your level of cooperation. Now start filling in the gaps.'

'Umm, I work for an employment agency. I'm covering maternity leave for up to twelve months… I think and—'

'Pull the other one, sweetie,' Trudy said, spikily. 'We've just watched you have an awkward conversation with a woman in the café by the station. Confessing to your appalling lack of professionalism were you?'

The astonishment on Ella's face seemed to strike Leonora as amusing. She laughed bitterly. 'What? Uncomfortable are we? How about you furnish us with the truth before we make life incredibly distressing for you?'

Ella visibly shrank. 'What do you know about Val?' The words had spilled forth before Ella had reviewed their weight, before she registered that, by saying them, her interrogators would have a name.

'Val? What do we know about Val? Well now, let's see ...' Trudy spoke with a whine. 'Could it be that Leo also saw you when you met up with her last week in the same greasy spoon cafe by the station?'

The barbed words continued as Leonora spoke, taking over from Trudy, steepling her fingers and putting her long gleaming talons on show, outstaring Ella. She was forced to look away within seconds of meeting her eye.

Leonora scoffed. 'And could it be that I had a little chat with the daughter of darkness, the slip of a thing that passes for a waitress?'

Seeing Ella's shoulders sag, Leonora pressed home the facts. 'The sour little cow managed a whole conversation. I know it's hard to believe, isn't it? But she did.'

Leonora reached for an apple and cinnamon muffin and passed it unceremoniously to her colleague. 'Once I had Val's full name and the name of her business, then the rest of the puzzle was rather easy to solve. I don't know who wants you to take incriminating pictures of our most generous client but that's not our business. Unfortunately for you this discovery that you are some sort of investigator creates a significant problem for us.'

'Are you going to report me?'

Trudy almost spat out the mouthful of muffin she was about to swallow. There was a pause while she chewed and gathered herself, holding one hand in the air, giving notice of her intention to pass comment. A final gulp preceded a lick of the lips and a long exhalation. 'Your lack of intelligence beggar's belief, child. Think about it. If we report you, then we are implicated in spying on our own customers. If we report you then, the club has to inform Mr D of a major security breach. If we report you we lose our lucrative income stream and you lose your job - both of them.'

'Then what is it you expect me to do?'

Ella could feel both sets of eyes scrutinising her every move, her choice of words and each inflection in her voice.

'We expect you to do precisely what we tell you.'

'How can I do that?'

'Act and behave like a hostess. Keep to the rules of the club and stay out of our way until we say otherwise. We don't know quite what you and your undernourished boss are up to but you'll have to think of something else. We suggest you plan to hand your notice in. Nothing too sudden. Don't draw attention to yourself, just give a week's notice and leave quietly.'

Turning to the window, Ella watched as large drops of rain began to fall onto the already damp tarmac of the car park. She could feel the burning in her eyes and the tightening of her throat as her own tears of anger threatened to tumble.

Despite the cacophony in MacDonald's and the ear-piercing screams of the snotty infant three tables away, endless possibilities raced through Ella's mind. At the forefront of her concerns were the threats and inconsistencies she had been presented with. Would Val have been sloppy enough to have talked with Saskia about their plans for

Harry Drysdale and Marcus Carver? Ella thought not. Unable to drag her eyes away from the rain now falling in an unforgiving torrent, she ignored the farewells from the two fat ladies of table eighty-eight.

'Merry Christmas, kid,' Trudy hissed as she stood to tie the belt of her overcoat.

'Yeah, and a happy New Year. See you on Wednesday and remember your future is in our hands and so is the SD card in here.' Leonora balanced Ella's black torch in one hand, flipped it into the air and caught it again before thrusting it into her coat pocket. Her wide grin was as ominous as the dark rainclouds outside.

26

THE WEDNESDAY AFTER CHRISTMAS

Marcus Carver used exhaustion as his reason to leave the fireside conversation and head to the bedroom in Lydia's parents' sprawling old Victorian town house. 'Please forgive me. I'm sure I'll be more sociable once I've caught up on a good night's sleep. We both will.'

His in-laws, Roger and Janette Limberg, exchanged worried glances but once he again declined their offer of a second nightcap and they bade him goodnight as he reversed through the living room doorway. The children had been put to bed hours previously, leaving him and Lydia to make a convincing show of their marriage to the most critical of audiences, and Lydia wasn't feeling well. She had dashed to the bathroom leaving him to fend off their probing questions.

Marcus had never developed a close relationship with either of Lydia's parents. They were nice enough people but rather dull and predictable. He didn't want to be there and he most certainly didn't envisage having to indulge in polite conversation with them on a Wednesday. Earlier in the evening Marcus had suffered the indignity of sampling

Roger Limberg's homemade tasteless beer as they stood in the workshop outside, whilst Roger regaled him with the virtues of owning a classic car. Marcus had no interest whatsoever in engines or indeed in any vehicle. As far as he was concerned they were merely a means of transport or an investment. He tried to nod in the right places and make appreciative noises, but his thoughts kept wandering. On three occasions after dinner he heard notification of messages arriving on his mobile phone and instinctively knew that Harry was playing with him.

In the privacy of the en suite bathroom, with the door firmly locked, and Lydia lying curled up in a ball on the bed, Marcus checked his messages. There was one photo from 'Mr D' - as his contact list recorded him - of Ella, in her uniform stepping through a doorway holding a jug of water. The door was held open by a smiling Harry Drysdale.

'You lucky bastard,' he whispered. Then realising that someone else in that room must have been taking the photograph, he scrolled to the next message. 'Please don't let it be Leonora.'

Despite his desperation at missing his weekly indulgences at Buxham's with Harry, the evening had panned out unexpectedly well for Marcus. Lydia had complained of indigestion, had vomited, and moaned in discomfort. His decision not to warn Lydia about the potential significance of these symptoms would have far-reaching consequences. However, Lydia's betrayal was his overriding current problem, and his answer to that problem would be to do nothing for now. Timing would be everything.

To avoid a catastrophic miscalculation, he determined to weigh up the options once more. Running through the checklist in his head, as he cleaned his teeth, he grinned at the prospect of such a simple solution.

'I think the change in routine has upset my digestion,' his

wife had said earlier that evening as they sat at the dinner table. Her parents had questioned why she kept rubbing her hand to her chest, just below her neckline. 'It feels like heartburn.'

'Perhaps a glass of milk would help,' her mother offered. 'Other than that I think I have some milk of magnesia somewhere in the medicine cupboard.'

'Do they still sell that old stuff?' Lydia queried, pushing her hands one on top of the other just below her sternum as she looked to Marcus for advice.

'I'm sure you're right. It's likely to be rich food and the alcohol. As your mother said, drink plenty of milk. It should help to counteract the acid.'

'It did when I was pregnant.'

'There you are then…' He had smiled pleasantly, although given Lydia's level of suffering he strongly suspected that there was an issue with her gastric band.

From the conversation at the dinner table it had become blatantly obvious that neither of Lydia's parents had the slightest clue that their daughter had resorted to weight loss surgery and Marcus had puzzled over exactly what lies Lydia had told them to cover up her extreme decision. He did the dutiful thing and checked on his wife when she disappeared to the bathroom to vomit, and he confronted her.

'Lydia, when you were in Tenby with your mother and the girls, after you had your surgery, what did you tell them?'

As the retching subsided, Lydia raised her head from the rim of the toilet bowl to reply. 'She thinks it was a gynae op for a uterine polyp. That's what I told everyone. That's what I told you too. Remember?'

He thought back with only a tinge of remorse as he recalled that he hadn't pretended to be sympathetic. Instead he had been irritated by her lack of interest in sex and her endless excuses as to why she didn't want to eat properly. Things between them were never the same after that.

Slipping into the bed beside Lydia he continued his play-acting. 'How's the pain now?'

'Much improved since I took those tablets mum found, but I feel shaky as if I've got the flu. I hope the girls don't catch it.' Marcus reached across and laid the back of one hand against Lydia's forehead, she was hot. 'No, you're fine. No sign of a temperature. Listen, if you're not feeling too good then we could perhaps go home. I could look after you there and the girls could stay here with your parents. That way they won't catch your germs. What do you think?'

Lydia nodded. 'Yes. That's a good idea. I'd rather be ill in my own bed. We could ask my parents in the morning.' She smiled at Marcus. 'Thanks for being so discreet.'

'I wouldn't want to spoil the relationship you have with your parents, I'm not a complete bastard.'

He should have warned her that her pain could be coming from an infection, a band intolerance, or oesophageal dilation and that a rupture could be on the cards. But he didn't tell her, and he failed to make any real reference to her gastric band being at the heart of her current pain and sickness. Not yet. When he did decide the time was right to reveal this, then Lydia would soon request, nay beg, for the band to be removed. Time would do the dirty work and Charles Broughton would be held accountable for insufficient monitoring of his patient.

'Goodnight Lydia, sleep tight.'

27

THE SEARCH

FRIDAY 26TH JANUARY

Quinn slouched on the edge of Carla Lewis's office desk.

'You seem to know much more about the case than we do, Mr Neale, and I get the distinct feeling that *you* are taking the piss. Shall we start again?'

'Keep up, DS Quinn, this isn't difficult. Harry is missing and you have CCTV footage that suggests he left here on Thursday morning the fourth of January with his friend Marcus Carver, and despite your efforts to find him Harry hasn't been seen since that day. The CCTV shows someone, presumed to be Harry, using the door pad, and this is recorded on the data for that security system. He is then seen at the railway station and you have made enquiries confirming him being sighted with Marcus Carver entering Carver's residence together, not too much later that same morning. A taxi driver gave a positive if I'm not mistaken.'

Quinn rubbed his hand over his stubbly chin. 'Is that right, Sherlock? As it happens you are pretty much correct. All the members at this here club have their index finger and thumb prints on record and it was most definitely Harry Drysdale that released the gate that morning.'

'Hmmm, I see.'

There was a pause as Quinn, statue-like, sat motionless staring at Konrad's face until he found his voice. 'You are suggesting there may be another explanation?'

'Yes. I am,' Konrad said.

Quinn leapt up from his seat and rushed to the door. Swivelling his head from left to right he spied a member of staff at the far end of a corridor and yelled a demand to see Carla Lewis immediately. Before she returned to face his questions, Quinn turned to Konrad once more for help. 'What else do you have?'

If Konrad divulged all the information he and Lorna had gleaned then his element of surprise, his full house, his golden egg of a scheme to save his career, could be lost to the judicial system. His only recourse was to feed Quinn with enough to avoid being accused of withholding vital evidence.

'I have to assume, being an intelligent man, that you will be questioning Marcus Carver again. He must be at the centre of this, surely. I mean, his wife died that very day and you have to ask yourself what was he doing at Buxham's if she was so ill?'

'More to the bloody point, if he and Harry Drysdale were together at his house then we should be searching there, rather than here, don't you think?'

'Quite. And if Harry was seen leaving here and entering the Carver residence, then where is he now if he never made it to Chamonix to see his old friends?'

'The airport records are clear. He never got on the plane.'

Their double act was brought to a swift halt by the arrival of a flustered Carla Lewis. 'Nula said it was urgent. How can I help?'

'I need copies of the fingerprints for Harry Drysdale and Marcus Carver from your security system. All of them please. Now. I need to email them through to forensics.'

'Certainly. Anything else?'

'Oh there will be a lot else, but this is all I need for the time being. If you would…' He waved a hand towards the computer encouraging Carla to take up her seat in front of the screen. 'Doctor Carver came alone on Wednesdays after the night of the third of January, did he? Please check carefully.'

'He's a mister Carver actually,' Konrad interjected. 'He's a surgeon.'

'Whatever you say,' Quinn responded rather irked by Konrad's manner.

Carla answered the officer's question. 'Yes. He's arrived alone for the last four weeks, sat at the same table with his usual guests. Mr Drysdale wasn't due to join him. He was supposed to fly out for a skiing holiday and then he had a big court case that was due to start almost as soon as he was back. We weren't expecting to see him until, well… the beginning of February at the earliest.'

Konrad looked on, deep in thought. He had already convinced himself that his own, more accurate, hypothesis was correct, and he was desperate to follow up his hunch.

'I'll wait outside for you, DS Quinn. I'll be in reception.'

'Yeah, yeah. Good idea. You shouldn't be privy to this information.' Quinn was distracted, watching intently as Carla Lewis retrieved vital data, he waved a dismissal.

The lady at the reception desk couldn't have been more helpful. Konrad shared a few snippets of relevant information; just enough to convince Nula that he had detailed knowledge and was seeking confirmation of the facts.

'I was hoping to have a word with Ella the restaurant hostess.'

'I'm sorry but she no longer works here.'

'She didn't last long then. That's a shame. I liked her bubbly personality and my wife has expressed a wish to take up art lessons, so I wanted to chat to her about where she recommends. Has she gone far?'

A stickler for maintaining the privacy of guests, the same standards did not seem to apply when it came to members of staff. Nula fell for the Konrad Neale double bluff as he continued. 'I do apologise. How thoughtless of me to ask. Don't worry yourself. I'm sure her old employer can furnish me with an address. I wouldn't want to cause you a problem.'

Nula grinned at him, somewhat star struck. 'You don't need to go to all that trouble, Mr Neale. I have her brother's business card; I'll give you his number. He'll be glad to help.'

'May I?' Konrad asked, taking the card from Nula and absorbing the details he read there. 'Mallory Fitzwilliam, data security analyst.'

'Keep the card if you like. He's been here a couple of times. Charming man. He collected her belongings for her.'

'*For* her? Not *with* her?'

'No. She left under rather difficult circumstances. I'd rather not say, if you don't mind.'

FOUR DAYS BEFORE HARRY'S DISAPPEARANCE

The smell was unmistakable. Hollberry Hospital with its shiny floors and bustling corridors where everyone walked so slowly, was not a popular destination for Ella. She had bad memories of her visits to A&E there.

She brushed past the frustrating dawdlers and made her way, according to the signs on the walls, towards the Albert Fawcett Surgical Ward on the third floor. The lift took too long to arrive and her impatience was spilling out in the form of foot tapping and muttered expletives. This drew a number of embarrassed responses from other hospital visitors who went out of their way to avoid eye contact with her. Unable to contain her irritation, she took the stairs instead, bounding up them two at a time.

'Oh, no, how long have you been like this?' Val enquired as she turned her head to see who her noisy visitor was. Ella sprung into the side room where Val was recuperating from surgery, and went to the bottom of the bed. She pulled out the folder containing Val's records in the shape of food and fluid charts, vital signs records, and her drug chart.

'Like what?' Ella asked, quickly turning the pages of the

red folder. 'Oh would you look at this chart. How fascinating. Total urinary output for yesterday was—'

'Do you mind you nosy cow? Put that down and come here where I can see you properly.'

Ella did as she was told and stood like a petulant child, twiddling her thumbs and fidgeting. 'What?'

Val groaned as she moved onto her elbow to glance up and down at what Ella was wearing. She shook her head in despair. 'Come on, kiddo. You know the bloody signs. How the hell have you let it get this bad?'

'It's not. Honestly, I just decided to brighten myself up a bit, like a tonic, putting two fingers up to the grey inclemency of the winter weather. My last-ditch effort to possess sunshine and flowers. I'm not over-excited, I'm not talking incessantly, I'm interruptible, I have little difficulty when it comes to insomnia, apart from the last few nights, I'm not eating that much more than is usual and—'

'Stop! Stop right there,' Val begged, trying in vain to sit upright. She fell back against the pillows of her hospital bed. 'Listen to yourself. You're talking at top speed in your posh voice and using la-di-dah vocabulary. You arrived here singing loudly and walking at the pace required of an Olympic event. On top of that you are wearing lime green trousers matched with an orange and black jumper. I need my fucking sunglasses,' Val complained drawing a deep meaningful breath. 'Taking a wild guess you have been on a spending spree on your way here.' Val flicked her eyes towards three large shopping bags that Ella had abandoned by the wall.

'It's the sales,' Ella said with an expansive waft of her hands. 'There's no benefit in wasting my day off. I have things to do.' Continuing to tell Val about which shops she'd been to and the details of her purchases, Ella drew items one after the other from the bags on the floor and flung them onto the bed.

'Has this been going on all weekend?'

'What, shopping? No, I've been at work. I covered breakfast, lunch, and dinner service on Friday, Saturday and yesterday which of course was New Year's Eve. It was most satisfactory. I'm really getting the hang of it now and I've been practising my surveillance skills to boot. I can tell the devious ones just by looking at them. Would you credit it, I caught a man red-handed with his mobile phone in the dining room, attempting to take a surreptitious photo of another guest. He was mightily put out because it was his brother's birthday celebration, but rules is rules, as they say.'

'Ella! For pity's sake, shut the fuck up for five minutes and listen to me.'

Ella stopped what she was doing and put both index fingers to her closed lips. Her gleaming eyes danced with excitement.

'Answer me with a nod for yes or a shake for no, but don't speak. Okay?'

Ella nodded vigorously.

'Have you, at any time in the last three weeks, forgotten to take your medication each night?'

Shake.

'Have you been sleeping less than seven hours on more than three consecutive nights?' Val drilled her eyes into Ella's. The fluorescently dressed girl standing in front of her, bursting with a need to speak, hopped from one leg to the other. Ella then held her hands out, palms upwards and jiggled her head to indicate how unsure she was.

'Shit. That's a definite maybe. Oh, God, Ella we are so close to stopping this guy. Don't let me down now. Here's the important question, be truthful. Have you been drinking more milk than usual, milkshakes?'

The floodgates opened. 'I have, and I've been having hot chocolate made with milk and a squirt of cream to top up. But honestly I don't think I'm that high. Not really, when you think about it.'

'Yes you are. You bloody-well are. You have to get this under control right now, do you understand? This very moment! There is no way I'm allowing you to screw this up. Get my bag.'

A vexed Val poked a bony finger towards the locker at her left-hand side. Ella rushed to pull open the doors and drag the small black leather rucksack from within. Without pausing, she unceremoniously dumped it on top of the pile of clothes, makeup and hair accessories that she had strewn across Val's bed.

'You know what to do,' Val said handing Ella two packets of tablets. 'One of my lorazepam right now and then increase your dose to three times a day. Have you got enough back in the club? Including the ones in case of relapse?'

Ella nodded.

'The chlorpromazine, only take at night and make sure you take it with double your usual dose of quetiapine. Get this sorted by Wednesday or they'll sack you before we get the chance to finish the job we came to do. You have to take incriminating photographs and then we can expose them for what they are.'

Val watched intently as Ella took a one-milligram tablet of lorazepam and popped it into her mouth, taking a slurp of water from a tumbler she found on Val's bedside cabinet.

Lifting the glass to her lips Ella caught sight of Val's bare arms. They were usually covered up, hiding her past. But in hospital with a cannula in the back of one hand and a blood pressure cuff attached to the other arm, her skin was on show. So were the crisscross raised lines of old scars that chequered the inside of her left forearm from wrist to elbow.

An understanding look passed between the two women as Ella swallowed the last of the water and handed Val the tumbler.

'I'm on the case. Truthfully,' Ella assured. 'These clothes… they're for my ingenious plan. I'll be irresistible. I'll capture the required evidence on film. How can I do this? It's simplicity itself. You've no need to worry. I bought this.'

Flapping around, pulling clothes from the pile on the bed, Ella eventually produced an oblong package and tore open the end to pull at the contents. It was a hair accessory for creating a bump, an accentuation of hair on top of the head.

'Brilliant. So you're arming yourself with a beehive hairdo.'

'No, a much closer inspection is required, chérie. What you can't see is a miniscule wireless camera and a microphone. I will be able to divest myself of all clothing and still film the activities of our two libidinous gentlemen. Aren't I the most resourceful private investigator of the modern era?'

'How much did that cost you?'

'I'll offset the cost against tax. This sophisticated little gadget has a micro SD card and pairs with my mobile phone, you know. Phones are allowed in accommodation so—'

'So don't you fucking-well fall asleep and let either of those two bastards get hold of your phone. If you do, you're on your own. Get it?'

'You have your alibi right here, of course,' Ella said, curtseying in an exaggerated fashion. 'Meanwhile, I'll avail myself of some calming music, partake of another pill or two and prepare for Wednesday. Don't fret, ma petite, it isn't my intention to disappoint.'

'Oh God. You're using French.'

'So I am. That's worryingly indicative of tribulations on the horizon. Unnecessary utilisation of French affectations is in my red warning zone. I'll take another lorazepam.'

'French, and that poncey voice and flowery words, the bright colours, the confidence...'

'I think the words on my relapse identification card are *an overinflated sense of self.* I think I'm normal.'

'Normal?'

THE DAY BEFORE HARRY
DISAPPEARED

The medication was finally slowing her thought processes down, and it had been helpful to reduce stimulation by listening to calming classics, by practising yoga and engaging in mindful meditation. All these had mercifully taken the edge off her wildest emotions and she had even managed some sleep, albeit induced by heavy sedative effects from the necessary, though evil, drugs.

Following her visit to the hospital there had been a series of dire warnings from Val, who had sent her text reminders. These were mostly about which pills to take and how often. Also, on the pretext of delivering a late Christmas gift from their fictitious parents, Mal had been sent to visit Ella at Buxham's, on the Tuesday. He had been bemused by her insistence that she couldn't go with him to the local café as usual.

'Let's just talk in your car. I can't allow myself to slip. Peace, quiet, stillness, and loads of drugs are the things that will help most. If I can get a few hours' sleep tonight, I may just avert a major crisis.'

'Come on. It can't be that bad, luv.'

'Yes, Mal, it can. Ask Val. She was there the first time I left the stratosphere, and it's not pleasant. Not for anyone, least of all me. The consequences are similar to those of a tsunami crashing through an idyllic beach paradise. I have to remain grounded to stand any chance of completing a restaurant service and then presenting myself as an irresistible additional dessert dish for Harry Drysdale and Marcus Carver. If anything else adds to the fire under my neurochemistry, then I'm pretty much done for and so is this whole charade. Val needs this to happen. She's sicker than she's letting on.'

Mal let out a long lingering sigh. 'I know.' He looked across at Ella as she sat in the passenger seat of a midnight blue Maserati. She stared out of the windscreen, breathing steadily, eyes fixed on the bare branches of the tree in front of the bonnet.

'What is it that ties you two so closely?' he asked.

'She saved my life.' A fleeting twitch crossed Ella's mouth as she recalled her first ever meeting with Val. 'I hit the most appalling wall of reality when my first manic episode subsided. I was in a psychiatric unit under a section; I'd alienated my family, my friends and plenty of other people along the way. I can't even remember half the things I did.' Ella rolled her eyes. 'To cap it off, I'd ruined my dreams of ever becoming a registered nurse, and I was lost. The depression, as a result of being confronted with this new and bleak world, was consuming me and no one, apart from Val, saw my despair. She adopted me as a pet project to keep her occupied, I think. Those places can be a hell hole of monotony.'

Mal was thoughtful. 'She told me she was in the nuthouse once. I just assumed she was making it up. To scare me like.'

'No, she really was there. I would never have spoken to someone like her in any other circumstances. We were opposites in many ways. She was Fat Val, and I was Skinny Ella.

She was brash, harsh and formidable; I was almost like a mouse once I was back to reality. It was only recently we discovered we had more in common than a trip to the asylum.'

Mal considered her words before speaking again. He modulated his voice, respecting her need for a tranquil approach. 'Why not call it a day? If you're risking a break-down, shouldn't you back off?'

Ella didn't hear the question, she was still reminiscing. 'No one believes just how fat Val used to be, but when her weight became dangerously high, she had surgery to save her life. As a teenager she was bullied for being different - for being a Tomboy. She self-harmed and ate to make herself feel better because bigger meant stronger, less of a target. Her tough outer shell still hides the victim inside.'

Mal nodded in affirmation. 'Yeah, she's a soft old thing, once you get past the thorny bitch act.'

'She was unlucky...' Ella's thoughts faded.

'Why knobble both men? I thought we were after Harry Drysdale?' Mal asked.

'Val is after both of them.'

'Why? Why now?'

'Marcus Carver got away with something years ago, thanks to his friend Harry Drysdale, and Val has been keeping an eye on him ever since. Why now? Me, I think. Marcus Carver is the other thing Val and I have in common.' Ella looked across at Mal and gave him a watery smile. 'Years ago, when I was a shy student nurse on placement with the bariatric service, he was the registrar to a surgeon by the name of Charles Broughton. Mr Broughton seemed like a decent enough man, but Marcus Carver was a slimy toad. Still is. Good looking, overconfident and arrogant. He cared little for any of the nursing staff apart from the senior theatre sister. Now I think back, she was on the large side.

The sort that threatened to escape from her uniform if it was put under additional strain. Anyway, Marcus Carver thought he was beyond reproach until I reported him for... well take a guess, Mal.'

'Touching up fat chicks?'

'That's one very politically incorrect way of saying it, yes.' Ella sighed. 'I saw the way he touched some of the obese female patients, pretending to examine them "just once more, to be thorough" he used to say. Naïve as I was, I could tell he was getting a kick out of his hands-on approach to patient care, it was excruciatingly inappropriate to witness. His sexual arousal was hard to miss.'

Malik launched his eyes towards the roof of the car. 'Nice'.

'At first I wasn't sure. There was something about his general unpleasant attitude that offended me deeply, it disgusted me and so, when I began to have doubts about his examinations, I made it my business to catch him out; to prove it. When I did, I blew the whistle and the investigation into my allegations against him was so stressful that it tipped me into my first horrendous life-changing manic episode. I was mad; so he was declared innocent. Not for the last time.' Ella looked down at her lap.

'That was back in 2010. So I know what he looks like, I know what he does. It now appears that he's in cahoots with his lawyer who enjoys the same perversion and who defends him instead of protecting the public. It's time to expose the truth, if I don't cock it up.'

Mal shook his head. 'I can't believe she never told me there were two targets.'

THE EVENING SERVICE had begun like any other, but the restaurant team knew it would be significantly busier than a usual Wednesday because of the special monthly Lensham and District Pudding Club meeting. Their Christmas invitation dinner had become a thing of legend, and Schubert had devised a dessert menu fit for a palace banquet, to delight the club members.

Adding to the general mood of excitement at Buxham's was news that television royalty had been invited as after-dinner speaker for the event. Ella had gasped when Carla Lewis informed her that Konrad Neale and his wife would be that year's guests of honour.

'I know. He's even more handsome with that eye patch, isn't he?' Carla had said, wistfully tucking stray hairs behind one ear as she proceeded to reinforce the additional security requirements. 'Be as subtle as you can. Treat him like any other guest, but be extra vigilant for over-enthusiastic members trying to bother him. The man is here to enjoy the evening just like anyone else.'

It spread like a warm feeling, starting in the pit of her stomach. 'Konrad Neale. I've watched every single one of his documentaries. He's brilliant.' The anticipation of talking to him, perhaps touching him, built rapidly as the thought of meeting such a famous personality rolled around in Ella's head. These fantasy moments threatened to undo the hours of concentrated relapse prevention strategies that she had employed over the previous forty-eight hours.

By the end of the evening, Schubert had resorted to swearing at her again because, according to him, she mismanaged the front of house service, rushing the kitchen brigade and creating unnecessary logjams of food orders.

'Take your fucking batteries out woman. You have messed with my service all night. You have lost control and I won't stand for another night of this nonsense.' He had shouted right into her face, and although he was being insulting, for some reason she found it impossible to be cross with him. He looked so amusing, red and sweaty, that she was compelled to kiss him, full on the lips. The big wet kiss had him reeling.

'Are you drunk, Ella? Well? Are you?' He slammed a metal serving spoon onto the pass, making a horrendous clattering, jarring the other chefs into reacting with synchronised jolts, their white cylindrical hats wavered. As Ella stood there grinning inanely, he raised the long-handled spoon above his head. 'I'll have you sacked for this, now piss off and sober up.'

Protesting her friend's innocence, Ada had dragged her away to a corner of the stores at the rear of the bar. Once there, they could see through a gap in the door as Spiros entertained the pudding club members with puns. 'Hey, lovely to see you all again, thanks for *pudding* up with me.' He laughed heartily each time he received a positive response. 'Make sure you come back because if you don't then I'm a gonna *tiramisu* so much!'

The effusive barman was handing out final nightcaps almost as fast as he was throwing one-liners at his customers. 'I have a couple of favourite pudding songs. It's true. Number one is *in the gateau* by Elvis, and number two is by The Beetles. You guess.' The bemused customers shook their heads, beaming. 'It's a very famous song. Yes, it's *yellow sub-meringue*! Yes. Now Spiros is a comedian, ladies and gentlemen.'

Ella began to laugh until Ada dug her nails into the back of her arm. This vicious action made Ella yelp, bringing her up short. Ada, seizing the chance, then marched her into the cold night air through the double service doors into the car park beyond. Ella chatted incessantly until they took up position by the huge waste bins that served the kitchen and bar, tucking themselves out of the chill night air. Without warning, Ada let out a yell of surprise. 'Bugger me. I thought that were a dead body.' She held her hands to her chest as her breath caught.

Ella chuckled at her friend. 'You silly individual.'

They looked at an untidy heap of items, each about six foot in length, wrapped in thick grey plastic, tied with brown hemp twine. Most had been thrown carelessly into the bin and the lid failed to close properly as a result. A couple of the grey bundles had been tossed to the ground.

'What a neat way to dispose of Christmas trees,' Ella said.

'Aye, but why wrap the bloody things up, for God's sake? They frightened the shit out of me.'

'Saves the needles all dropping to the expensive carpets, I expect.'

'I think you could be right. They must want to see the back of Christmas, getting shot of this lot so soon.'

'Yes. It'll be Valentine's day before you know it. So, what have I done? Why have you brought me outside into the freezing cold?' Ella demanded, rubbing at her arms.

'Because you have been a right good mate to me and I'm worried about you, my little chicken. You're losing it. I've never seen you so wayward. You can't shut up. You're running about trying to do your job at breakneck speed and if you don't slow down a bit, you'll end up exhausted. I'll finish up down here. Don't even think about arguing with me. Go.'

'Don't be so melodramatic, Ada. I'm possibly the best senior hostess this place has seen in years.'

30

THE SEARCH

SATURDAY 27TH JANUARY

Lorna placed her mobile phone back into her jacket pocket as she updated Konrad with news about Lydia Carver's untimely death.

'The funeral was yesterday and Katie says it was one of the most tense affairs in her ten years of directing services at the Lensham crematorium.'

'Oh?' Konrad was doodling. He had written a few random pitch ideas on a piece of blank foolscap paper plucked from the printer in Lorna's home office. Despite appearing studious, he had stopped being productive several minutes before Lorna dialled the number to talk to her tame funeral director. Glad of an excuse to procrastinate, he lay down his pen.

'Katie says that Marcus Carver was in an absolutely dreadful state.'

'Not unexpected in the circumstances.'

'Granted, but she was shocked at how badly he reacted to the sight of one of the mourners. There was an embarrassing fracas between Marcus and a tall older man before the service even began. Marcus spied the man, who turned out to be none other than a surgeon by the name of Charles Broughton, and went ballistic, shouting at him and accusing him of being responsible for Lydia's death.'

'What? What did Katie say happened?'

'Charles Broughton left, on the face of it deciding that discretion be the better part of valour. Marcus ranted and raged, and rumour has it he breathed alcohol fumes over those closest to him, which included the pallbearers. Lydia's family were appalled by the indignity of Marcus' actions and asked Katie to call the police unless he restrained himself. They had refused to speak to him since details of the cause of death had become public and they have effectively excluded him from family matters. Apparently they have yet to come to terms with Lydia's decision to have surgery and are blaming Marcus for not realising she was in a critical condition before he called an ambulance on the day she died.'

Konrad looked deeply into his wife's eyes. 'They have a decent argument for being angry with him, I would say. He's an eminent surgeon and didn't happen to notice how close to death his own wife was? He knew she'd had the gastric band surgery by then and must have realised she was in pain. Despite this, he went to Buxham's to meet with Harry and two fat ladies for fun and fleshy frolics. What does that say about the man?'

'That he's a bastard?'

'Perhaps, but is he enough of a bastard to withhold treatment deliberately for his wife and to kill Harry? And if he is, then *why* has he killed Harry?'

Lorna sat in her office chair and swivelled it left and right as she pondered. 'Maybe they had a falling out over that girl. Ella, the hostess with the mostess. You saw the rivalry and how far their tongues hung out whenever that lovely woman paid them any heed. It was very entertaining to watch if I recall.' Lorna stiffened and ceased her chair swaying movements. 'Hang on. The last time Harry was seen, he was with Marcus entering his house. According to the taxi driver they walked through the front door together, right?'

'Yes.'

'Then less than an hour later Lydia Carver is taken in an ambulance and rushed to hospital where she died. So what happened to Harry in that time?'

Konrad stood up. 'I think you're on to something. I'm going to follow my original hunch and track down the other missing person - Ella Fitzwilliam. I shall start by getting in touch with her brother.' He reached into his pocket, pulled out his wallet and rifled through the main section until he found the business card given to him by the receptionist at Buxham's. 'That girl may well hold the key to this mystery.'

31

PAST MIDNIGHT, THE DAY OF HARRY'S DISAPPEARANCE

Visualisation was working and, repeating bingo calls, she had begun to drift into a relaxed state. She held the medication pack against her chest and as her breathing became deeper, she could feel the pills were taking effect. When an insistent knocking entered her head she sat up in the half-light of her room. She flung the packet of tablets across the bed before staggering unsteadily towards the noise and taking hold of the door handle. Ella knew she should feel concerned, it was late, and the club had settled for the night, therefore the odds were that her visitor was not going to be a welcome one.

Knock on the door, number four.

She had barely turned the handle and pulled it towards her when a foot appeared.

'How the hell did you find me?' she asked. 'Why are you here?'

'We were expecting you forty minutes ago at the very latest.'

'I'm sorry, I was told to cancel any arrangements for tonight.'

Marcus Carver stared at her, examining her closely as she

stood in the doorway, hair in disarray, wearing a towelling bathrobe, slightly groggy and disorientated.

'I see. How unfortunate. Mr D and I have been waiting for you in room eleven.'

Legs, eleven.

His expression, as he took a step backwards was hard for Ella to translate, it was almost business-like. 'Who told you the arrangements were cancelled?'

'Reception said your guests had informed them to cancel because you were both tired. They were on their way home.'

'Trudy and Leonora?'

'Yes.'

Ella had been so entranced by the presence of celebrity in the restaurant that evening that she'd barely given table eighty-eight much thought as the night progressed. Dutiful in her role as a hostess, she had dealt carefully with the two men and been wary of Trudy and Leonora. With stern flashes, they reminded her of her vow to remain within the parameters of their agreement. She had to back off. Paradoxically this resulted in Mr D and Mr C flirting with her more openly, requesting her presence more than strictly necessary, playing against each other as they sought her notice.

Val's words had repeated in her head, 'Whatever you do, don't get caught.' There was little possibility of that happening. She didn't have any intention of taking a risk and countermanding the instructions from two very formidable women who had made their aims transparent to the extent of actual intimidation.

'I don't think your lady friends approve of me spoiling their party. I'd rather not cause a fuss,' she said to Marcus who impassively waited for her excuse.

'Nonsense,' he replied. 'Anyway, whatever they think, they've eaten well, had some fun and gone home. I have Mr D's late Christmas present for him and you are part of the gift, which is why I made a request for you to attend Mr D's suite this evening.'

A chance.

A heavy weight dragged at Ella's chest preventing her from taking a reasonable breath and the surge of accompanying adrenalin hit like a shot of stimulant. This was her one and only opportunity to come good for Val.

'Was the request for a life drawing sitting?'

'Something along those lines.'

She caught a wisp of a greedy smile.

'Not unexpectedly there's food; a hamper of special tasty treats for you to share with us. You'll be surprised at what I've put together. So you'll come? Now?'

'I'll just put on some clothes and brush my hair. Wouldn't want to be a scruffy gift. I'll be along in ten minutes. Room eleven, you say? The VIP suite.'

In her wardrobe was a dress she was saving for a special occasion. She'd bought it on a whim during her recent spending spree and it called to her. Cut low, front and back, it relied heavily on internal scaffolding to mould her breasts and cinch her in at the waist like a corset that could be fastened at the front. No need for a bra.

Ella looked across at her trusty goldfish. 'It's no good relying on you to zip me up...' she said, breathing in and hooking the last metal clasp into place. She tied the wide belt and swayed her hips from side to side in admiration, checking her handiwork in the mirror.

Then came the matter of hair and makeup and attempting to hide the minuscule camera and microphone within the hairpiece she had bought for that very purpose. Ella checked the instructions, turned on the tiny gadget and her heart plummeted. 'Separate battery included? What sort of shit equipment is this?' Swearing, she tinkered with the round disc and inserted it as instructed into the main body of the surveillance camera. 'Is the light supposed to come on?' She had no idea whether the device was working or not when she secured it in place with some last minute ingenuity involving a piece of hotel tinsel and the majority of a can of hairspray.

In her head a battle was taking place. The sedation of the tablets she had taken earlier was being undermined by the sheer thrill she felt at having a favourable set of circumstances in which to complete her objective.

'Gordon. I have one last chance to collect ironclad evidence and I must sharpen up.' Gordon swam about in his glass bowl, ignorant of the stress in Ella's voice as she talked him through her strategy. She overlooked sharing this with anyone else in her life. No text to Mal, no message to Val. She was acting on her own instincts and heading into the unknown without back up. Again.

She'd taken a huge risk and put the second and only remaining camera torch into her clutch bag, in case the one in her hairpiece failed to capture the action. Realising that taking her mobile phone would be a step too far and would tempt fate, she left it on her bedside table attached to the charger cable.

Time against her, Ella left the attic room in a muddle and headed across the top floor before descending via the stairs to the suite on the first floor.

Room number eleven was larger than some peoples' executive apartments. It was palatial. The sparkling tinsel in Ella's hair, and her green and gold lamé dress complemented the amber brocade of the swag and tail curtains at each window. Wearing her brightest red pashmina, she looked every inch the Christmas parcel, ready to be unwrapped. Marcus, still dressed in a traditional dinner suit, opened the double entrance doors in answer to Ella's knock. Once a few feet inside, Ella gawped at the splendour of the suite.

On a carpeted dais to the left of where Ella stood mesmerised by the splendour, was a magnificent four poster bed, white with gold ormolu detail. Draped in fine shimmering toile, the bed reminded Ella of a scene from a Disney film. Emperor sized and imposing, it was set like a stage. On it lay Harry Drysdale, also wearing his formal dinner attire, with burgundy cummerbund at his waist, black bow tie at his neck. The only item missing was the jacket.

To Ella's amazement she saw that he was tied at his ankles and wrists to the base of the four upright ornate posts using braided silken tiebacks, pulling each of Harry's limbs taut. At the end of the bed, between his legs, was a wicker basket, lid open, content on display. From where she stood, Ella could make out fine chocolates, an array of delicate amuse-bouche, a finger buffet of cake and desserts and a bottle of champagne. A Buxham's special festive hamper.

'Come closer, Ella, so that my friend can appreciate the delightful present I have arranged for him.' Marcus directed Ella to stand to one side of the huge bed where Harry Drysdale turned his head to see her. Although he was gagged, his eyes flickered with elation as he saw her. The anticipation was palpable.

'Hello, Mr D. Happy New Year. I'm sorry I'm late. I didn't realise—'

'Stop chattering.'

Marcus approached her from behind and, without asking, took her clutch bag from her as he directed her to stand still. Despite her protestation, he removed her pashmina from around her shoulders and allowed it to fall to the floor. Raising one of her arms at right angles, he squeezed at the folds of pliant flesh beneath her biceps.

'Look, Mr D, how tender she is. I could eat her up.'

Harry thrashed his head left and right with eyes imploring Marcus not to continue. When Ella caught his despair, she recalibrated her thoughts in a flash. Something was wrong.

'I'll put this one back down and see what else I can find to entertain you with shall I?' Marcus crooned. Ella felt Marcus Carver press himself against her as he leered placing two sweaty hands on her bare shoulders. 'What a simply divine dress you're wearing, so flattering in all the right places. Shall we take a peek at what's underneath?'

'No. I don't think so,' she said, hoping desperately that the interaction was being captured and recorded by her hairpiece and that she could make her move and extricate herself, preventing Marcus from having his wicked way. 'I get the distinct feeling you're not much of an artist, Mr C.'

'That's where you're wrong. I have created a masterpiece of suspense for my friend here. Look at him. He's bursting with desires he can't act on. Now then, young lady, before I position you for the finale, you really should have a treat. Go on, make a pig of yourself from the hamper and Mr D can watch that too.'

One fat lady, number eight.

The food was beyond delicious and Ella had almost forgotten about Harry as she tucked in to the feast. Marcus had laid a plate on the bed next to his friend, in front of Ella, refilling it every few seconds as she devoured the morsels of luxurious fulfilment in rapid compulsive succession. Marcus laughed as Harry squirmed. He seemed to be trying to tell Ella something but with the gag firmly in place she had no way of interpreting his dancing eyebrows, reddening face and thrusting pelvis.

'Hold still, Mr D. The food is slipping off the plate and making a mess.' Marcus Carver's words sounded cruel, almost sadistic. Unable to force another morsel into her mouth, Ella took a sip of fizzy wine, prosecco or perhaps champagne she assumed. Marcus took the cut glass flute from her and placed it on the table next to her clutch bag.

'Now to business. Put your hands on your hips please,' Marcus requested from behind her, his voice deeper and more resonant. He stood so close that she could feel his hot, red wine infused breath on the back of her neck and it sent shivers across her shoulder blades. Trying not to react, holding onto her racing thoughts as best she could, she stared ahead. When she noticed that the posts of the bed were made of cut glass, she almost cried out. Alleviating some of her fears, this was a breakthrough of pure luck. For although the images were fractured, she could make out her own outline and that of the man behind her. If she could see him, she could film him.

Clickety-click, sixty-six.

The numbers and the rhymes began to enter into her mind, unbidden, nonsensical. Unstoppable.

'Mr D is finding this most exhilarating, aren't you, Mr D?' Marcus said as he placed one hand on Ella's shoulder, watching his friend writhe. 'I'm going to carry out a simple medical examination, nothing invasive.'

Doctor's orders, number nine.

He stepped to her side and produced a stethoscope from around his neck. 'I shall palpate your magnificent assets as if they are made of the finest dough and listen to the sounds of your bowels. Mr D loves to knead, to feel the rise and fall of the flesh. Isn't that true, Mr D?'

It was a most peculiar experience for Ella. She didn't object. She stood patiently allowing Marcus to prod and put his ear to her heaving chest using the stethoscope. As he did so, she called out bingo numbers in her head to distract her from the degradation. After a short while she got stuck on a repetition of the same call. *Two fat ladies, eighty-eight. Two fat ladies, eighty-eight. Two fat ladies, eighty-eight.*

When Marcus had completed his first task she was ordered to face in the opposite direction, away from the bed, her back to Harry Drysdale whose muffled groans continued.

Treat 'em mean, thirteen.

Marcus had his hands in her cleavage trying to examine how the dress could be undone. He was greedy, licking his lips, panting.

'Is this what you do to your patients, Dr Carver?' The question from Ella was spoken clearly, loudly and with emphasis on the word *doctor*. These words were in her head and that was where they were supposed to have remained, but she couldn't manage the pressure. 'Dr Marcus Carver who gets off on big women but is too embarrassed to admit it. Too ashamed to be seen admiring decent sized women, so instead he helps himself when they are at their most vulnerable, you should—'

The reaction was instantaneous.

'What?' Marcus stepped back, stethoscope swinging at his neck.

'You heard me,' Ella said tossing her head in Harry's direction. His eyes were wide. Was it fear that she saw there?

'You shouldn't know my name,' Marcus growled.

'But I do because we've met before. I've seen what you do to women like me. Women who need you to help them, not to abuse them.'

'Have I treated you?'

'If you did I'm not a good example, Dr Carver, am I?'

In the background Harry was grunting, and a strange sobbing emanated from the gag as he thrust his head back and forth trying in vain to attract attention.

'Are you a journalist?' Marcus challenged. 'Undercover reporter? No. I think not. You hardly blend into the background. No. You are something else.'

'I am a private investigator.'

'Pull the other one, dear.' Marcus was sneering at her. Scornful.

'I am. I work for Valerie Royal.'

'Who the hell is that?'

Where was his defeated look? There should have been a moment of shock, a confession of shame and a hiatus during which Ella could hear the declaration of his guilt as she made good her escape, but it didn't arrive. Marcus Carver held her defiant stare, and she witnessed a nebulous fury build in him.

'I've never heard of Valerie Royal. Don't take me for a fool. You're trying to claim that you are here to take revenge for women who tease me with their bodies just like you are now? Is that what you mean?' He closed the gap between them and held her wrists against her waist. 'I don't think so. You have willingly come along to a man's suite in the night, dressed for sex, expecting to take off your clothes for money. I suppose you'll be anticipating a handsome payment in return because you're nothing but a common whore. A fat prostitute taking advantage of my wealth and my desires. Don't try me. You were gagging for this.'

Marcus was rough and the grip on Ella's wrists tightened as he thrust his pelvis against her. 'You flirted with us both, playing one against the other. You wanted in on the lucrative deal the other girls have. Can't blame you. They get paid a hell of a lot more than a waitress does.'

Ella sucked in air through her clenched jaw, and, shifting her weight onto her left leg she raised the knee of her right with as much force as she could. Marcus released his fingers from her wrists and made a guttural groan of agony as he bent forward, clutching at his groin. Ella staggered backwards and pushed Marcus away towards the bed where he fell, poleaxed, landing on Harry Drysdale's head before rolling off to bend his knees, coiling up in response to the pain.

Ella leant down to gather her pashmina from the floor, but as she turned to the table to retrieve her other belongings and flee, the atmosphere in the room changed.

'What have you done?' Marcus squawked from his foetal position on the bed where he was staring into Harry's lifeless eyes.

'Is he hurt?' Ella asked.

'Not anymore,' Marcus replied in a hollow voice.

THE SEARCH

SATURDAY 27TH JANUARY

'Hello, I'm enquiring about a quote for a security system,' Konrad said holding the card that Nula had given him on one hand, his mobile phone to his ear.

'Certainly sir, domestic or industrial?'

He had been following his lead, his hunch, but Konrad had not been expecting the number to be for a legitimate security business and he blustered slightly until it came to him. 'Well, it's both. It's for a garage and service station but part of the premises is residential.' Barney wouldn't mind and Netty would be wonderful in the role of sceptical customer, Konrad decided.

He discussed and agreed a date and time for a site visit. 'That's great, my friends have struggled with petty crime and several drive-offs. I've finally managed to persuade them to have a proper security system fitted. So who shall I tell them to expect on Monday?'

'Malik, sir. Malik Khan. I make all the site visits in person. Can I ask how you found me? Only Lower Marton is a bit outside my normal patch.'

Konrad, on hearing a note of concern in Malik's voice,

quickly saved the situation. 'I was given your number by the reception staff at my club. They recommended you.'

'No problem, mister?'

'My name is Neale. Konrad Neale.'

THE FOLLOWING MONDAY ANNETTE called Konrad. 'Well, he'll either turn up out of curiosity and the magnetic draw of meeting a celebrity, or you will have frightened him off completely. What time did he say? Eleven-thirty? He's late.'

Annette Ribble was never impressed by tardiness, and although she was keen to meet Malik Khan, his late arrival had grated. 'What with people who answer every bloody question with the word "so", people who don't tuck the chair under the table when they get up after a meal, drivers who fail to say thank you…' She was about to reel off a further list of things that irritated her in life when she heard a big litre car engine as it rolled onto the forecourt of Ribble's Garage.

'He's here, Kon. We'll fill you in with the details once he's gone. Bye.' She ended the call as Barney appeared from the workshop, wiping his hands on an oily rag. He approached the car with his familiar rolling gait and broad grin, his warm breath vaporising in the freezing air. Pulling on a woolly hat, Annette prepared to step from the entrance of the small convenience store adjacent to the workshop where their assistant June was manning the till.

'Bloody flashy car. One of Konrad's film buddies is it?' June asked in a flat indifferent tone. 'I 'ope not. Can't stand them lot. And that boring wife of his is bad enough.'

'No. I think this might be the chap about the security system.' Annette cast her patient reply over her shoulder as the door swung shut on June's disdainful response. 'He'll charge too much.'

Mal parked a glacier blue BMW M4 in front of Barney's

workshop, away from the fuel pumps. 'Hello, mate. Mr Ribble is it? Is Mr Neale here?'

'Sorry to disappoint young man, but Mr Neale is in London today. You took a risk driving that high performance beast in this crap weather.' Judging by the sheepish expression, Barney guessed that the BMW had been a means to impress Konrad. Emphasising the foolhardiness of driving a pricey sports car in late January, a few flakes of snow descended.

'Never mind. My wife is Kon's film editor, she has a studio upstairs and she'll be the one dealing with you. She knows more about this sort of thing.'

A flicker of uncertainty crossed Mal's face as he was introduced to Annette. 'You're Konrad Neale's film editor?'

'Yes. What were you expecting? Some lush dressed up to the nines swanning around in a lavish studio full of famous actors all tripping over themselves? Sorry, sunshine, but reality is so much more mundane. Follow me.'

'This is it? This is the entire business premises?' he asked as he was led around the perimeter of the building. They walked through the compound containing a vast collection of mechanically unsound vehicles in various states of disrepair, piles of old tyres, discarded oil drums, and a hillock of hardcore that Barney used for filling pot holes in the yard. Having escorted him on the grand tour of the business, with Malik expounding the virtues of CCTV and motion sensor equipment, Annette was getting rather irked by his overuse of the familiar term "luv". The word peppered the end of many a comment from the sharp dressed Asian man with a pseudo East End gangster persona. Cocky and irritating were the two words that sprung to Annette's mind as they completed the circuit of Ribble's Garage.

She eventually paraded a shivering Mal through to the

small convenience store that served the village of Lower Marton.

June honoured the visitor with a surly nod. 'Come far 'ave you?'

'Not too far. Crewsthorpe.'

'Should have hopped on a train in this weather.'

'Er, yes. Maybe I should,' Mal replied brushing snow from the lapels of his suit and wiping his shiny black leather shoes on the doormat.

'Forgot your coat, did you?' June asked without any sympathy linked to her enquiry. 'Still, I don't s'pose you need one where you come from.'

'June!' Annette was about to step in with an apology when Mal responded. 'I was born in Crewsthorpe, luv. It's just as cold there as it is here in the sticks.'

Hustling Mal to the door at the back of the shop, Annette took him into the homely residence attached to the garage business. 'Sorry about June. She's not very worldly wise.'

He stared about him, underwhelmed and momentarily silenced at the sight of mediocre furnishings past their best and décor from another era.

'Shabby chic,' Annette said ignoring the disappointment present in Mal's tone when he asked if they had only recently moved in. She found herself laughing at his judgemental approach to life. 'Your place is a bit swanky then is it?' He didn't need to reply, she knew as much already.

Mal tiptoed around the kitchen furniture, holding his hands away from any surfaces or chair backs as if touching them would result in contamination. Annette directed him to follow her upstairs and into her film-editing studio. No larger than the average double bedroom it was kitted out with monitors, mixing desk, computer and an ample supply of snacks to keep Annette provisioned with additional calories between meals.

'Have a seat, young man.'

With a resigned sigh Mal placed himself on the edge of one of the office chairs in front of her desk as Annette squeezed her backside between the two arms of her well-worn seat.

'From all your sales patter it seems you are a bit of a whiz-kid when it comes to CCTV security systems. So, as you will have noticed, there are a number of cameras around the premises which cover the forecourt. We have them linked to record any flagrant breaches of the law. You know the sort of thing: break-ins, drive offs, scallywags after nicking themselves a motor.'

'Right, so what do you need me for? Staff theft?'

'No, bigoted she may be, but June's as honest as the day is long. We have a tricky problem and I was hoping you could shed some light on this.' She pointed towards one of the monitors to her left and pressed a button on a keyboard illuminating the screen with an overhead shot of two people making their way through a secure gate. One was wrapped up against the weather and wore a baseball cap hiding their face, the other was plain to see, dressed in a single breasted Chesterfield style overcoat, scarf tied neatly, cravat style, at his throat.

'Where is this exactly, luv?' Mal asked.

'Recognise it?'

'No, not immediately.'

Annette gave her visitor a sideways glance to check his level of interest. He was staring intently for several seconds before his facial features stiffened. 'Hang on. What is all this about, luv?'

'You obviously recognise the taller of the two, but can you help us to identify the one in the cap?'

Mal sat back moving his chair from the desk and he

tensed, ready to stand up and leave. 'This is not what I'm qualified for.'

'You'll get your money. Don't fret about that. Konrad contacted you because we are looking for Ella Fitzwilliam in connection with a friend's disappearance.'

'I don't see what that's got to do with me.'

'Don't you? That's a peculiar thing to say. Staff at Buxham's, where that film was taken, say you are her step-brother, and that you collected her belongings from there when she lost her job. Konrad was keen to ask you about where we can find your sister. She seems to have gone to ground.'

Mal stood. 'I think you've made a mistake. You must be looking for another Malik Khan. It's a popular name, luv. Very common.'

Annette swivelled her chair around to face Mal. 'We weren't looking for a Malik Khan, actually; we were directed to contact a Mallory Fitzwilliam. He seems to have the same telephone number as you.'

'As I said, I can't help you.'

'Can't or won't help?' Annette raised one hand, palm facing her anxious guest who had blanched at the sight of Marcus Carver on the screen. With her other hand Annette pressed another key and a picture of a Mercedes A class appeared. Through the windscreen the driver could be seen, an Asian man wearing a flat cap. Blurred indistinct outlines of two female passengers in the rear could barely be made out.

Annette could feel the moment when Mal stopped breathing. He shook his head. 'No I'm sorry, you've got me there. I've no idea why you are showing me these pictures, luv.'

'So that car doesn't belong to your cousin Dinesh Khan?'

'Look, lady, it may belong to someone called Dinesh

Khan. How the hell would I know and what are you doing with these pictures anyway?'

Annette had him where she wanted him. He couldn't leave. He would have to find out why she had these shots of him and of Marcus Carver, and how she had them in her possession.

'Oh dear. It seems Kon and I may have made a terrible mistake. I'm so sorry. I can't apologise enough, Mr Khan. Please forget that you ever saw these pictures, forget the name Ella Fitzwilliam.' Rolling forward, Annette put both hands on her knees and extricated herself with some difficulty from her chair. She grunted, risking a brief glance at Mal for his reaction.

'I'm editing tomorrow's Crime Watch programme for the BBC, you see. The police are keen to know where our friend Harry Drysdale has disappeared to.'

She sighed dramatically, hoping that he would accept her story.

'Such a shame. We honestly thought you were the man we were looking for and you do look just like the bloke driving that taxi. We think young Ella is in deep trouble, but then, if you don't know who she is, you can't help...' Annette suddenly put a hand to her mouth before dropping it again, eyes wide. 'Oh, my word. How stupid we've been. The police would surely have spoken to the real Mallory Fitzwilliam by now, unless they don't know about him yet.'

Mal had moved to the door but lingered there. 'Why would the police want to talk to him?' he asked.

Finally, Annette had him where she wanted him. 'What's it to you... luv?'

THE DAY HARRY DISAPPEARS

'Yes, he's definitively dead.' There was no sense of panic in her tone. She sounded almost matter-of-fact as she held her ear to Harry's mouth and looked down to his chest for signs of movement, of breathing.

Marcus sat in an elegant gilded chair, holding silken curtain ties in one trembling hand, a stethoscope in the other. All strength sapped by fear, he let them dangle there as he stared at Ella examining Harry Drysdale's limp body.

'This can't be happening… You killed him.'

'Me? I don't think so Dr Carver. You killed him. I was merely trying to protect myself when you sought to rape me. See?' Ella held her wrists in the air and the red welts on her flesh were plainly recent.

'You pushed me. I fell.' Marcus felt cold. His throat closed as if suddenly swollen.

'Is that what you're going to tell the police?' she asked.

His hastily thought out stunt to make Harry suffer in repayment of his teasing photos and videos the previous week, had backfired completely. To add to his state of panic, the girl in front of him was acting as if she was in a television drama. Her response to the whole diabolical situation had been most bizarre, and she was becoming increasingly agitated and restless. Wasn't she supposed to be in a state of shock too?

'Can't we leave him to be found in the morning? As if he died in his sleep?' she said, shrugging.

'He doesn't exactly look as if he died in his sleep does he?' The words had come without thinking. 'No pathologist will fall for that.' Marcus unsteadily levered himself from his seat and made his way towards her. 'How the hell are we going to clear up this mess? I can't be involved.'

'That's a thought. We could throw him out. Put him in the skip with the Christmas trees.' Ella's eyes sparkled like the tinsel in her hair.

Marcus stopped suddenly, startled as Ella leapt up and began to jump on the spot, clapping her hands in gleeful applause at her own inventiveness.

'Shut up, woman, and for God's sake stop bouncing about, if someone makes a complaint we'll be discovered and I need time to think what to do.' His voice quavered as he touched at his clammy forehead. 'Fuck. Fuck...'

Ella couldn't hold back. She was bursting with delirious levels of anticipation. 'Two little fucks, twenty-two. Gone to heaven, thirty-seven. Devil's door, number four. He's gone blue, number two.'

Incongruously, Ella produced a guttural laugh and Marcus stepped towards her to place a silencing hand over her mouth, when suddenly his mobile phone vibrated its way across the table in the middle of the room.

Releasing a gasping but bemused Ella, he walked across picked it up and stared at it, freezing.

It was Lydia.

In the time it had taken for him to glance at the number of missed calls and at the texts he found, Ella had moved at an alarming speed and pounced back onto the bed. She was now wrapping a dead Harry Drysdale in the bottom sheet.

'Stop. What are you doing?' Marcus called out in a stage whisper.

'What does it look like? I'm tucking him up in a shroud. Then I shall proceed to the waste bins outside, unwrap a Christmas tree and bring the plastic up here. Then you and I will transport Mr D back down in the lift disguised as an unwanted tree and dispose of him with the others. The waste collection is in the morning, monsieur.'

Marcus shook his head in a pathetic effort to clear it. 'What the bloody hell are you talking about?' The girl was behaving as if she was drunk or on some weird cocktail of drugs. One moment she was elated and rambling the next animated and coherent.

'We can't leave him here. And if we are as equally guilty for his death as one another, then we have to move him. Why, what was your brilliant notion, monsieur?' Ella asked, speaking rapidly. Marcus didn't reply. He was stumped. This wasn't supposed to have happened. He had wanted to punish Harry for his cruel stupidity, not to kill him.

With his brain working through a furious jumble of tangled possibilities, he mulled over the girl's outrageous proposition. Disposing of the body had to be preferable to calling the police and losing everything. If the police became involved, he would be exposed in the press as a pervert. His past would return to humiliate him, he would be marched in front of the Royal College and suspended, even if they believed his side of the story. He swallowed hard.

Sitting in a lavish suite with a dead barrister and a mad woman he grappled with the outrageous conundrum of finding a way to cover up this appalling catastrophe. He didn't have the luxury of time. The messages on his phone had been unnerving. Lydia was at home in terrible pain, the children were due back from her parents in the morning and she was asking for his advice. He was desperate to avoid her calling for an ambulance too soon; people would ask why he wasn't at home. At the same time he was afraid that if she left it too late to seek help, she could be risking her health if not her life.

'What are you suggesting?' he asked Ella, who replied with speed.

'We'll use the service lift. The kitchen and bar have closed ages ago and the staff have gone, all apart from reception and the waking night manager who'll be in his office. I'll confirm when I go down to retrieve the plastic and twine. You remain here and begin packing his bags, and then you need to pack yours before we go.'

'We should throw his bags out too.'

Ella laughed scornfully. 'Hypomania rules, Dr Carver. It sharpens the mind.'

He looked at her, not understanding.

She explained, exasperated. 'I have Bipolar Disorder. It has its up sides,' she said tapping her temple with a forefinger. 'If we throw the bags in the bin with the body, they will be found together. If the bags leave the club with a person carrying them then it will be assumed that the person is the owner of the bags. Comprenez-vous?'

He did understand but a cold feeling of dread was threatening to incapacitate him. His breathing was deep and rapid, leaving him light-headed, reeling. Amid the madness this girl was as bright as she was bonkers, if there were such a thing, and he realised that she was right. They had to hide the body. Although she was the one exploring possible solutions to their plight, they were both implicated in the death of Harry Drysdale. Whatever the decision, he needed to return home to Lydia as soon as possible to avert another crisis of his own making. The walls were closing in creating a tunnel, a single pathway with no room for U-turns.

He sent his wife a text.

I'll be home in a few hours. If the pain gets any worse, then call an ambulance.

Pacing around the suite, Ella dressed herself in a cardigan she found in Harry's wardrobe. It was a little snug, but she managed to button it up at the waist. Marcus gathered together the rest of Harry's belongings. He found a suitcase and began to throw items in haphazardly. Thoughts were spiralling. If Harry had been a true loyal friend, then he wouldn't have been cruel and teased him and this would never have happened. If Konrad Neale had not called to Harry as he made his way back from the gents' toilets earlier that evening then Harry would still be alive.

Harry had broken every rule and introduced Konrad Neale to the occupants of table eighty-eight, showing off, inadvertently sealing his own fate.

'We love it here,' Harry had said to Konrad. 'Bloody amazing place, very discreet.' Marcus had watched in stunned silence as they threw their heads back laughing and patting each other on the back. The giveaway moment had been Harry's parting comment. 'As I always say, there's no fun without flesh.' Konrad had then left to re-join his friends, chuckling. Marcus knew who he was instantly, just like everyone else in the restaurant had done.

'What if he had recognised me, you bloody idiot?' Marcus had spat those words in Harry's ear. He knew that he could never forgive the thoughtlessness and began, at that very moment, to make a plan for revenge; a punishment for Harry's teasing and for that idiotic breach of trust.

DISAPPEARING HARRY

Entering the service lift their chests heaved with exertion as they struggled to manage the awkwardness of the body now wrapped in thick grey plastic sheeting, tied with brown hemp twine.

Once inside the relative safety of the elevator, Ella pressed the button to take them to the ground floor and to the loading bay at the rear of the stores. She lifted the soft woollen cuff of Harry's cashmere cardigan to check her delicate dress-watch and was relieved to see that time was on their side.

Cup of tea, number three.

Not quite three o'clock in the early hours of the morning. Plenty of time to make preparations to depart before the hotel came to life. She felt astoundingly smug about how well her strategy for disposing of Harry's body had gone, so far. It was physically tiring but not impossible.

With the lift descending at a snail's pace, Ella leant against the dull sheet metal of the interior, trying to recuperate. The head end of the bundle lay over her feet. Harry Drysdale was dead, and Ella felt vindicated. It wasn't her fault he was dead, but the means of his death put her in an unassailable position as far as manipulating Marcus Carver. Val would have her day. One down, one to go.

Marcus held on to his kneecaps, gasping for air, preparing for the next few minutes of exertion. The lift shook more than anticipated, and steadying himself he looked up at Ella, somewhat baffled. 'Back in the room, you said we'd met before. When was that?'

Deep in thought, she didn't answer. The lift juddered to a clattering standstill and there was a gut-wrenching delay before the doors eventually began to part. When they did open to their fullest extent, only the light from within the lift illuminated the stark concrete of the rear service area. The air was chill. To their right were lengths of clear plastic strips, beyond that the stores door, firmly padlocked. Left was an area containing metal cages on castors and large plastic laundry baskets on wheels, waiting to be collected for use by housekeeping in the next few hours. Ahead, and with only a faint green glow from the fire evacuation lighting showing their outline, were double doors with a push bar across them.

In a most unladylike fashion Ella stepped over Harry's body, pressed the lift button to hold the doors and skipped to a panel next to the exit. 'I need to disable the door alarm. We do it all the time. Don't worry.'

'What about the CCTV?'

'Shit.'

'Great plan,' Marcus moaned.

Momentarily, Ella considered the advantages and disadvantages of the first notion that popped into her head. Without more than a second's hesitation she hoisted her dress up and pulled down her briefs. White and accommodating, she hoped they would help to give the illusion of frosted glass, should reception care to look too closely at the changing screens on the monitors set behind the desk.

'Oh, my God...' she heard Marcus mutter in disbelief as she forced open the doors with a sideways heave of her hips, catching a breath in her throat at the bitterness of the freezing air. He made no further objections once she had flung her knickers, with the accuracy of an international netball player, at the camera where they landed perfectly, obscuring the view from the lens.

Stuck in the tree, fifty-three.

She was cock-a-hoop and gave herself another round of applause. 'Yay!'

'Shut the fuck up!' Marcus whispered, frowning with urgency.

Ella stopped immediately and raced back to where he was pulling at Harry's wrapped feet, sliding the body bag from the lift and across the concrete floor to the doorway. Ella helped him to drag Harry to the base of the large yellow waste bins at the rear of the bar area. They made some much-needed space by removing three similar shaped parcels from the bin. Then, using empty bottle crates, they managed a two-stage manoeuvre to raise the bundled Harry high enough to roll him over the rim. Ella, teetering in court shoes, saw Marcus wince as the body landed with a gentle bounce on top of kitchen waste and broken Christmas decorations. Silently and speedily they replaced the Christmas tree parcels on top. Ella had the final one in her hand when she stopped in mid flow. 'Wait.'

They consulted with each other in hushed tones, avoiding their voices travelling upwards to wake any staff member or resident from their slumbers.

'What?'

'We need to prove that he has left the building, otherwise

they'll search everywhere for him when he doesn't appear in the morning.'

'How the hell do you suggest we do that, Miss Know It All?'

'You're a surgeon, aren't you?' she asked quietly, knowingly. 'We need a fingerprint to use on the security pad when we leave with his bags.'

'We?'

Thee and me, twenty-three.

'Yes. We.' Ella was buzzing with the intoxication of the deception she had devised. 'Come on back to the lift. I'll explain on the way.'

Ella pulled the fire escape doors closed behind her and, in order to enable an easy return, she deliberately failed to secure them properly. In sharp contrast to Ella's liveliness, Marcus was pale and shaking. 'You want me to do what?' he asked, eyes-bulging, mouth agape.

'Would secateurs be the right sort of implement to do the job? That's all you need to answer. Yes or no?'

Ella let Marcus back into room eleven with the swipe card she had tucked into a deep pocket of her borrowed cardigan. He seemed drained of an ability to act, so Ella gave instructions to him as if he were a toddler.

'Answer the question please.'

'Well, yes... probably.'

'Good. Sit down. Eat something sweet. I'll be back just as soon as I've broken into housekeeping. Actually, I'll have one of those Danish pastries if you don't mind. Keep my strength up.'

Baker's bun, sixty-one.

She reached across the dessert trolley that she guessed had been used earlier by Leonora and Trudy and grabbed the nearest pastry. 'Yummy.'

In the main housekeeping department on the ground

floor, they stored vases, ribbon, oasis, mesh, and many other items necessary for the floral arrangements throughout the club. Ella could access these without alerting reception as long as she wasn't seen by anyone else. Instead of creeping along the corridors like a seasoned cat burglar, listening for signs of life, watching for movement, she walked purposefully and with absolute confidence.

Straight on through, eighty-two.

After several minutes she returned and knocked gently on the door to Harry's suite. Marcus must have been standing just the other side waiting impatiently because there was no delay before he opened the door wide enough for her to slip back into the room. She held aloft a pair of sturdy secateurs.

'Grubby but good quality,' Ella announced.

Dirty Gerty, thirty.

'I debated whether to clean them, but then realised that as he's already dead, he can't die of an infection.' Ella laughed at herself. 'Don't look so appalled Dr Carver, I nicked some surgical gloves too. Thought they might come in handy. We go back to the bin, I jump in, rummage around and free an arm, you cut off the digit and we wrap him back up again. Oui?'

'It's such a bloody risk going back a second time.'

'Well, we can leave it and hope the rubbish collections haven't changed again this week. Christmas and New Year cause such a lot of disruption to normal schedules.'

'No, you're right. We take a finger and use that to open the side entrance when we leave together with the cases I've packed.'

'Have you left some of Harry's clothes out for me?'

Marcus crumpled. 'No. I didn't think.'

Ella let loose a disdainful laugh. 'No. Clearly not, monsieur. Best leave the thinking to me. I have a superior brain and a mind for problem solving you can only dream of.'

She bounded towards the open suitcase and extracted some items. A shirt, black trousers, a blue baseball cap with a white Ping logo on it. 'I never knew he was into golf. How odd,' she said placing the hat backwards on her head. It perched on top of her hair. 'I need a coat and a scarf to tuck my hair into. Oh dear. Shoes. What size are his feet?'

Buckle my shoe, thirty-two.

Holding the trousers up Ella released a long groan. 'So much for that idea. I'll never fit into these.' Discarding them she reached for the shirt. 'Nor this. Go and get me some of your clothes to wear. I might stand a chance of doing the buttons up.'

Waiting for Marcus to make his way to and from his suite two doors away, Ella returned to the issue of footwear. Using three pairs of socks she managed to make use of black ankle boots belonging to Harry Drysdale, they had a Cuban heel, to add height. 'How do I look?' she asked as Marcus stepped through the door, overcoat slung in the crook of one arm, suitcase pulled behind him. He glanced down at her feet.

'Disturbing.'

He opened his suitcase and handed her a pair of suit trousers, the jacket to match and a navy-blue roll-neck sweater. 'This may stretch enough to accommodate your…'

'Breasts, Dr Carver. Big fat mammary glands. Bags of fat. That is what they are. Not so thrilling now we have to disguise them, are they?'

Marcus turned to face the opposite direction as she stripped off her dress and forced her way into the jumper. It appeared he could not trust himself to look at her. Once on, the trousers were held together by the hook and top button alone and were a little long in the leg, but once the jacket was in place Ella became an entirely different shape.

'Now, can we go and harvest a finger then leave?'

'We can't leave too early. That would be suspicious,' Ella responded, slipping on Marcus's long tweed overcoat and pulling the collar to make it stand upright at the neck. She posed in front of a large mirror.

Marcus was pacing again. 'Oh, God. I have to get out of here. The stress is too much to bear and my wife is ill. I have to get home.' He was forcing the words out.

Something clicked within Ella's mind and she rounded on him. 'Why were you here if your wife is ill?' She took the back-to-front cap from her head, remembering that she was still miraculously in possession of the hairpiece welded onto her head with hairspray, several pins and the length of tinsel.

'Come off it. You know damn well that I come every fucking week to get my rocks off with a big woman.'

Two fat ladies, eighty-eight.

'Like an addiction is it?' Ella asked, pushing for the elusive confession.

Marcus looked to the floor. 'Something like that.'

'Would you have raped me?'

'Rape?' Surprised, Marcus stood wide-eyed. 'Good God! No. I wanted to make Harry jealous. He likes to indulge in his passion for art, especially naked women. The flesh as it moves excites him, so I was going to treat him to yours.'

'I don't understand. Don't you have sex with Leonora?'

'Yes, but not necessarily… look, Ella, not now, okay? We can discuss this later. Let's get that finger and get out of this place before we get caught. There's a good girl.'

35

THE SEARCH

TUESDAY 30TH JANUARY

'Cousin Dinesh runs a legitimate taxi,' Lorna confirmed, looking up from her iPad and across at Konrad, who was making scribbled notes as she spoke. The kitchen table was awash with printed pages, the result of the morning's searches into Malik Khan and his connection with Ella Fitzwilliam.

'At least one of the family is kosher then.'

'I'm not sure that's an appropriate turn of phrase when referring to a Muslim. I take your meaning though. On the surface, the Mal we see is a flashy git, who says he works in cyber security, prefers to be seen in designer gear, driving sports cars and playing fast and loose at the casino. Now and again he reverts to type, becomes an invisible Asian man and does some other security work for a previous colleague in her fledgling investigations firm. He collects debts for her, scouts out places, follows the odd mark and has been babysitting Ella Fitzwilliam at Buxham's club by pretending to be her brother.'

Konrad drummed his fingers on the pine table. 'Yeah. What the hell is that all about? Tell me about her.'

'Valerie Royal? She's a dyed in the wool lesbian, hard faced, bitter and resourceful. Unfortunately, she's also terminally ill. Strangely there is a strong link between her and Ella. Val employed her less than a year ago and she recently started paying the rent on Ella's bedsit, keeping it going despite the fact that Ella got a live-in position at Buxham's.'

'Lovers?'

'Maybe.'

'Shall we pay Val a visit?'

'In hospital?'

'Well, if she's that bad we'd better go soon before she pops her clogs. Don't you think?'

'Kon, where is your humanity? Let me phone the hospital and ask if she'll agree to meet us.'

'On what grounds is she likely to do that? Forget calling ahead. We'll take Malik Khan along for the ride. He's not daft. He knows Val hasn't been truthful with him and something has gone hideously wrong for young Ella wherever she is.'

Mal had been most helpful when Annette had grilled him about his part in supervising Ella's first real foray into the world of private investigations. He had caved in and divulged much needed information about his involvement.

'He was told to follow Harry,' Konrad said aiming a finger at Lorna, 'but my money is on Marcus Carver being the real target. So what have Val and Ella got in connection with him? Were either of them on his patient list, past or present? I wonder.'

'I can answer that. Neither of them have any connection with Harry, none whatsoever, but Valerie Royal was a patient of a certain Marcus Carver back in 2012.'

'Don't tell me, she was one of the three women in the case against him who were discredited and vilified in court.

Curious then that she should be stalking him now, never mind that she's about to die; at last knockings.'

'Maybe that's *exactly* why.'

Two hours later Malik Khan phoned Lorna's mobile number. 'I got your message asking me to call. What do you want, luv?'

She cringed. Annette had been correct. It was bloody annoying being referred to as 'luv'.

'Konrad and I wondered if you would arrange for us to go with you as visitors to the hospital.'

'Strike a bleedin' light! How did you find out so quickly? She's only just this minute spoken to me.'

Lorna shot a look across at her husband who was sifting through information and pretending that he didn't need glasses. His remaining eye was getting old with him and reading was becoming more of a challenge when the print was small. Konrad had a sheet of paper at arm's length and was squinting when Lorna's change of tone alerted him.

'Oh, it was an educated guess,' Lorna said, hesitantly. She had no idea whether Val's health had nose-dived or whether Mal was referring to something else entirely.

'You must have one hell of an education to work that out, luv. I've been phoning all the psychiatric units this side of Watford. I'd never even heard of Flemenswick. It's bleedin' miles away from here, luv. Miles away.'

Lorna removed the mobile phone from her ear to silently mouth the words, 'Malik Khan has found Ella,' towards her husband whose head had popped upright. She grabbed a pen and scribbled the details down, trying to convince Mal she already knew the facts. Konrad stood to look over her shoulder as she responded, 'Yes, Flemenswick, we'd never come across it either...'

Konrad stepped to his left, tapped the name into Google and slid the iPad to his wife. 'Derbyshire is a long way for her to have been admitted... unless she's on a section and the local beds were full.'

'Yeah, that's what the nurse on the ward just said. I'm the only family member they had details for and I'm not even her real brother.' There was a lull. Lorna could hear Mal breathing and determined that he was buying thinking time. He sounded uncertain, softer. 'Do you really want to come with me to see her?'

Lorna shot an enquiring glance at Konrad before pushing the advantage. 'Erm, well, we were wondering whether it might be best to speak to Valerie first and find out exactly what Ella had been doing while she worked at Buxham's. We think Valerie may have a connection with Marcus Carver.'

Mal's unexpected reply caught Lorna by surprise. 'Not just Val, luv. They both knew him - for all the wrong reasons by the sounds of it.'

'Ella too?'

36

THE SEARCH

TUESDAY 30TH JANUARY

'What was your great scheme to bring about the professional destruction of Marcus Carver? And why has Harry Drysdale done a disappearing act?' Lorna asked.

Valerie Royal, face painfully drawn, pallid and debilitated, rested her head against the hospital pillow, eyes darting between Lorna and Mal, seeking assurances. 'Is she okay? Did he hurt her?'

'We dunno, mate,' Mal replied. 'We're going to see her tomorrow. The Old Bill are on their way to pull in Marcus Carver for questioning about the other bloke's disappearance. Harry Drysdale. They don't know anything about Ella's connection. Not yet. They will though, cos they're asking all the staff at Buxham's about the two fellas and the fat birds.'

Lorna wrapped her slender fingers around what she could of Mal's muscular arm and, taking the hint by moving away from the bedside, he allowed her room to question his friend in more detail.

'Please, Val, try to be very accurate. What was Ella asked to do and what were your ultimate aims?' Lorna asked.

'Incriminating photos or video footage of him engaging

in sexual deviancy with obese women. That was the assignment.'

'By "him" do you mean Marcus Carver or Harry Drysdale?'

'Both if we could, but it was Marcus Carver I was after. I couldn't prove what he was doing in his professional life, so the aim was to show his wife and destroy his private life, but, as it turns out, she already suspected. Instead, with Ella's help, I was going direct to the press to prove I was right all along and to stop him from doing more harm to his patients.' The effort of explaining was too much. Val closed her sunken eyes.

'Did you meet his wife then?'

Val spoke quietly and her breathing became increasingly laboured as she tried to explain to Lorna the chain of events. 'Yeah. The poor cow was completely taken in by her husband - the tosser. After their sham marriage I watched her getting fatter and fatter until she barely had enough strength to walk her own children to school.'

'Were you stalking her?' The familiar sound of Mal's voice roused Val into opening her eyes again. She gave a weak smile.

'I was observing. Not stalking. Eventually I introduced myself and told her my story. At first she was fuckin' outraged. Not with the truth, but that I'd dared to accuse her husband of such terrible things. She said he'd been cleared of any such wrongdoings and she threatened to report me to the police.'

'Did she?' Mal asked.

'No. Don't be dappy. It was all bluff. She knew deep down he was a perv, so I didn't badger her. I didn't even need to follow her anymore. As she wasn't the type to respond to an aggressive approach, I just gave her a card with my thera-pist's name and details, and suggested she make some changes for her health and the future of her children. I never saw her again after that.'

'A generous act,' Lorna said.

'It wasn't. Not really. She went the whole hog and lost huge amounts of weight. I knew he'd go astray if he couldn't get it at home and then he'd help himself at work. Which he may well have done, I don't know. Assuming that he was being true to form, I followed him and discovered how often he met with his lawyer, Harry Drysdale. Then I sent Mal on a mission to keep tabs on Mr Drysdale and that was when we found out about Marcus Carver's weekly fat feasts at Buxham's.'

Mal stood by the window, staring out into the bleak winter sun that bounced from the metal of a smoking shelter in the car park below. He breathed heavily against the window causing condensation, obscuring his view. 'You could have told me about him.'

'I didn't want you to treat me, or the job, any differently to what you normally would. It was better that you didn't know.'

The door opened gently accompanied by a knocking. Konrad poked his head into the room apologising for the interruption. He held his mobile phone aloft, waggled it and beckoned to Lorna, indicating for her to join him outside in the corridor by tipping his head in that direction.

'It's a damn good job I took that call,' Konrad said, taking Lorna to one side. They stood next to an information board that held a patchwork of posters and leaflets about healthy eating. 'It was the mighty DS Quinn. They've located Marcus Carver at his home address, they had a warrant to search the place too and they're taking him in for questioning.'

'Have they found Harry?'

'No, but they're on to something.'

Lorna inclined her head towards the ceiling, her mouth turned down at the corners. 'God.'

'He didn't give a great deal of detail. That's all I know.'

'And?' Lorna had spotted Konrad's body language giving a suggestion that more revelations were in the offing. He looked awkward.

'I think there's been a bit of a balls-up. It seems some evidence was found in his house… They want me in for questioning about the last time we saw Harry with Marcus Carver at Buxham's club.'

Lorna scratched at her hairline. 'I thought you'd answered all their questions about that night. Did he say whether they re-checked the security fingerprints held at the club against those of the thumb found in the refuse lorry on January the fourth?'

'No. Why are you asking about that?'

'Because, if that thumb does belong to Harry then their theory doesn't make any sense. If Harry left the club with Marcus and if he accompanied him home, why, for goodness' sake, would Marcus kill him, *then* chop off his thumb and throw it into a dustcart? And, what's more, that dustcart provides a service in Lensham, nowhere near Marcus's home address.'

'Which means that Harry had his thumb cut off on his way there.'

'Yes, before he arrived at chez Carver…' Lorna's eyes sharpened. 'Alternatively, Harry never left Buxham's with Marcus. His thumb did.'

'Then where the bloody hell is Harry?' Konrad asked.

After a short debate, Lorna agreed to keep the latest turn of events a secret and she sidled stealthily back into the hospital room where Mal was chatting animatedly to Valerie Royal about old times. 'I saw Screw McBride last week,' Mal said. 'He was a horrible little scrote. Remember how far we managed to fling him that night?'

Val's lips formed a wide slit. 'Yeah. Right from the top step through the air and into the middle of Archway Road he went. Screamed like a sissy.'

'Sorry to interrupt,' Lorna said. 'Kon sends his apologies. He's been called into the office on an urgent matter. I know you are both keen to see that Ella is okay, but I don't know too much about her, so it might help to have a few pointers before we see her tomorrow.' Lorna took a seat next to the hospital bed. 'I know she worked for you and I know from Mal how you met, but can I ask when it was that Ella lost her job at Buxham's and how? It's important.'

HARRY IS NO MORE

Standing precariously balanced within the enormous yellow waste container, condensation whooshing from her nose and mouth like a dragon, Ella reached out. With one arm extended she took the secateurs from a tremulous Marcus who held the bin lid open. Even through two pairs of surgical gloves the handles felt slightly warm from his touch.

'Hold the torch still and tell me where to cut,' she whispered placing the blades either side of Harry's right thumb.'

'A smidgen lower, on the second joint where it hinges.' Marcus stared at her as she sited Harry's dead hand against her own thigh and, with one blue gloved fist encasing the other, she applied downward pressure through the weight of her shoulders onto the grips. It took four cuts to free the digit, after which Ella placed it into a see-through disposable shower cap. She'd had the foresight to salvage one from the bathroom in Harry's suite, and had quickly rammed it into the pocket of Marcus's borrowed tweed coat.

Kneeling amongst the detritus, decorations and grey plastic, she managed to tuck Harry's arm back inside the bundle. With no heart to pump it, there wasn't too much blood to be seen, only some gravity-driven leakage. Ella stood on Harry's grey polypropylene body to lever herself over the rim of the waste container, and with help from Marcus she landed elegantly on top of the beer crates where he stood, the torch held in his teeth.

'Switch that off now. Let's go. Time's getting on and we need to prepare for an un-dramatic getaway,' Ella said in a hushed voice as she removed the outer pair of surgical gloves. She threw them into one corner of the bin and then, having twisted the end and taken the batteries out, she tossed the torch into the container. 'One broken flashlight, discarded.' Gingerly they closed the lid, accepting the fact that the overflowing waste prevented it from sealing.

Gathering their bags Ella and Marcus carried out one final sweep of both hotel rooms and headed in the central lift to reception. Nothing remained to imply that an abnormal night of antics had taken place. The dessert trolley and special hamper were left, ravaged and cluttered with used crockery, cutlery and table linen. Beds were unmade, towels in bathrooms used and placed carelessly back onto heated towel rails.

'Where is Harry's mobile phone?'

'In my pocket, I turned it off,' Ella replied.

'Good, his Oyster card is in its case. You can use that when we get to the station.'

With general chitchat, Marcus distracted the night manager who had been left to man the reception desk on his own. He stood at the desk, barring the view as Ella strode past rolling Harry's suitcase behind her, in as manly a fashion as she could produce. She made her way to the exit where she stood facing the locked doors, waiting for their release. Watching with intense satisfaction, she witnessed the borough council's waste disposal lorry as it reversed through the gates to the car park. 'Beep, beep, beep,' the alarm sounded, warning stray pedestrians to remove themselves from harm's way.

Since her first week at Buxham's club Ella had become painfully familiar with that sound on a Thursday morning. It would wake her up and disrupt much needed sleep. The imposing wooden main gate slid gracefully closed once the truck had entered.

'My turn to pay for last night's dinner, I'm sad to say,' Marcus announced picking up a pen from its onyx holder on the gleaming wooden counter of the reception desk. 'But we have to forfeit breakfast this week. An early start for both of us. We must catch the next train to London.'

'Yes, sir. Table eighty-eight. On account? Here please.'

The sallow-faced manager was a model employee; polite, efficient and willing, but, at the tail end of his energy after a long uneventful night, he paid scant notice to the two departing residents other than to request a confirmation signature and fingerprint.

Marcus obliged by placing his forefinger onto the small screen of a hand-held device offered to him by the manager who thanked him and said, 'Have a safe journey, gentlemen,' before pushing a button beneath the desk to release the lock on the entrance doors.

Ella tripped in her oversized footwear, but somehow managed to catch the handle of the large door to prevent a fall.

'Steady there, sir.'

Marcus tutted. 'Mr D may still be suffering from rather too much wine at dinner last night. The fresh air will soon put him right.'

Ella smirked as Marcus ushered her through the door. She was surprised at how well he was managing his nerves. More amazingly, she had somehow remained silent and been able to stifle the giggles that threatened to escape from her throat when the intense nature of their escape had resulted in childish thoughts. It was as if the whole episode was a fanciful notion come true; a dead body and two desperate fugitives trying to hide from the law. What a caper! What a game to play! Who would win? Who would live and who would die? Who would betray who first?

They stepped from the doors, down a ramp and towards the pedestrian exit. Knowing that the CCTV was filming her, Ella kept her head down, the large peak of the golf cap pulled low on her brow, squashing her hair. Not wishing to touch her own skin against lifeless flesh, she continued to wear a pair of blue Nitrile gloves. With her right hand she felt for Harry's thumb within the confines of the coat pocket. She manipulated it, partially unwrapped the plastic of the shower cap until she held it in her curled fingers, beneath her own more slender thumb. Approaching the security pad she turned a shoulder to hide her actions as best she could. As she aimed the dead thumb against the pad and pressed firmly but evenly, she was holding her breath. She exhaled long and loud as the mechanism clicked into life and the door swung aside.

The dark winter morning was icy cold and still. Their passage was lit by a half moon and a series of yellow street-lights that led them to the avenue where the bare branches of the lime trees cast unwavering monster shadows across the pavement.

Despite the bitter chill, Ella began to feel physically tired for the first time in over two weeks. But, as fatigued as her body was, her mind was still racing with random intrusive connections and she held court with herself through endless internal rhyming bingo dialogue as she walked along.

All the trees, thirty-three. The trees know, and they're looking at me. Kelly's eye, number one. Did anyone see what we have done? Under the thumb, fifty-one. Nobody saw what we have done. We're clear and free, number three. Nobody knows because they didn't see me. Garden gate, number eight. The damage is done, and it's too late.

Neither of them spoke to each other. The eerie stillness of the morning was peppered by the sounds of early travellers heading to work, by car or bus, interspersed by the endless drumming of suitcase wheels on tarmac.

They were rounding the final bend to head for the station when a deep rumbling cacophony of engine noise made them turn to investigate. The purple and yellow council waste lorry was passing, accelerating noisily as it made the right-hand turn. Checking rapidly right and left, Ella dashed across the road behind it, heading for the opposite pavement. Her clown shoes flapped like flippers and her suitcase, pulled in her left hand, made the journey skidding on one set of wheels. As she flip-flopped her way across the road and past the open jaws of the heavy-duty rubbish eater, she pulled Harry's thumb from her pocket and lobbed it. The shower cap floated into the gutter.

Hopping onto the pavement like a penguin, she turned to see Marcus's facial expression change from one of admiration to a frown of concern. He ran across the road to join her. 'It didn't make it.'

'Yes, it did.'

'No, it didn't,' he asserted, pushing her to proceed along the pavement in the direction of the bright station lights. 'It landed on the footplate. The platform where the workmen stand.'

'Bugger. Really? I was hoping to reunite it with its owner. Never mind.'

Marcus looked down at his strange companion and shook his head, clearly baffled by her lack of concern.

The station was brightly lit and Ella caught sight of her distorted reflection in long glass panels of the modern structure as they headed through the automatic sliding doors and into the ticket hall. She resembled a tramp who had happened upon a bag full of expensive clothes, none of which fitted correctly, but she consoled herself with the certain knowledge that she didn't look like Ella Fitzwilliam.

She watched as Marcus fiddled with his phone, sending texts and eventually making a call to his wife. 'Why haven't you called them? How many painkillers? I'm on my way. I'll be there in twenty minutes.' He looked across at Ella who was sitting opposite, huddled into his oversized tweed coat. Her nose poked over the top of the burgundy coloured scarf she wore.

'More problems?' she growled, in an effort to mimic a male timbre.

'Not as bad as some,' Marcus answered, cryptic in tone. 'You come home with me, change into your own clothes, I'll lend you a coat, one of Lydia's old ones, then you head back.'

Ella nodded emphatically once. She didn't need him to tell her what to do. It had been *her* plan, not his. She wiggled in the train seat forcing herself not to speak more than a few words in case she was overheard by other passengers. She kept her hands wedged into her pockets and played in the depths of the coat where she touched her glove against the leather of the mobile phone case. As she registered its feel between finger and thumb, a series of interlinked notions formed.

Marcus Carver deserved to be punished. He had led a charmed life; an inherited wealth, a public school education, university, medical school, Royal College of Surgeons, a Harley Street consultancy and he risked it all and abused his power to take advantage of the vulnerable.

Watching him bite nervously at his fingernails, Ella registered his desperation. He was unprotected. No lawyer to help him evade the consequences, to shelter him from accusations, or to play with. Harry Drysdale was dead and Marcus had instigated the cause of that death. He had tied Harry to the bed. He had groped and prodded Ella as she stood as an offering to Harry for a present. Sexploitation.

Such a shame Harry had died, because apart from that, the evidence, which she hoped had been captured on film, would have condemned both men as deviant and devious. Members of the press would have been competing with each other to run the story and the lives of two unprincipled men would have been destroyed. Job done.

However, having been involved in the accidental death of Harry, she convinced herself that she could be accused of manslaughter or at least as an accessory after the fact. What was the expression she had used? 'The cock-up of all cock-ups.' It was indeed.

Only when she stared into her lap did she realise that the blue gloves she was still wearing, inside the pockets of the tweed coat, could be her salvation and the end for Marcus Carver. How ironic. Surgical gloves.

38

THE CARVER RESIDENCE

The taxi could be heard pulling away on the gravel at the end of the drive and silence greeted Marcus and Ella as they carefully closed the glossy front door to Marcus's elegant house. The white hallway was brightly lit by a central chandelier and the black and white squares of the floor tiles helped define the style of the house. It was lavish, traditional Regency, with a sweeping stairway leading to a galleried landing. A show home, clean and neat.

Hurriedly, he directed Ella into a small sitting room 'We don't use this room often. No one comes in here.'

'The cleaning lady?'

'She doesn't start until eight... er, and she doesn't do Tuesdays or Thursdays.' Marcus was thrown by Ella's ability to think with clarity.

'That's lucky,' she replied, surveying the pristine room like someone who was viewing the property with an estate agent.

'Your clothes are in there,' Marcus said, aiming a hand at his own suitcase. 'Get changed as quickly as you can and put my clothes back in my bag. I'll sort them out later.' He left the luggage with her and closed the door having told her to wait for his return and to remain hidden and, most importantly, to stay quiet. The girl seemed increasingly wired, wild-eyed and prone to emotional excitement. A most incongruous reaction to the predicament they were in, he thought. She was a liability indeed, but his wife was a major catastrophe in the making and thus she took priority.

Throwing his jacket on top of the oak newel post, he raced up the carpeted stairs, stumbling in his haste, praying that Lydia had already called for an ambulance and left for hospital. He was drained. Nervous energy was the only thing keeping him going. Breathing heavily, he opened the door to the main bedroom and with hollow legs giving way at the knees he launched himself at the bedside telephone.

Lydia lay in muted sweaty agony. Soft groans emanating from her throat. Hair carpeted to her head, knees tucked up.

He dialled for an ambulance then retched violently next to the bed.

'Oh, God, what have I done? Lydia. I'm sorry. I shouldn't have left you last night. I'm so very sorry. Please hang on.' He touched her shoulder not daring to rouse her, believing his own lies about remorse.

He had a matter of minutes in which to send packing the mad girl downstairs. She was unhinged. He'd seen her muttering and laughing to herself on the train journey, and what's more she'd caused him to kill his friend and had then mutilated him without so much as one fit of the screaming abdabs; no hysteria, nothing. What was wrong with her? This was more than her professed bipolar disorder, surely? She was so bizarre. Whatever it was that ailed her and however odd she became she *must* return to the club and act as if nothing untoward had occurred. He had no time to think of a different plan of action.

Marcus flung open each door of the fitted wardrobes in

Lydia's dressing room until he found a brown faux-fur coat, suitable for sending Ella back to Lensham in. Searching wildly, he mumbled insincere prayers, 'Please, God, don't let Lydia die. Please don't let her die. I'll never sin again, so help me.' His mouth was dry.

Lydia hadn't put on the brown furry coat since the day he informed her that she resembled an obese grizzly bear. She'd lost so much weight the coat didn't fit her anymore anyway, so she wouldn't miss it. 'I'll tell her a charity auction was looking for donations.'

Excuses in order, he located a pair of cream leather boots in a long box, tissue paper protecting them. He couldn't remember Lydia ever having worn them. They had high heels and appeared new. From a hook on the door he snatched a cream shoulder bag that would match the boots near enough and he thundered back downstairs.

'I'll need money for the train,' Ella said, stuffing Marcus's jumper, trousers and suit jacket back into his suitcase. She had removed Harry's boots and socks and these lay next to his much smaller case on the beige carpet of the sitting room. She was back in her dress, resembling a dishevelled party-goer who had woken up from a drunken slumber behind someone else's sofa at a house party.

Marcus tried to absorb the scene. 'Yes. Good. Here's a coat.'

'Boots. Thank goodness for that, I'll freeze in these if I have to walk all the way back to the station. It's bad enough having to go commando.' She grabbed at the shoulder bag, opening it she placed her own shoes inside.

'Why are you still wearing those surgical gloves?'

'Fingerprints. Idiot. You don't want anyone to know I was here do you?'

'How come you thought of that?'

'I didn't - until we got to the station and I had to use the

Oyster card. What do I do with his phone? It could be traced. Pass my clutch bag I'll put that in with my shoes.' Ella sat on an upholstered chair and forced her bare feet into the leather boots.

Marcus shrugged. 'You're the one with the brain, get rid of the phone on your way back. Launch it from a train window. I don't know. I've enough on my plate. My wife is very unwell. I've called an ambulance so you have to leave right now.'

'These boots are a bit on the tight side, but I'll cope. Can I have a drink of water? I'm really thirsty. Please.'

With every second that ticked by on the antique gilded French clock on the mantelpiece, the risk was increasing for Marcus. The ambulance would arrive, sirens blaring, and the neighbourhood would twitch their curtains to witness the events unfold. Ella must not be seen in the vicinity.

'Be quick.' He ran to the kitchen and by the time he returned with a tumbler full of tap water she was waiting by the front door. He saw her as she finished primping her hair in the mirror and then, using a tissue from a box on the hall table, dabbed at the smeared makeup that had found its way under her eyes.

She drank in gulps, both blue-gloved hands holding the glass as Marcus pulled a wad of notes from his jacket. 'Here. Money. Now go quietly. I'll sort the clothes.' He watched in despair from the open door as she ran across the frozen lawn to avoid the dreadful scrunch of her feet on the gravel drive. A conspicuous pattern of footprints could be identified in his front garden, two sets with toes aimed towards the house and a smaller set making a return trip. They left a different shape in the frosted grass and there would be no way of disguising the fact that a woman had left the house. Marcus could only pray that no one would be interested enough to take note.

Dawn was not due to break for another forty minutes, but the streets were a great deal busier than when they had arrived. Marcus could hear the sounds of his neighbours' cars being started, warmed or defrosted before leaving for work. In the distance the wailing of an ambulance could be heard increasingly loudly as it approached.

39

THE SEARCH

WEDNESDAY 31ST JANUARY

'Mallory Fitzwilliam, I'm here to see my sister Ella. We rang yesterday.'

Lorna smiled encouragingly at Mal who brushed his palms together impatiently waiting for a voice on the intercom to acknowledge his reply. 'I'm glad you're here. I have no bleedin' idea what to expect,' he said.

'I'm not sure I'll be much help. I haven't been in one of these places for a while and, to be frank, I've no clue what we're in for either.' Lorna pulled at her gloves in anticipation that she and Mal would be entering the unit shortly. She began unwrapping her scarf as a buzzing noise and a metallic click heralded their permission to proceed. Mal pulled the door towards him and allowed Lorna to step through the entrance where she was met by a further door. She tried the second door, only pausing to read the sign once she found it to be firmly locked.

'Oh, I see. We have to wait for the first door to close before the second is released.' Sure enough, as the outer door clunked shut the mechanism on the internal door sounded. Once within the unit they approached a reception hatch. A glass-fronted office held a number of staff, none of whom seemed interested enough in the visitors to pay them much attention until Mal tapped on the window.

'Have patience. Be with you in a minute. Sign in.' The accent was unusual and the wave of the hand was from an indifferent West Indian man wearing a black tunic and trousers, name badge obscured by his greying dreadlocks. Without getting up from his seat, he directed them to an open visitors' book with a nod. Mal scowled. 'Any chance of something to write with?'

Lorna looked about her. The place was stark and institutional. Noticeboards held the obligatory information about how to contact the Patient Advocacy Liaison Service, what the visiting hours were, who the nurse in charge was that day and who had won the employee of the month award for December. Despite the personal touches of patient artwork on the walls of the otherwise utilitarian corridors, the place had no soul. Lorna shuddered. She heard Mal's voice take on an edge of frustration and offence. 'If you want us to write in your bleedin' book, then maybe you should leave a pen with it, mate.'

'Sorry *mate*, no can do, in this place a pen is a risk.'

'Give over.'

'No. Not kidding. They can be used to self-harm or as a handy little weapon,' the man said. He handed Mal a biro, then carefully placed it back in his breast pocket once the details had been filled in on the requisite page.

'A few rules for you, as this is your first visit, keep your belongings with you, and don't give money out to patients.' He eyed the large suitcase that Mal had dragged through the entrance doors and placed by his feet. 'If you have items to give to a patient whether it's food, drinks, bathroom products... anything, then check with a member of staff first. Cigarettes have to be handed in, and especially lighters. No using mobiles either. Enjoy your visit.' The disinterested man turned away and headed to the opposite end of the office to open up a filing cabinet.

Mal glanced across to where Lorna was standing, his eyebrows raised. Aiming his next enquiry towards the back of the man in a black uniform, he coughed. 'Excuse me for interrupting your busy schedule, squire, but could you give us a clue where we have to go. Where is my... er... my sister, Ella Fitzwilliam?'

There was a sigh as the drawer to the metal cabinet was rolled shut. Without acknowledging Mal, the man took a couple of shuffling steps to a door, opened it and shouted. 'Fran. Visitors for Ella. They can use room four.'

'Righto,' came the reply from a young woman who appeared to be in her early twenties. She was dressed in a similar uniform but instead of black she wore a grey tunic top and her dark hair was tied in a neat twirled bun. With a disarming smile she approached Lorna and Mal and led them down a long corridor, pausing to unlock each set of double doors with a fob. 'I'm Fran. I'm a student nurse. If you need anything, please ask.'

Mal was quick to take up the offer. 'Your receptionist, is he always so rude?'

'Attlee? He's a staff nurse, not a receptionist. He's okay. He's a bit snowed under with paperwork from the morning's ward-round I expect.'

Lorna grinned at Mal's expression on hearing this news. 'Blimey, I thought nurses were good with people. My mistake,' he said, shaking his head in disbelief. 'A staff nurse you say. Well, fancy that.'

'We all get a bit grumpy when we're stressed, don't we?' Lorna added, trying to defuse the tension. She could see how awkward the observations had been for the student nurse who had diplomatically tried not to agree with Mal's opinion of Attlee the staff nurse.

'How is Ella doing?' Lorna asked.

'I can't tell you much, because of confidentiality, but she's better than she was. She's a bit down.'

'Understandable,' Mal chimed in. 'It's hardly a laugh a minute round here, is it, luv?'

Fran unlocked and opened the door to a side room where four matching orange chairs were sited at a low coffee table. 'I'll fetch her. Can I take that suitcase? One of the staff nurses will have to go through it and make an inventory before we can let your sister have her belongings. She'll be so relieved to have her own clothes to wear though. She came to us with nothing. Literally nothing.'

The minutes passed slowly in the silence of the square room until eventually Lorna heard the soft tones of Fran as she encouraged her charge to meet with the waiting visitors. 'He seems lovely…'

When the door opened, Mal stood and Lorna held her breath as his face transformed from a welcoming brotherly grin to one of hurt and anger as he looked from Ella to Fran.

'What have you lot done to her?' He reached out and took Ella into his arms and held her against his chest as she sobbed. She wore a pair of baggy, unflattering grey tracksuit bottoms and an equally shapeless beige T-shirt with a faded logo on the front.

Lorna began to wish she hadn't joined Mal in the room. Ella Fitzwilliam looked markedly different to the last time she had laid eyes on her. At Buxham's she had been a picture of health, a vibrant, curvaceous, glossy-haired beauty who had exuded happiness and fun. Lorna had been struck by her capacity to engage so many guests in conversation, manage the waitresses and flirt with the men. She had remarked to Konrad about the sheer energy that flowed from her.

In the psychiatric unit at Flemenswick four weeks later, weeping, was a shell of that person. It was as if her personality had been sucked away. Ella wore her hair dragged into a tangled ponytail, her face somehow bloated but at the same time ashen and haunted.

Pulling herself from Mal's protective embrace, Ella eyed Lorna with suspicion. 'What's going on?' she asked, glancing up at Mal.

Lorna looked at him and tried to give an imperceptible shake of her head as a warning not to divulge the true reason for her presence. Before Mal had a chance to fabricate a plausible response, Ella's eyes widened in recognition. 'Mrs Neale? Why have you come here?' The voice was weak and laboured.

With no choice left other than to tell the truth, Lorna began her explanation. 'Please don't worry. I'm trying to help. You see, we - my husband and I - are friends with Harry Drysdale and we're trying to find out what happened to him.'

The lengthy pause was disconcerting, as was Ella's reaction.

She smiled but only with her mouth. 'I wasn't expecting *you*.'

'Sorry?'

'They didn't tell me you were coming too. They just said they'd found my brother, and he was going to visit. I don't know you. I want to speak to him on my own.'

It had been a serious error of judgement. Lorna was cross with herself for being inconsiderate, for making the quest for answers about Harry take precedence over that of Ella's wellbeing.

'You're right. I'll wait somewhere else. I do apologise for intruding. It was very rude of me.' She picked up her handbag, scarf and gloves and headed for the door. In the corridor outside the room, sitting on a chair, was Fran. She gave an understanding nod before directing Lorna to a dining area. 'Cup of coffee? It's not Starbucks, but it's warm and wet.'

'No, thanks. Fran? Can you tell me anything about how Ella was when she was first admitted here? Was she depressed? How did she get here?'

Fran gave a sympathetic response. 'I appreciate how frustrating this is, but I can't tell you anything.'

'Please. It's really important.'

Fran shook her head. 'Sorry. You understand my position.' She then tilted her head in the direction of a table in the corner where two women were quietly playing a game of cards. One was an elderly lady in a floral dress and heavy cardigan, the other was most likely Chinese in ethnicity, Lorna guessed, younger and dressed in jeans and a hoodie. Both concentrated on the laying of the next card before moving the ones held in their hands, rearranging them until satisfied with the order.

'Please feel free to chat to Cheryl and Ling, they don't have many visitors, and they really enjoy a conversation.' Fran winked at Lorna and gave a cheeky grin. 'I can't help what *they* say, now can I?'

40

HOW ELLA LOST HER JOB

The passengers on the train shied away from her. She was only talking. Why they reacted like that was a mystery and she was becoming increasingly irritated by their sullen expressions and inability to respond to her.

'Did you do anything wildly exciting last night?' she asked three people in turn. 'Well? Did you?' Finally, she backed a bespectacled man into the nearest carriage doorway. Reprimanding him for his churlish attempts to ignore her, she almost missed the name of the station. 'Is this Lensham?'

'Yes. Yes, it is.'

'Don't look so bloody petrified. I'm merely making a straightforward enquiry.' She squared her shoulders to the commuters squashed into the stale, airless carriage. 'Mesdames et Messieurs, you are all excessively ill-mannered. Adieu ignorami. Au revoir.'

Her annoyance was overflowing as she strutted along the platform and headed to the turnstile with a dozen or so other passengers who were about to commence a day at work in Lensham. She held them up as she fumbled for her ticket. 'It was in my possession when I alighted the train. Un moment s'il vous plaît.'

A guard called her to one side. 'Please let the other passengers through, madam.'

'Mademoiselle, if you don't mind.'

He eyed her with doubt. 'Do you have a ticket?'

'Yes. I do possess a ticket, Herr Oberstgruppenfuhrer.' Ella proudly brandished her ticket in his face. She had discovered it that very second inside the pocket of the fake fur coat she was wearing. She clicked her heels, gave a Nazi salute and goose-stepped past the astounded man.

'Pissed, by the looks of things,' she heard him remark to the stunned group of onlookers who had stood by to witness the exchange. 'That is one of the most brazen walks of shame... what a sight.'

The disparaging words faded away as she marched through the glass doors, coat flaps flying, head tossed back, leather handbag swinging by her side.

Lights were on in the Old Station Café, the windows were fogged up, and, catching a waft of coffee and fried bacon aromas, Ella had a sudden urge to step inside.

'What size was the cat?' Saskia asked, as she served a cup of coffee to an elderly gentleman huddled at a table just inside the door.

'Cat?' Ella asked.

'It must have been a fuckin' whopper to have dragged you in,' Saskia said aiming her words at her own feet.

'One can determine from your demeanour that you, my dear Saskia, are not a morning person. How's your love life? Jolly spiffing? Très bien? Je ne regrette rien ...' Ella reeled off several more stock French phrases and threw herself into a window seat. Saskia advanced with an obvious lack of enthusiasm.

'Non-existent. You know that. I went to see her at the

hospital, I know she's dying, and I know why, I've said my goodbyes so I'm expecting you to tell me when she finally carks it. Alright?'

'Don't look so incredibly forlorn. I'm sure she'll bounce back. Can I have a hot chocolate with whipped cream on top and a chocolate flake to dip in? Also, I'll perhaps have—'

Saskia glared at her, glued to the spot, and tried desperately to interrupt as Ella continued to talk, not registering that a conversation was happening around her. 'Bounce back? Val's not going to bounce anywhere, she's dying, you stupid bint.'

'—some of those pancakes with bacon, but I want them American style with maple syrup. Au contraire... it may be prudent to avoid too much bacon. I can't decide if I'm going to become a vegetarian today. And then—'

The beleaguered waitress threw her order pad and pen onto the table in despair. 'When you've made up your soddin' mind, write it down. I'm too busy to listen to you prattle on and on and on. What the hell is up with you? On the snow? Had a dabble with some spice, did we? You're acting like a fuckin' nut job. I'll get your drink if you promise to turn your volume down.'

Saskia ambled off in the direction of the kitchen, shooting a perplexed look over her shoulder at Ella who continued to ramble about potential breakfast choices.

A scruffily dressed gangly man in his early thirties sat in the next booth, hiding himself in the corner as he ate a slice of toast and waited for the rest of his order to arrive. He read a newspaper as it lay open on the Formica table in front of him. Having wiped his buttery fingers down the sleeve of his blue overalls, he intermittently took a sip from a mug without taking his eyes from the page. His slurps alerted Ella to his presence, and she honed in on him. There were half a dozen other people in the café and none of them dared to be caught staring at Ella. They risked brief glances from hooded eyes.

The thin man mumbled a brief 'mornin' ' in response to her demands for a reply to her greeting. This wasn't good enough for Ella.

'I'm on a special mission, you know,' she barked at him.

'Are you now?' The man still declined to make eye contact.

'I am standing up for the rights of real women everywhere.' A barrage of information spilled like a torrent from Ella as she ranted. 'Over a quarter of all adults in the UK are obese. Did you know that? One million of those can link their obesity to bullying in childhood. I bet you never knew that either?'

Ella stood on the bench seat and spread her arms out wide. 'Down with diets, kill the bully!'

Every customer sat back in his or her seats to gawk in shock. Saskia ran through the swing doors, her face contorted with annoyance. 'Get down and get out. Go on... piss off. Go home and sober up, you're a bastard disgrace.' She pulled at the sleeve of the brown fake fur and Ella stumbled towards her, laughing.

'Steady... the last person that grabbed me like that killed someone.'

'You are talking utter shit. Now fuck right off back to your weird world and don't come back in here again. Got it?'

'What is your problem, scrawny? Don't like the fat girls taking control?'

As Saskia pushed her forcefully from the door of the café and into the street, Ella was laughing loud and hearty. She sang to passers-by, 'Fat bottomed girls they make the rockin' world go round...' and the pavement on her side of the road emptied as pedestrians crossed the road to avoid her. She didn't mind, it made her progress all the more rapid. People were too slow, and they got in her way.

Reaching the side road leading to Buxham's she stopped and leant against a wall. 'These boots are crippling me.' She undid the zips and pulled them off one at a time. The frost on the ground restored and refreshed her aching toes and she dashed on towards the gate where she placed her forefinger on to the security pad.

'Hi honey I'm home!' she shouted when she approached reception.

Nula had recently arrived on shift and was about to take up her seat behind the desk when she spied Ella. A hand shot to her mouth. 'Oh, my God. What the hell happened to you?'

'Me? Nothing at all, I'm fine and dandy, thank you. I'll be down in a minute to help Ada with breakfast service. Le petit déjeuner.'

Boots in one hand, Ella skipped to the stairs and, as she ran up them, she sang. 'I ain't gonna bump no more, with no big fat woman ...'

Nula reached for the phone.

Arriving at the door to her room, Ella rooted around in the shoulder bag, found her clutch bag and emptied it onto the carpet. She couldn't recall if she'd taken her room key card with her when she'd left in a rush, many hours earlier.

'Balls.'

Leaving personal items strewn in the corridor outside her room and divesting herself of the heavy coat, she headed for the back stairs to the restaurant and sprinted, barefoot, down three flights. Bowling into the stores area, she bounced off the chest of Schubert who was making his way back to the kitchen with a clipboard in one hand, a pack of bacon in the other.

'What the hell?' he shouted, looking down at where she had landed on the concrete floor, crashing against an empty metal trolley. Legs akimbo, her dress had flipped up exposing her nakedness beneath. The chef averted his eyes. 'Oh no. That is too much. Shame on you, Ella. You are a fucking drunk; an unprincipled tart and you are flashing your gash. Get out of my kitchen! Disgusting.'

On hearing the clattering noises and raised voices, Ada and Flora had made an appearance and rushed to assist Ella, who was now howling and baying with laughter. She brushed them away as she stood to confront Schubert.

'I'm not a drunken whore. I'm on an assignment to save the children from bullies and to promote the benefits of vigilante-ism. Death to the bullies, long live big fat beautiful women!'

Ada stepped in. 'She's not drunk. She might look it but she's not. She doesn't even drink alcohol. Do ya, chuck?'

'And I am the King of Spain,' replied Schubert, sarcasm dripping from his tongue as he threw the clipboard onto the trolley in order to take hold of Ella's upper arm. He had to raise his voice to be heard over her preaching.

'The law is an ass. A scrawny inadequate ass. Fat people have rights; the right to eat what they like, when they like, the right for reinforced toilets seats to be made available, the right not to be called *porky* or *lardy lass*, *chunky chick* or *blimp*. The right to be seen as beautiful.'

News had spread. Carla Lewis arrived in a fluster, but as the scene before her registered, she became rigid, stopping in mid stride.

'Ella,' she shrieked. 'Are you intoxicated?'

'Intoxica*ting*, maybe, but not inebriated. S'il vous plaît. I am gorgeousness, fabulous, and downright amazing.' Ella was trying to gesticulate wildly, but the chef had one arm firmly grasped in his beefy hand. He dragged her in the direction of the service lift.

'Chef. You are one of the nicest fat men I know,' Ella said

turning to face him and aiming a kiss at his mouth which he dodged with the speed of a boxer. 'We could make brilliant big bouncing babies together. Come on let's do it now.'

With Ella's ample bosom being thrust at him, Schubert faltered, and, in his bemused state, Ella ripped her arm free and bolted for the kitchen, wafting her dress like a flamenco dancer. She ran for the head chef's office where she leant against the doorframe, sliding her hands up and down her thighs. 'Show me your pudding, Schubert, and I'll make sure we have it with cream,' she purred, licking her lips.

Without warning she screamed in anger. 'Get back the rest of you!' She directed an outstretched arm and forefinger at the chasing group. Ada, Flora and Carla looked at each other, halting as ordered and then retreating slowly one step a time until they were out of Ella's sight.

'Hands off, he's mine,' she rasped.

Schubert, rolling from side to side and gasping for air, made his way forward and gestured for Ella to make her way inside. Instead of following her, he snatched at the door handle and pulled his office door shut. He held on tightly as he instructed Carla to call urgently for police and ambulance.

'Raving mad. Stark raving fucking mad,' he declared, sweat pouring down his face.

Ella was infuriated. Through the part-glazed door, she could be heard and seen swiping the desk clean of its contents, banging the filing cabinets, dragging books from shelves and hurling a chair at an internal wall. When it went eerily quiet after several minutes had elapsed, Schubert released his grip on the door handle to peep through the glass. He couldn't see her hiding behind the desk and unable to satisfy himself that she was safe, he turned the handle and pushed the door inwards.

In a whirlwind of nudity Ella launched herself at the opening and wrenching the door towards her knocked Schubert off balance and into a wall. She escaped, leaving her dress in the doorway, and began prancing around the kitchen, smearing herself with foodstuff: sauces, scrambled eggs, flour, plum tomatoes, and marmalade. 'Breakfast for the fat King of Spain,' she yelled.

By the time the police arrived she was completely deranged. Two burly chefs had barricaded her into the dry goods store where she rampaged for forty minutes. The emergency services had no choice other than to unceremoniously bundle her into the back of an ambulance, wrapped in a blanket where she was handcuffed for her own safety. It had been impossible to silence her and even as the ambulance departed she could be heard shouting in fury at the injustice meted out. 'If I wasn't fat, they wouldn't have treated me like this. Black people have it easy. You fuckers...'

41

ELLA

FOUR WEEKS LATER

The sight of Mal, standing waiting for her as she walked through the door to the small meeting room at the unit, resulted in a crescendo of emotion pouring out in gulps and sobs. All she wanted to do was to stand within his embrace and wish the rest of the world goodbye, but why on earth was he with Mrs Lorna Neale? What the hell was going on?

Ella had been expecting the police, but so far they hadn't put in an appearance and none of the staff members had mentioned that she might need a solicitor for anything other than to appeal against her detention under the Mental Health Act. This was now a moot point as she was an informal patient ready to be discharged. She could only think that there was another reason behind Konrad Neale's wife being with Mal but at that moment it didn't make sense and she could do no more than ask her to leave. It simplified matters.

Once Lorna had closed the door, Ella took several minutes to compose herself enough to cope with Mal's questions. She sat. He took a seat opposite. It took a gargantuan effort to concentrate on what he was saying. Her thinking was slow, stultified, shackled by neuroleptic medication designed for that very purpose. Her emotions had plummeted and for the past ten days she had been shadowed by an insidious depression that threatened her very existence.

'Ella? What have they done to you?' Mal asked, as he looked her up and down in dismay.

There was a long pause between each question and the answer which, when it came, was hesitant and weak. She had to assimilate the meaning and then search for the words with which to respond.

'They've given me lots of drugs to dull my mind. I feel like I'm not in my own body.'

'Are you eating? You look like you've lost weight.'

'Don't feel hungry.'

'What happened? Why didn't you contact me until now?'

'My parents live abroad, so I had to have an advocate to help me instead of a nearest relative. I didn't want to tell the hospital about you because you're not my real brother. I don't know. I wasn't thinking straight.'

'What happened that night with... you know who?' Mal was whispering, looking at the corners of the ceiling to check for cameras. He found none.

Ella scratched at her left knee. 'I don't know.'

'What do you mean?'

'I mean I can't remember it. Only flashes of memories.'

'Shit. Really?' Mal inhaled steadily as if steeling himself for what he was about to say next. 'I caught up with your friend Ada. She says you were... out of control. They had to call the police.'

'So I've been told. I can't remember that bit. I know that at one moment in time I was standing in a refuse bin, the size of an American dumpster. It was cold and dark, a light was shining at me and I was balancing on Christmas trees wrapped in plastic sheeting. God knows what I was doing there.'

'If only God could tell us the rest of the story…'

There was a difficult silence. Mal had pity in his eyes and Ella wore a cloak of resignation. 'I might have killed Harry Drysdale,' she said.

'You don't know that.'

'No I don't, but I could have done. I decided to call the police and tell them everything. Have they found his body yet?'

'Why are you so convinced he's dead?'

Ella began to shiver. 'I see pictures of him.'

'Covered in blood?'

'No, cocooned in plastic tarpaulin, like one of the Christmas trees. I pulled his arm out and it flopped.' Ella gazed into space. 'Someone was with me. I spoke to them and they held the torch so I could see what I was doing.'

'Man or woman?'

'Man. I'm pretty certain it was a man.' She looked down at herself. 'I was dressed like a man. In men's clothing.' Checking Mal's reaction she realised that he was doubtful of her story.

'What did the old bill say?' he asked, bracing himself for the answer.

'I'm not sure they took me seriously when I said where I was calling from.'

'Hmmm. I think you're getting yourself muddled up.' He changed the subject. 'Try not to worry. I brought you some of your own clothes. Good job. I can't say what you're wearing does you any favours, if I'm honest. Who did you borrow those old rags from? Someone called Waynetta?' A fleeting grin washed across Mal's face as he tried to alleviate the sad reality of the moment. 'I collected everything from your room at Buxham's. Most of it's back at your flat. I let myself in with your keys. I hope you don't mind.'

'Thanks. The goldfish?'

'My cousin's kids have adopted him.'

'Good.' Ella glanced up, a spark of life appearing in her eyes. 'Did you get my mobile phone?'

'Yes. It's in the suitcase. The staff have to make a list or something before they let you have it.'

'Can you get it back from them? You keep the phone. Keep it safe. I'll tell them. Give my permission. You have to guard it with your life. I filmed everything. I think, I, I, filmed everything.' Stammering, Ella reached out to Mal and grabbed one of his hands. 'I, I, I used a micro-camera hidden in my hair. I don't know where it is. I lost it.'

Mal patted her and stroked her arm as he spoke. 'It won't be on your phone, luv. What you recorded will be on the SD card in the unit itself. You can watch live pictures on the phone, but the recordings will be on the card. Where do you think you lost it?'

THE SEARCH

THE NEXT DAY

'Mad as a box of frogs then?' Konrad asked.

'So they said,' Lorna replied. 'Ling, the Chinese girl, saw Ella when she was admitted and says she was covered in sticky sauce, cornflakes, tomato ketchup... everything you could think of. According to her, our girl was practically bouncing off the walls shrieking about Christmas trees and calling bingo numbers in French of all things. I was horrified to think the poor mite had been in that state from here to Derbyshire.' Lorna sighed as she fumbled in her bag. 'Both ladies said she was a nightmare for about eight days. Then the medication kicked in and she slept for a good forty-eight hours, finally emerging as quiet as a lamb, doped up to the back teeth. She's being discharged tomorrow. We tried to ask if we could bring her back with us yesterday, but the bloody system is so immovable. Cooped up in a hospital for weeks on end and the best they can manage is for her to be given a travel warrant to come back by train, on her own. There's care for you.'

Konrad stirred his coffee, an old habit. He no longer took sugar, but the action of circling the spoon in the cup helped him to think. 'I take it you didn't tell her the latest about Marcus Carver.'

'What do you take me for? I'm not an insensitive oaf like some people I can mention.' Lorna smirked at him before returning to the seriousness of the subject matter. 'I didn't tell either of them, but Malik twigged that something shocking had happened. What a stroke of luck you called when we were at the motorway service station. Imagine if you'd blabbed on hands free when I was driving.' Lorna shook her head, recalling Konrad's staggering announcement the previous night. 'It's not been disclosed in the media so far, has it?'

'No, thank God, but we can expect it any minute. How was our Asian Romeo when he saw Ella?'

Lorna gave him a knowing grin. 'You were so right. He's really soft on her, but the whole experience has shaken him. He was dreadfully quiet on the journey home.'

'I'm not surprised...' Annette added, pulling open a kitchen cabinet door. 'I give up. Where do you keep your biscuits these days, Lorna?'

'I never said we had any. You asked where I keep the biscuit tin... which is right in front of you.'

Annette turned, holding a lid on one hand and a red biscuit tin tucked under the other arm, a horrified look on her face. 'What? I've just looked in here and it's empty,' she said incredulously. 'This is my idea of a sick joke. You offer a cuppa but no cake or biscuits? What is the matter with you two?'

Feeling sorry for her, Lorna gave up her search for the item she was seeking and crossed the kitchen to where Annette was standing and staring inside the tin in the hope that magic would happen.

'Will toast and jam do you?' Lorna asked, a sympathetic tone apparent.

With a lengthy blow of relief, Annette relaxed and toddled back to a chair at the kitchen table where she plonked herself down next to Konrad. 'If you haven't got scones, then toast would be lovely.'

'I can't resist a biscuit, so Lorna has stopped buying them,' Konrad explained, patting his midriff. 'Got to stay trim for the viewing public. You know how it is. Now then, Lorna, what is it that Malik Khan gave you?' he asked his wife, who was busying herself placing slices of granary bread into the toaster.

Lorna indicated to where she had left her handbag. 'It's on my phone. There's a number of voice recordings he made.'

'Oh, I know what that will be,' Annette chirped, grasping Konrad's forearm. 'When I collared him in my studio, he confessed to hijacking his cousin's private hire contract with Buxham's. Same cab, different driver and the customers never seemed to notice any difference. Cocky Mal dresses down and becomes a stereotypical Asian taxi driver who then spies on the escort women from the XL Agency. He listened in to their conversations and simply made whatever recordings he could. A belt and braces job of surveillance and helpful in terms of keeping an eye on what Ella was dealing with inside the club.'

Lorna raised an eyebrow at Konrad who had reached into her handbag and pulled from it her mobile phone. He weighed it in the palm of his hand. 'Why is he letting us have this?'

'He thinks it might help to explain what Harry and Marcus were up to and why Ella was out of her depth. Those were his words, roughly.'

A wry smile appeared on Konrad's lips. 'If this is as juicy as I suspect it is, then we may have been handed a career life-line. I have to see the executives on Tuesday. If I can't rustle up a decent proposal for the first episode of this new version of *The Truth Behind the Lies,* then I may as well eat what I like, get fat, and be a happy-has-been.'

'It beats thin, miserable and rich any day,' Annette said, grabbing a large roll of flesh beneath her knitted top.

Stillness settled in the kitchen, interrupted momentarily by toast popping up, being buttered and slathered in jam before being presented to Annette on a plate. 'Right. Shall we listen?' Lorna asked, taking her seat.

The toast remained untouched. Annette only noticed its presence when Konrad pressed the pause symbol after hearing the first recording.

'Thirteen minutes of dynamite, Netty,' Konrad announced. 'Absolutely bloody earthshattering.' He sat forward in his chair and closed his mouth, elbows on the table he slowly placed the tips of his fingers to his lips.

'There are five more, some shorter, some longer and I wonder if you would have time to transcribe them before… say… Sunday evening?' Lorna looked directly at Annette who had taken the first bite of her toast. She nodded so enthusiastically that her hair swung forward and brushed against the jam as she rushed to chew the sugary slice and reply. Crumbs escaped and landed in an avalanche down the mountainous front of her top and she waved one hand in a small circular movement as she swallowed. Taking a slurp of tea, she then ran her tongue across her mouth before speaking excitedly.

'It would be a pleasure. I can't wait to hear the rest of this stuff. Bloody hellfire and buckets of blood.'

'Quite,' Konrad said. 'Feeders and gainers, what's that about?'

'Found it,' Lorna said, raising her eyes from her ever-present iPad. 'Adipophilia, to give its proper name, is fat fetishism. According to Wikipedia it is a sexual attraction to overweight or obese people to the exclusion of other body types.' She paused before reading on. 'Goodness me. I think we might need to explore this in more depth.'

'Over to you, wife,' Konrad said with a cheerful smile. 'Netty, do your thing with these recordings and I'll speak to the XL Agency about the price of buying an escort girl.'

'What?' Lorna queried, eyes wide, arms folding.

'I want to sound out just how much they may charge for a full and frank interview...'

'Oh... good,' Lorna said, appeased. 'Maybe we can find out what might have happened to Harry, while we're at it, or had you forgotten about him?' Lorna remained seated with her arms crossed while Konrad scratched the back of his neck considering his wife's words.

'I know you thought he was God's gift to the justice system, but, underneath the seriousness and the tailored suits, our Harry was a cheeky scoundrel, a pocket Casanova, a party animal and a maverick. I talk about him in the past tense because from what police have uncovered, it looks as if Harry may be as dead as his own thumb.'

Lorna's face fell. She stared at Annette waiting for her to disagree. Annette said nothing and, with a slice of toast and jam half way between plate and mouth, she too waited for Konrad's explanation.

'While you were gallivanting up north with your new buddy Mal, talking to potty women and playing cards, my love, I was hanging around in a shitty pub in the back streets of Crewsthorpe plying DC McArthur with beer until his tongue ran away with him. He's a sorry excuse for a copper, that one. He boasts. By the time he's had a few ghastly lagers he's gagging to blow the gaff about how important he is and how he knows better than DS Quinn. Anyway, the upshot is that blood found on an overcoat belonging to Marcus Carver was discovered during a search at his home. There it was hanging in his cloakroom as plain as day and covered in claret. The blood stains have been matched with the thumb and the thumb belongs to Harry.' Konrad spread his hands wide. 'Add to that the discovery of Harry's mobile phone in a conifer bush in the garden and police have decided that Marcus Carver is the killer. He strenuously denies it of course.'

Lorna and Annette were watching Konrad. Taking in his every word, each turn of phrase. They both kept their questions brief, instinctively knowing that Konrad hadn't finished sharing the facts he had cajoled from DC McArthur.

'How wonderfully obvious,' Annette said. 'Why did they suddenly decide to search his house?'

'They had a phone call from Ella Fitzwilliam wanting to give information and telling them enough to set the wheels in motion for a possible murder investigation.'

'I'm surprised McArthur was so detailed,' Lorna chipped in.

'So was I, but he couldn't wait to tell me the best bit. By all accounts even the hardest nosed coppers had a job keeping a straight face when they marched in to the Carver residence, warrant at the ready, only to be confronted by scenes of celebration. Marcus had been so grief stricken at his wife's death that he'd arranged a dinner party in order to feel better. Would you believe the cops barged in to a scene of gluttony, hedonism and voluptuousness the like of which they'd rarely witnessed before? McArthur's description was peculiarly poetic. He said that Marcus Carver struck him as a perverted bastard and that the whole sight was reminiscent of a porn film he'd once watched involving a woman called Big Bertha. Quite an astute observation.'

Lorna agreed. 'Maybe he *is* a better detective than Quinn.'

'That's unlikely. He certainly can't keep his trap shut. Fortunately for us, McArthur let slip another intriguing fact. When they re-examined the security records at Buxham's,

Ella Fitzwilliam showed up as returning from a night out at nearly nine in the morning of Thursday the fourth of January. That was the day she went bananas and the day Harry was last seen. Interestingly there was no record of her leaving the premises the night before and no sightings of her until she made a nuisance of herself on a train returning to Lensham station.'

Konrad's blue eye twinkled with anticipation as he waited for a response.

'Shit,' Annette hissed. 'So Marcus has been arrested for what? Murder even though there's no body?'

'Interesting scenario, Miss Marple. It appears so. But what if he didn't do it? What idiot would leave a coat covered in blood for the police to find?'

Annette raised her eyebrows. 'Sloppy.'

'Or a clue deliberately left by someone else,' Konrad said.

'Such as?'

'Ella Fitzwilliam.'

'Don't be ridiculous. Why would she kill Harry?' Lorna asked.

'Think about it. We know she's working for Valerie Royal. Val is dying from pancreatitis brought on by gall bladder problems and she has a massive smoking habit. One or the other was bound to send her to an early grave. We also know Ella is sent to gather damning evidence that will finally vindicate Val and prove the case that Marcus Carver is a risk to women - overweight women. Harry defended him in court even though he's almost as active a pervert as his client. The motive is revenge for her friend Val. If we are to believe the story, when Ella and Val first met, in a psychiatric unit not a million miles from here, Val was enormous to the point of downright obese. Shortly after discharge she underwent radical surgery to remove part of her stomach to enforce weight loss and save her from premature death.'

Konrad adjusted his eye-patch. 'She drew an unlucky hand of cards that woman. Her surgeon, checking on how she had faired afterwards, misjudged the level of sedation when he decided to grope her and help himself to handfuls of flesh in which to amuse himself.'

Resting his forearms on the kitchen table, he said, 'It turns out Val wasn't a one off or a momentary lapse of morals, but she *was* the first victim to report Marcus Carver to the police and to bring charges against him. Now she's dying, and Ella wants Marcus and Harry to pay. So, acting as if of unsound mind she whacks Harry for defending Marcus. Then sets up Marcus to take the blame. Plain and simple,' Konrad confirmed, stretching back and raising both arms, interlocking the fingers of each hand behind his head.

Lorna had remained silent until that moment. She fiddled with the handle of her mug, long since emptied. 'No. It can't be that straightforward.'

'There's blood on a coat, and just because there's no body, so far...' Konrad said, tailing off, keeping his true thoughts from his wife.

'What do the police think?'

'I told you. They are convinced it was Marcus who killed Harry and disposed of the body. Not only that but they are reconsidering the facts surrounding Lydia Carver's early demise. Police view her death as suspicious.'

'Do they? I can see he might have wanted Lydia out of the way if he was obsessed with the girls at Buxham's but murder by force-feeding is still stretching it a bit. Killing his wife is unlikely, but if the police are correct then what is the motive Marcus had for killing Harry?' Lorna asked, still unconvinced.

'Envy,' Konrad replied. 'According to the astounding genius that is DC McArthur, texts and pictures on Marcus's phone show a dangerous game being played out, a rivalry and a race to see who could entice sweet Ella into bed first. It was such a draw that Marcus Carver left his sick wife at home to participate in the shenanigans. Your Ella, in her amateur attempts to win private investigator of the year, seems to have caused catastrophic friction between the two men. If those voice recordings are anything to go by, she would have been in for more than she bargained for. I wouldn't like to hazard a guess as to who came off worse.'

Konrad stood, his chair making a scraping sound on the kitchen tiles. 'Time to chat to the two fat ladies of table number eighty-eight, see if we can't piece together a real time line of events, because the police have got it wrong,' he announced. Facing Lorna, animatedly he added, 'Ella killed Harry, set up Marcus to look like the guilty party. She black-mailed him into helping her to hide the body and… you need to find out what else Mal was told. We have to know what Ella said to him when they talked at the hospital. She is our killer.'

43

TUESDAY 6TH FEBRUARY

The grey darkness of the rainy afternoon did nothing to make the task any easier. Mal drove Ella in his cousin's taxi and parked on double yellow lines directly outside The Old Station Café. Lights were on and the foggy windows prevented passers-by from recognising the blurry shadows of the customers within.

'She'll want to know. Let's go in together, sit her down and break it to her as gently as we can. You okay, luv?' Mal asked. Ella wanted to run away and not to have to tell Saskia about Val.

'Not really. What if she's not here?'

'I phoned. She's here 'til six this evening. I told her boss we have bad news, and he's ready to let her go home early. We'll take her.'

Ella unclipped her seatbelt and reached for her handbag in the footwell of the car. 'I wish I could remember where I got this bag from. It's very expensive but I can't recall buying it. I can't even find a receipt. Mind you, it's irrelevant in the great scheme of my overdraft. God only knows how I'm going to pay that back. I bought so much...' She swung her head towards Mal. 'And don't bother offering to help. You've done enough. I can never repay you.'

'You don't have to.'

Malik pushed the door open for her and the sound of the familiar tinkling brass bell clanked above the gurgling noises of the ancient coffee machine. Nineteen eighties pop tunes were playing on the radio which stood pride of place on the counter. Saskia spied them and strode towards them before they could decide where to sit. She raised her hands, palms front, and said, 'Hold it right there.' With a fierce glower she spoke to Ella through gritted teeth, and her tangled hair shook loose from the impossibly large untidy bun on her head. Mirroring her body language Mal also raised his hands but spread them wide in an open placatory gesture. Saskia ignored him, boring into Ella, trying to herd her back towards the door.

'What is it you don't get about the words "piss off and don't come back", eh? No druggies, no alkies and no whores. Got it?'

'Right…' Mal answered, somewhat uncertain. He looked at Ella, she raised both shoulders and pursed her lips, eyes wide.

'No. We don't get it. Can we please speak to you in private? It's a delicate matter,' she said.

Saskia faltered. 'Brilliant. Alcho-zheimer's, is it? Conveniently forgotten what a fuckin' disgrace you made of yourself, have ya?'

'What?'

'Still got the boots to match the 'and bag as well?' Saskia was scornful, almost venomous and Ella could only stare at Mal for support. He waded in.

'Listen, luv—'

'Don't you *luv* me, you arrogant tosser. Some friend you

are. Last time Val allowed me to visit she said you ain't bovered to see her more than once.'

Voices became raised and inquisitive customers had their heads inclined in the direction of the conflict. Saskia now had a forefinger aimed at Mal's chest and in defence he raised both hands higher as he backed away. The scene resembled that of an old fashioned, childhood game of *stick 'em up.'*

Mal smiled. 'You've got this all wrong. Can we please talk? Sensibly like? It's taken all her guts just to walk through the door, so the least you can do is to listen to what we've come to tell you. It's not good news, luv.' This time the unwarranted term of endearment was overlooked. Saskia appeared to sag, unable to hold herself upright. Mal stepped forward, taking an elbow and guided her to the nearest seat. Ella joined them.

'I'm so sorry. We've just come from the hospital. Val named us as next of kin. Goodness knows why.' There was no need for Ella to use the actual words. Saskia began to shake and allowed Mal to take her hand, all animosity dispensed with. She didn't cry. 'Poor cow,' was all she said.

Ella, face pale, no make-up, dressed in a brown jumper and jeans, waited. She tried to feel sorry for the waitress because a broken heart was always painful, but Saskia hadn't been that much in love. Her reaction was muted, so perhaps it was only lust after all, Ella decided. Sympathy only went so far and Ella's driving need to fill in the blanks, from the night and morning that Harry Drysdale had disappeared, had to take precedence. What did the girl mean about the matching boots? Why had she been so angry?

Saskia must have possessed amazing powers of intuition because she sought Ella's eyes. 'S'pose you wanna know what ya did?'

'Yes, please. I had a craft moment, I'm afraid.'

'Craft?' Mal queried.

'CRAFT - Can't Remember A Fucking Thing. Usually strikes in middle age, but not in my case.'

'Oh, I see.' He managed a short-lived grin at her quip.

Ella turned to Saskia. 'I'm so sorry if I caused any trouble. What did I do?'

The description of Ella's behaviour the last time she'd been at The Old Station Café had most impact upon Mal. He lowered his eyes and, having let go of Saskia, who didn't revel in the touch of another human, he began to rub at his cheeks with the tips of his fingers.

'Val should never have sent you in there,' he murmured.

'I volunteered. Remember? She gave me a job when most other employers wouldn't give me the time of day. She saved me. Again. I owed her.'

'Did Val tell you they met in a psychiatric unit?' Mal asked, staring at Saskia, his eyes sad.

The bird's nest bun on the waitress's head bobbed as she confirmed.

'Did she also tell you I live with Bipolar Disorder and I have to take medication and limit stressful situations and get enough sleep, all to avoid a relapse?' Ella asked softly.

'She did mention it.'

'Good, then you'll understand that what you saw was not a drunk or a druggie, it was me in the middle of a full-blown manic episode. I can't remember much because my brain goes haywire preventing me from storing memories correctly. I can't recall what I don't file away.' Ella looked around her. 'Can you tell me if I said anything about a murder?'

Saskia looked horrified. 'Don't be bleedin' stupid…' Her words faded. 'Hang on though, when I was dragging you down from that bench over there you said something proper weird.'

'Like?'

'Like... "be careful, the last person that did that to me killed a man", that was it, I think.'

'What were you doing to make me say such a thing?'

'Pulling at your clothes, that stupid fake fur coat thing.'

'And I had this bag with me?'

'Yeah and matching boots, like I said.'

'Where the hell did I get them from?'

Nobody had an answer for her.

The sight of a police car pulling up behind his cousin's taxi aroused Mal's attention. 'Shit. Hold tight, I'll get rid of them then we'll give you a lift home if you like,' he said to Saskia. 'I've cleared it with your boss.'

'No, thanks. I'd rather keep busy.'

'Your call. Give me a sec, Ella, then come out as if you're my fare. Good luck, Saskia. See ya.'

'Yeah, see ya,' she replied. The corners of her mouth moved slightly as if a smile may finally escape, but before one could blossom the familiar sour dolefulness returned.

Ella watched with interest as Mal headed through the door with a cheery greeting to the officers who had walked to the rear of the Mercedes. One was talking into the radio clipped to his uniform, ducking his head down.

Wrapped up against the chill of the winter weather, Ella put on a tatty duffle coat and coiled a beige scarf around her neck. 'Bye, Saskia. Again, I'm sorry for the trouble.'

'Don't worry. I've dealt with scumbags much worse. Take care of yourself. Let me know when the funeral is, will ya?'

Ella didn't reply. She headed to the door looking up at the bell as it rang out announcing her departure.

Mal wasn't making his usual impact.

'So, this isn't your vehicle,' the tallest policeman said. 'This vehicle is registered to your cousin. What's his name then?'

'Dinesh Khan.'

'That checks out, Pete,' his colleague answered, poking a finger to hold the earpiece of his radio in place, allowing him to hear over the passing traffic. 'Malik Khan?'

'Yeah, that's right.' Mal looked uncertain. 'Who wants to know?'

'We do, sir.'

The officer greeted Ella. 'Hello there, would you be Ella Fitzwilliam, by any chance?'

There was no reason for her to lie. She had been expecting them to track her down as soon as Harry's body was discovered. It was all over the news. Marcus Carver, renowned plastic surgeon, had been taken for questioning. It was her turn. She'd given the police enough indication that the best place to search would be the local waste disposal site and that Harry Drysdale's body would be wrapped up to look like a discarded Christmas tree. How hard could it be for them to decide she was the guilty party?

'We've been looking for you two. DS Quinn would like to speak to you both in relation to an incident that took place at the beginning of January.' He wafted a hand towards the vehicle in front of them. 'Your cousin will have to pick his cab up from the police station, Mr Khan. It can't stay here. Miss Fitzwilliam, if you would come with us please.'

Mal tried to salvage the situation, and in an effort to protect Ella said, 'Does she have to go? We've just come from the hospital, our friend died today.' He reached out for Ella's hand, but she held it stiffly, not grasping at him for comfort. 'Look officers, Ella hasn't been well herself and she has to avoid stress. Can't this wait?'

'Sorry, Mr Khan, but we have been asked to bring you both in for questioning. It's better to volunteer information than to wait for an official demand, if you get my drift.'

'I'm sorry, Mal. I've caused you so much trouble. I'm

sorry.' Ella's voice sounded full of self-reproach. 'Let's get this over with, shall we? *I* can't help any more than I already have but *you* might know something that will help the police. What more have we got to lose now that Val's dead?'

Nothing showed in her face because despite being on the verge of tears, her emotions were flattened, and her senses controlled, but gnawing away inside was a steely determination to get to the dreadful truth. The police could give her pieces of the jigsaw puzzle that were missing.

44

LATER THAT EVENING

'What do you mean she still can't remember?' Konrad boomed into the phone. Barney turned to Annette who shrugged and took a sip from a glass of red wine. The regulars at The Valiant Soldier fell silent.

'He's not a happy bunny this evening. I thought you lot were celebrating,' Rob the landlord said as he passed a pint of beer to Barney.

'We thought we would be,' Annette replied. 'But Eliza called to say her mother has been in a fantastic mood all afternoon during their annual girls shopping spree for Delia's birthday. That was our first clue that Kon had neither rescued his professional backside nor enhanced his reputation. He's keeping quiet and bluffing his way through, like he always does, but you can tell he's wound up tighter than his ex-wife's knickers.' Annette leant towards Rob. 'I have a mole on the inside at Channel 7 who says Kon's pitch to the executives received lukewarm and polite applause. He was asked to wait for their decision, which should come by the end of the week. Dino Ledbetter seemed impressed by all accounts. But, I'm told Dastardly D.L.C. wore a smug grin, like the happy toad he is. He and his sidekick Muttley conspired together during the presentation, making comments about *familiar concepts being overused* and that the show needed *a younger more dynamic presenter such as Stacey Dooley or Simon Reeve.* Quite a-stitch up job.'

Briefly Annette placed one finger to her lips before adding, 'Kon doesn't know we are party to this information, so keep schtum, Rob. He's got to go back on Friday for the verdict and until then he's acting as if he was a roaring success, mostly for Lorna's benefit. She'd be worried sick if she found out, you know how bloody fragile she can be.'

'So what's the problem now?' Rob asked watching as Konrad escaped through the main door to talk more privately in the entrance hall, away from prying ears. His protestations could be heard as the solid wooden door closed and the cast iron latch clicked into place.

'Dunno. I'm not sure if he's talking to Lorna or someone else. I guess we have to wait to find out. Chuck us a couple of packets of peanuts would you, Rob? Thanks.'

Both glasses had been presented for refilling by the time Konrad stepped back into the public bar. He looked pensive.

'Well?' Annette asked.

Accepting a pint of amber coloured ale from Rob, he sipped delicately at the froth on top and placed it back on the bar as he spoke. 'That was the mighty Quinn. He seems incapable of running an investigation without my help these days.'

'Perhaps you forgot to tell him the most pertinent facts when he questioned you? Saving them for your own personal use, maybe.' She shot a look at her husband, but her reproach went unnoticed by Konrad.

'It's hardly my fault they can't think for themselves. The thumb was the key, as was Ella Fitzwilliam, who, by the way, remains convinced that she killed Harry at Buxham's on the night of January the third. This is just like I thought originally, but there's not enough evidence to prove it. Other than a few hints at moving the body, she still insists that she can't remember any more of the events that took place that night.'

Barney frowned. 'But I thought they found the body at the rubbish dump this morning and he'd got a broken neck, that he was done up like a parcel still wearing his dinner suit. Like she said to Malik Khan at the hospital.'

'Correct, old pal, she said the same to the police but there is no evidence to show how the neck was broken or by whom. You can't lock someone up just because they've confessed. More's the pity. Loads of nut jobs own up to things they haven't done.' He inflated his cheeks before allowing the air to escape through a puckered mouth. 'It's an inconvenience I could do without. She's no good to me if she can't remember a damn thing.'

'That poor girl,' Annette said. 'Fancy thinking you've killed someone and having no way to prove it, or disprove it come to that. How awful. She's come out of hospital and has pretty much gone to the police straight away and they can't help her either. What a mess.'

'I think it's deliberate,' Konrad said, tapping his fingertips against the pint glass.

'Really? You think she knows but is pretending?' Annette asked, sitting more upright, her puzzlement making itself plain by the look on her face.

'If forensics can't help piece together the chain of events, then police will have to decide who to prosecute for what. Did she kill Harry? Or was it Marcus Carver? Or will they both be charged with preventing the lawful burial of a body? She can't clear her name, so wouldn't the best way be to feign memory loss and pretend to be wracked by guilt at the possibility that she committed an offence for which someone else could be charged.'

'What a load of old bollocks, Kon.' Barney scowled at his friend. 'You've convinced yourself she's guilty and you're making things fit your hypothesis so you can make a sodding documentary about fat fetishism more titillating by throwing a deranged buxom female murderer into the mix. Shame on you. Give us fat wankers some credit. You want to be careful, you could upset the wrong people.'

The heavy oak door opened again and Lorna slipped in to the pub brushing fine droplets from her raincoat before hanging it from a brass hook on the beamed wall. She headed straight for Konrad and gave him a hug from behind followed by a kiss when he turned to greet her. 'Well done, hubby. I knew you'd knock 'em dead.'

Barney and Annette raised weak smiles as they welcomed Lorna. She failed to notice the tension.

'Thanks. I quite enjoyed it when I got going,' Konrad said. 'They loved the theme, and I'm sure we'll get the green light for the first show. Have you had any luck with Ella?'

Lorna stepped back. 'Luck? By which I take it you mean have I signed her up for your first episode. No, why would I do a thing like that? We haven't even seen the contract yet and, besides, she's in no state to think about giving an interview.' She looked askance at her husband. 'Since when did you become such an insensitive berk? What has happened to the man I married?'

Barney, standing with hands stuffed deep into his trouser pockets, snorted. 'I was asking myself the same question.'

'Yeah, me too,' added Annette.

Konrad Neale looked from one to the other of his friends, a sheepish expression arising as he did so. 'Have I become that bad?'

'Yes you sodding-well have,' Barney said, leaning forward, his eyes never leaving Konrad. 'You have been like a dog with a bone. Me, me, me. The famous Konrad Neale treads over the little people to get his story and please the puppet masters, and shits on the person least able to defend herself. Ella Fitz-whats-it. Why don't you accept that Marcus Slice-'em-Up Carver did it? That's what the police say, it's what the papers say, and it's what Hugh Thingy on the BBC News says and he's always right.'

Konrad sucked his lips tight together and glanced at Lorna who shrugged. 'I might as well tell you,' Konrad said. 'Marcus Carver, with all the evidence pointing at him, has insisted that Ella was with him and Harry, in a bedroom, late at night behaving like a mad woman. He says that she attacked them both with such viciousness that Harry was killed when he fell dodging a wild blow to his head. Quinn tells me that Carver made a valiant effort at telling a comprehensive story, most of which could not be proven, but which makes sense. He panicked and went along with Miss Fitzwilliam's plan to hide the body. They've released him pending further investigations.'

'And where is Ella now?' Annette asked in hushed tones.

'She was with Malik Khan, police pulled them in to help with their enquiries,' Konrad said.

'What, even though she's already volunteered information that resulted in Harry's body being found? That doesn't sound good.' She rounded on Barney. 'Maybe she's not as innocent as we assume.'

Lorna sank onto a barstool. 'It's shocking. She could be a killer but, imagine… what if Ella is not guilty? Given her mental state, how much more can she take?'

THE EARLY HOURS OF THE FOLLOWING DAY

DS Quinn couldn't have been more forthcoming. He spouted detail after detail about Ella's movements on the morning of January the fourth, including the address of Marcus Carver's home.

'Did you, on the morning in question, accompany a Dr - I mean Mr - Marcus Carver to The Manse, 109 Laburnum Grove, Colts Hill, arriving there by taxi from the Colt's Hill station?'

Ella concentrated hard, holding the address in her head. 'I don't know.' *The Manse, 109 Laburnum Grove, Colts Hill,* she repeated silently.

There was a slight cough from the man sitting on her left. 'Do you mean that you don't remember? Or are you implying that you decline to answer, in which case you should reply with the words *no comment.*'

The weary social worker who had been dragged in to act as the appropriate adult under the requirements of PACE, had repeated this stock remark several times. Ella wished he would bloody-well sit silently to allow her to concentrate. He wasn't a solicitor after all. She snapped at him. 'Mr Rogers, I appreciate your time and efforts but I'm not a halfwit. I know the difference. I am unable to recall these events because of my mental state at the time. If I *could* remember them I would be telling the detective the facts because, strangely enough, I want to know what happened to me. Sorry to be a nuisance but please...'

The Manse, 109 Laburnum Grove, Colts Hill,

DS Quinn stifled a yawn. 'Miss Fitzwilliam. You have given us nothing new to help clarify the events that took place at Buxham's or at the home of Marcus Carver. Your recall becomes incredibly patchy regarding the evening of Wednesday the third of January and you do not recover your faculties, for want of a better expression, until approximately three weeks later. Carver insists that you assaulted him and his friend. How do you account for this?'

'I don't. How does Doctor Carver account for the fact that in my memories of that night, sketchy though they are, he is there? He is helping me do something with a dead body. Harry Drysdale's dead body.'

'I ask the questions, Miss Fitzwilliam.'

'Yes, but how could I have made him do that? Why didn't he phone the police?'

'These are questions that have been put to Marcus Carver. Now answer the one I put to you please.'

The Manse, 109 Laburnum Grove, Colts Hill.

'Whose clothes were you wearing when you left Buxham's club in the early morning of January fourth?'

'I'm not sure. They were men's clothes. I know that much. A tweed overcoat, shoes that were too big, a scarf... I think.'

'Is this you in these CCTV pictures? For the purposes of the recording, I am showing Miss Fitzwilliam the security camera still photograph taken at oh-six-twenty-seven on the morning of the fourth of January this year.'

Ella studied the footage.

'I've no idea.'

'We believe it is. We also believe that you accompanied Mister Carver to his home because you were working together as a team. Did he pay you?'

The questions continued, and Ella answered truthfully where she could. After hours spent at the police station she had what she needed. The police didn't, and they were obliged to release her.

She thanked the desk sergeant, she thanked DS Quinn, she thanked the uninspiring social worker, and she left as a free woman; pending further enquiries.

Despite the hour, she didn't go back to the hideous bedsit. She didn't phone Malik Khan. She caught a train to Colt's Hill station where she revived her flagging energy levels with three cups of espresso from an all-night kiosk. She switched her phone off; it was superfluous to requirements.

The February sky was gloomy and dismal when she took a taxi to Laburnum Grove paid for with the last few pounds that Mal had given to her in loose change. It was nearing seven in the morning when she stepped onto the frosty lawn at the side of the gravel drive of The Manse.

What had made her do that? Why walk on the lawn and not the driveway? She gazed at her sturdy black boots, cheap versions of Doc Martens. Rather like déjà vu, vague impressions of having done the same thing before, intruded. She stared at the house. The gardens were neat, stark at that time of year but the evergreens lining the sweeping borders were well tended. The glossy front door, so familiar to her, made her think about how best to approach. 'The cleaning lady comes on Wednesdays.' The certainty of her knowledge was disconcerting. 'I *have* been here before.'

A petite dark-haired lady arrived driving a battered Fiat Panda, her head barely visible above the steering wheel. The dented car made its way slowly around the driveway and pulled up at the rear of the house. Carrying a large shoulder bag, the driver took a key from her pocket and entered. Once inside, she put down her bag on the kitchen table and threw a tabard over her head, patting it down and placing her mobile phone into the large front pocket followed by a selection of rags and dusters. Ella had watched her through the kitchen window, unseen in her drab coloured clothing against the tangle of thorny leafless roses that lined a pathway pergola.

It was a short while before the droning din of a vacuum cleaner began, but when it did Ella recognised it as her cue to enter. She stepped in through the unlocked kitchen door and followed the noise until she determined which room the cleaning lady was servicing. Was Marcus Carver at home? Casting her eyes across the ornate and airy entrance hallway at the front of the house, Ella spied a padded jacket slung on the bannister rail at the base of the stairs. To her this was a strong clue that the owner was indeed within the house, probably in bed.

The sight and smell of the hall, its chandelier hanging above the reflective tiled flooring, had a peculiar impact on Ella. A flashback. In her mind's eye she saw the door to a cloakroom, a brass handle, and she saw herself hanging a coat inside it, and a hat, a peaked cap, like a baseball cap. Unable to resist the urge to check, she listened for the continued sound of the vacuum before heading across the black-and-white tiles turning a doorknob and pulling it to her slowly. A light came on. This was the closet she remembered.

A row of various jackets and waterproof coats hung on wooden hangers suspended on a brass rail. She flicked the shoulders of each, searching, but there was no coat like the one seen in her head. Deciding it was all nonsense and brain trickery she was about to close the door when her eyes caught sight of a blue peak on top of a row of shoes. She stepped closer and bending down she made a small gasp. 'Ping. Golf. Harry played golf. I wore *this* hat.' She put her hand to her mouth, realising that she'd spoken aloud and that, suddenly, the house was unnervingly peaceful. There was no drumming hum of the vacuum cleaner.

Ella could not afford to be seen or heard until she had decided how best to make good her promise to Val. As there was no solid plan forming in her head at that time, she decided to make the best of staying where she was. Silently she regarded the hallway through the fine slit in the door where she had not closed it properly. The automatic light had gone off after one minute. *How clever,* she thought.

In the darkness she smiled as voices echoed across the hall and she heard the unmistakable sound of footsteps thudding down the staircase. Fearing discovery, Ella reversed into the far corner of the walk-in cupboard and crouched, partially hiding herself by placing an old striped beach windbreak across at an angle. Propping it silently against the wall inside and taking off her own coat, she hid inside, her hood covering her head.

'Thelma. I'm going out. Lock up and don't forget to set the alarm this time. Just the doors and windows, otherwise the bloody cat sets off the motion sensors. I'll be back before lunch.' The rounded vowels and public school intonation were confirmation. It was Marcus Carver.

'Yeees meester Carver.' The accent was foreign. Filipino perhaps. The timetable was clear enough, so, once the front door had slammed shut, Ella made herself as comfortable as she could. Fortunately, Marcus must have taken the jacket he had left to hand because she hadn't been disturbed in her hideout. To rest her back, she moved to a more comfortable position, still camouflaged in amongst the coats and shoe racks, she sat on a metal toolbox.

It was a secure feeling, huddled in the dark, planning her moment of glory. The drug-induced depression had lifted within days of her discharge from hospital and her energy was creeping back at last. She would need it. The tablets she was supposed to take had been left in a bin on the train she had travelled in from Flemenswick. Good riddance to them. She was better off without them. They held her back, hobbled her, and undermined her ability to think creatively. Preserving her strength, she meditated. Mindful meditation. It enabled her to disengage the gears in her brain and detach from the reality of what she was about to do. She floated in her cotton cloud until awoken by a high-pitched tone and three beeps. The alarm had been set. The house was empty.

46

BUXHAM'S CLUB, THAT EVENING

Barney and Annette held their spoons at the ready.

'Welcome to February's Lensham and District Pudding Club. Tonight's menu is a tribute to winter. Yes, my pudding loving friends, tonight we eat suet!' There was a wave of enthusiastic whoops at the announcement by the jovial and portly chairperson with jowls spilling over his shirt collar. What followed was excited chatter while the menus were handed around the table and discussed.

Annette had been looking forward to escaping from Lower Marton and from their habitual trips to the pub. However, that particular evening the enjoyment, derived from eating until barely able to walk, had been marred by events surrounding Harry Drysdale's disappearance and subsequent death.

Buxham's had a different feel to it. An undercurrent of mystery and notoriety that made it a more exciting place to be. It should have been exhilarating, but Annette didn't crave excitement. She would have been quite content for her night out to be ordinary and selfishly indulgent, but, as friends do, she and Barney were on a quest to help solve the unanswered puzzle of who killed Harry. They listened in as the talk around the table turned to the events of the last pudding club and what the members had seen of Harry Drysdale that fateful evening. There was a debate between two amateur sleuths as they put their differing theories to the test; grasping at various possibilities but not realising that two amply proportioned, beautifully dressed women sat at booth eighty-eight, thankfully out of ear shot.

The fact hadn't escaped the notice of Barney and Annette who kept an eye on table eighty-eight and the two fat ladies that sat there.

'There's the black woman that's always with you know who,' Barney said, careful not to breach club rules.

'Mr C.'

'No sign of him tonight, by the looks of things.'

'Kon will be proven wrong then. He reckons the manageress woman said that Mr C continued to come every Wednesday, rain or shine, even though he knew Mr D was dead. The ruddy balls of the man.'

Annette made her excuses and left the table as if requiring a trip to the ladies toilet. She took a circuitous route and aimed for the restaurant reception desk where the new hostess was checking the screen of her terminal.

'Hello, Ada. How are you settling in to your new role?' Annette asked. A broad smile lit up Ada's face as she recognised her customer.

'Not too bad, madam. How are you?'

'I'm very well. Hungry and salivating at the prospect of spotted dick and custard.'

They laughed.

'Is there any news on how your predecessor is doing? Is she any better?' The accepted story, told to club members, was that Ella had left because of a sudden illness. Not a lie as such. Annette watched as Ada wrestled with her response, a note of true sadness could be heard in her voice.

'Coincidently,' Ada said, 'I tried to call her again this morning but her phone's switched off. I've been a bit worried about her, there was something in her voice that wasn't quite natural but when I spoke to her a couple of days ago, she sounded brighter somehow. She kept apologising for being a nuisance. My poor little chicken,' she said wistfully. 'Silly old thing, eh?' Ada shook herself. 'I'll let her know you were asking, shall I?'

Annette smiled. 'That would be nice.' She glanced across at the booth containing table eighty-eight and its occupants. 'Have they been stood up?'

'It certainly looks like it,' Ada said. 'They won't be too impressed with that, I don't s'pose.'

'No. Unusual.'

'Very. I would have bet my wages on him being here by now.'

Annette made a noise, humming in agreement and then continued on her way. No Marcus Carver. Why hadn't he turned up, she wondered.

'Barney, we have to alert someone,' Annette said on her return to her seat, whispering as close to her husband's ear as she could get.

'Can't you tell Kon later?'

'I'm not sure. I think this could be a police matter. Ella's off the radar. Lorna tried calling her this afternoon and her friend Ada over there hasn't been able to get in touch with her either. Malik Khan hasn't heard from her since before he left the nick late last night. He rang Kon and Lorna asking for help.' Annette bit her bottom lip. 'You don't think she'd do anything stupid, do you?'

Barney shook his head and Annette could tell that he wasn't really listening to her. He was watching the waitress place a bowl of steaming chocolate sponge pudding onto the tablecloth in front of him. Taking a long sniff, he said, 'Cor bugger me, that smells cracking.' He lifted his spoon. 'Do you need to deal with this right now, my lovely? Aren't you over reacting?' he asked plaintively. 'Malik Khan will no doubt be with the young lady somewhere. He's bound to have found her by now. Stop worrying. They've had a rough time, so perhaps they don't want to be found... nudge, nudge, wink, wink, know what I mean?'

'Is sex all you think about?'

'No. I'm generally more obsessed by food and motors... oh, and beer. That goes without saying.' Barney squeezed his wife's knee. 'Let it drop. Time to indulge ourselves instead of getting dragged into other people's problems. Eat up.'

47

EARLIER THAT WEDNESDAY

Ella climbed the last step of the loft ladder and crawled onto the chipboard that lined the attic space. In amongst the suitcases, dusty forgotten board games, Christmas decorations, and a doll's house, a coil of white coaxial cable caught her attention. That would do the job, she thought, turning on the light; a single bulb in an industrial fitting secured a few feet away at the apex of one of the roof timbers.

The length of white cable looked strong, but was it flexible enough not to snap? It was long enough to secure to a roof truss and have spare for her requirements, so she picked it up and tugged hard at one end, it stretched a little. Perfect. What she had in mind was simple enough to execute if only she could time it correctly and accurately judge the drop, but the loft ladder was going to get in the way.

Peering over the edge of the opening she examined the hexagonal heads on the bolts that secured the wooden ladder to the hatch. The door was no obstacle. Once she had unscrewed the fittings that held the ladder in place, it would swing out of the way to hang vertically, but the ladder itself would have to be dealt with.

278 | A B MORGAN

'Why is everything in this house such good quality? Just for once couldn't he have made do with a step ladder like other people?' Ella eased herself back over the edge and onto a creaking rung. Taking her time, she tested the strength of each rung, and noted its distance from the hatch above. When satisfied, she landed gracefully on the carpet and padded back down the stairs.

Ella returned to the cloakroom cupboard where she was certain to find the tools she needed. 'Aha, electrical tape. That will come in handy,' she said pushing a reel of black tape into the pocket of her jeans before picking up the metal toolbox.

By the time she had pushed it into the loft space, away from the opening, she was panting. It had been awkward to undo the fixings at the joint where the two halves of the ladder folded, without breaking it completely, but it was important. She wanted the retractable loft ladder to look just as it should be. Complete.

Safely back in the loft, she scrabbled around in the toolbox for the right implement to undo the bolts at the top of the ladder. After three failed attempts she finally found the correct size of socket in a small set. She undid the nuts and removed the bolts, taking care not to dislodge the ladder from resting in its usual position.

Looking around her she spotted the blue golf hat where she had placed it carefully in the angle of a cross member. 'Bugger. I should have left the cap downstairs before I did all that,' she said, berating herself for not thinking each step through properly. There was no real disaster. She would sort it out once everything else was in place.

It was a matter of waiting for Marcus Carver to return home. She had a surprise for him. Cross with herself for getting the order of events wrong, she spent a few minutes going through the plan in her head one last time as she sat fiddling with the Ping golf cap, running her fingers around the edge of the peak. Her fingernails were short, unpainted and practical. Looking at them she reflected on how unusual that was for her. Where had her colour disappeared to? It was a rhetorical question, she knew the answer.

Preparations were nearly complete. The coaxial cable, left over from the fitting of a TV aerial, she guessed, wasn't too easy to wrap around the cross member above her head, but she managed. Each end was tied tightly, knot upon knot, and she used black electrical tape as added insurance. She did not want to get this wrong, so she rehearsed, again and again, visualising the moment she would take that final irreversible step.

She didn't hear a vehicle, and it was only when the door opened downstairs in the hallway far below, that she poised over the square hatch, keen to hear confirmation of the return of Marcus Carver. Hurriedly, she tugged the light pull, extinguishing all but the faint glow coming up into the loft via the open hatch.

The house alarm put her on full alert with a series of beeps as Marcus punched in the six-digit code to neutralise the system. With precious time in hand, Ella leant over the gap of the loft hatch, holding the golf cap upside down before allowing it to drop onto the carpeted landing. It wavered and floated erratically like a sycamore seed, eventually coming to rest about four feet from the spot she had intended. It was close enough. Satisfied that she could do no more, she readied herself by coiling three loops of cable and holding them between her hands rested them on her legs, waiting for the right moment to launch. Peering out of the darkness, rigid with concentration, her senses were gathering vital clues as to his whereabouts.

She could hear him moving from room to room below, whistling a random set of notes as he strode across the hallway towards the stairs muttering. 'Pack a bag. Must call Lionel. Check the trains...' He continued his *to do* list as he climbed the stairs. 'Re-read the press release, sue the police for defamation of character, find the—' He stopped mid-sentence. Ella looked down from her high vantage point, glaring at his back and shoulders as he stooped to pick up the golf cap.

'Fuck. Where the hell did this come from?' He threw his head back scanning up the ladder into the darkness. 'Who's there?' he bellowed, a slight quaver undermining his efforts to sound brave.

He gingerly stepped to the bottom of the loft ladder. 'Who's up there? Thelma?' Placing his hands either side of the wooden ladder he put one foot on the bottom rung and hesitated. He peered upwards again but hearing no sound, seeing no light, he took the next step, then the third and the fourth. He got to half way and placed his left foot onto the upper ladder, beyond the join.

'Hello, Dr Carver,' Ella said, placing her feet on the edge of the hatch.

Marcus stiffened.

As the coiled cable dropped over his head onto his shoulders, his right foot gave way beneath him taking him off balance and cutting short a yelp as the whole ladder collapsed. He dangled by his neck, fighting to grasp at the cable with his hands, scratching at his own skin, swinging his legs madly as the coils tightened. Ella, with legs braced across the hatch, held the two lengths of cable together in her clenched fists, pulling backwards into the loft. Taking the strain. She grunted.

'This is for Val from me with love. Goodbye.'

48

THE APOLOGY

He'd spent many hours in various prisons in his career, interviewing murderers and deviant minds. Thus, for Konrad, this was not his first time inside a special psychiatric forensic unit. However, on this occasion it was an uncomfortable, if not unnerving, experience. He had travelled there on his own, no film crew, no sound technicians, no director.

The "clop-clop" of his handmade leather brogues sounded on the concrete path as he and the consultant psychiatrist headed towards a single storey building in the grounds of the hospital. There was no telltale jangling of keys, and with an absence of iron bars at windows and a distinct lack of anguished cries from the patients, he could just as easily have been strolling around a posh conference centre. The general peacefulness of the place was undisturbed, apart from the sounds of the birds in the gardens, flitting from the hedges and shrubs that lined the walkways.

'How did she take the news?' he asked.

The consultant, Dr Yellnow, wasn't what Konrad had predicted. For a start, she dressed more like a teacher than a doctor. Comfortable but smart trousers, topped off with a neat blouse and sensible shoes. A name badge and ID were the only indicators of her role and status. She was slight, dainty and softly spoken. Not at all the type of person designed to manage patients detained under strict Home Office orders; psychopaths, scoundrels and miscreants, all of whom had a diagnosis of mental illness to boot.

'It's always rather difficult to say when it comes to Ella. She's not easy to read. On the whole she was relieved to have her name cleared as far as one death is concerned, but it doesn't undo the fact that she murdered Marcus Carver. In fact I doubt it will make a difference at her next review tribunal or the one after that.'

'Do you have any advice as to how I should approach the subject?' Konrad hadn't felt this unsure of himself for a while. He had an apology to make and he wasn't familiar with humility. Lorna had demanded that he make good his gross error in person, face to face with Ella Fitzwilliam, before he made a public one on national television.

After a lot of internal wrangling, the executive board at Channel 7 had granted him free rein on his series of documentaries about secret private members' clubs. Dino Ledbetter in particular had been delighted with the initial broadcast. The first programme of the series not only exposed the peculiar world of adipophilia but also recounted the tragic events surrounding barrister Harry Drysdale and his friend Marcus Carver the eminent surgeon. Konrad had expounded his theory about how Ella Fitzwilliam had killed them both.

He had been wrong.

Dr Yellnow thought for a while, considering Konrad's question. 'Shall we sit for a moment,' she said, extending one arm towards a wooden garden seat. Konrad sat to her left to see her better as she sought to reassure him. 'I'm not sure why you are so nervous about this meeting. Ella isn't a wildly unhinged nutcase who's going to fly at you in a rage. She's well maintained on regular treatment and she's a bright intelligent lady for whom a tragic set of circumstances unravelled around her and tipped her into a manic episode. We all have our limits.'

'It's good to hear that she's doing well.' Konrad relaxed against the bench. 'I'm afraid I've been left with images of her being dragged from Carver's home, screaming and kicking after a police siege of nearly four hours' duration. It wasn't easy persuading her to leave the loft. Frankly, I'd never seen a detective sergeant wearing a doll's house on his head before then.'

'I didn't realise you were there at the time. Why was that?'

'Her friend Malik called me. We put two and two together and by the time we'd made four it was way too late. When we worked out what her intention might be, we called the police and got to the house before them. I flipped open the letterbox on the front door and when we heard Ella's wailing, Malik broke in through a window to get to her, and we scrambled up the stairs towards the noise. There he was, Marcus Carver, as dead as a proverbial dodo. The electrical flex round his neck had stretched until it snapped and he was in a heap on top of a set of pine loft steps, limbs at most unnatural angles. She was in the roof space laughing. I've never heard such a laugh. Apart from the wicked witch of the west...'

The diminutive psychiatrist had allowed Konrad time to reminisce about the day Ella had lost her personal battle and won a war, but interrupted his reverie by making an unexpected statement. 'She watched your documentary with interest, although she didn't think much to the title.'

'Table eighty-eight and the two fat ladies - what's so wrong with that? The marketing boys loved it.'

'She thought it was derogatory. She said the ladies in question were strikingly good looking as well as overweight. However, you failed to explore the reasons behind why men who have relationships with big women are viewed as perverted when it's nothing to be ashamed of. Making it a deviancy only encourages people like Marcus Carver to go underground, to take advantage and to abuse. I think you disappointed her.'

Konrad was bemused. 'Wasn't she angry?'

'No. She still can't remember what happened the night Harry Drysdale died or most of the days after that, so she accepted your version, until ...'

'Until now.' Konrad bowed his head and cast his one good eye downwards as he rubbed his tacky palms down his thighs, hoping the material of his suit would absorb the sweat.

'Do you mind me asking how the evidence came to light?'

Konrad let out a derisive snort. 'It's a great story but a bit long-winded so I'll give you the short version. A waitress by the name of Saskia helped herself to a customer's hairpiece. That customer was Ella, who lost it the day she also lost the plot after apparently killing Harry Drysdale. Believe it or not, in that hair accessory was hidden a tiny surveillance camera. The waitress eventually discovered the device when its existence was mentioned in the documentary. Are you with me so far?'

'I think so,' nodded the psychiatrist. 'The waitress had been using the hairpiece but handed it in because of your TV show.'

'Pretty much.'

'You played back the recording, discovered the truth and gave it to the police.'

'Correct.'

'You are now asking to see Ella to apologise for assuming that she killed Harry Drysdale, and to invite her to take part in a second film.'

'Yes. Will she agree?'

'Shall we find out? Follow me.' Dr Yellnow sprang to her feet and Konrad had trouble keeping up with her as she trotted at full tilt towards the main door to the modern building nearby. The sign on the door read *Creative Arts and Social Entertainment*.

'How long will she be kept here?'

Dr Yellnow stopped to answer him. 'At this unit? Oh, maybe another six months, then she'll join the mainstream prison population. Not that she'll thrive there. I hesitate to predict what will happen to her in the long term.' The doctor cast her eyes towards the door handle, breaking Konrad's inquisitive stare.

As they entered the building, the doctor put a cupped hand to one ear. 'Listen. You can hear her. This is her speciality. She's brilliant at it and the other residents love it. Twice a week she does this.'

Through a thin oblong panel of glass in a grey painted door to his right, Konrad could see Ella, standing in the room, smiling, conducting proceedings. Her face was instantly recognisable as was her long chestnut hair. She wore a bright headscarf holding it back from her face. Konrad stared, taking in the scene, knowing it was her, but shocked to see how much she'd changed since he saw her last.

'She's put on a few pounds,' he whispered.

'It's the medication I'm afraid. An unfortunate compromise; mental stability achieved for now, a physical health time bomb on the horizon.'

The pair stood in the doorway listening to the sounds drifting from the room.

'Two little ducks …'

'Twenty-two!'

The End

WITH THANKS

To each and everyone who gave time and valuable opinion in reading the draft versions of Fat Chance. It would not be the book it is without you all.

To Junction Publishing for taking on what others were not brave enough to consider.

To my long-suffering husband for helping with research into the strength of coaxial cable and coping with my vagueness as I plotted this one.

To Ampthill Writers' Group for a warm welcome and a safe place to witter on about all things writing.

To Marika, editor extraordinaire.

Thank you all.

ABOUT THE AUTHOR

 Alison Morgan lives in rural Bedford-shire, UK, with her engineer husband and bonkers dog. Life is never boring and they are usually planning the next adventure. Alison spent several decades working on the front line of mental health services as a specialist nurse and latterly as manager of an early intervention service for first episode psychosis. However, when a heart problem brought her career to a juddering halt, she had to find a way of managing her own sanity, so she sat down to write some useful clinical guidelines for student nurses. Instead, a story that had been lurking in her mind came spewing forth onto the pages of what became her first novel. Since then she has been unable to stem the flow of ideas and writes full-time from a luxurious shack at the top of the garden. Alison writes under the name A B Morgan and. within her story-lines, she continues to make good use of her years of experi-ence in mental health services, where the truth is often much stranger than fiction. www.abmorgan.co.uk

SOME SUGGESTED BOOK CLUB QUESTIONS

• How did the opening chapter capture your interest?

• What are the key themes within the story?

• How did the writing style and structure support the overall feel, flow and pace of the book?

• Who was your favourite character and why?

• As a reader, which issues provoked the most uncomfortable thoughts?

• What did you learn from reading this book?

• What are your opinions regarding the ending?